The Longest Distance

The Longest Distance

A Novel

DAVID SCOTT

The Longest Distance

Library of Congress Catalog Number: 2013922401
ISBN: 10-0991301404
ISBN: 13-97809913014-0-9

Edited by Lizzie Harwood (editordeluxe.com)
Cover design by Alexandria Ramon

Permission to use the poem 'The One Thing You Must Do' was granted by Coleman Barks. The poem is from *A YEAR WITH RUMI: Daily Readings* by Coleman Barks © 2006.

Published by:
HESPERIDES PUBLISHING
Wong King Industrial Building
Block G 4/F
2 Tai Yau Street, San Po Kong
Kowloon, Hong Kong

Printed in the United States of America

DEDICATION

I dedicate this book...
To all who have shown me Love...
And have received Love in return.
You know who you are.
You are who you know.

'There is one thing in this world which you must never forget to do.
If you forget everything else and not this,
there is nothing to worry about,
but if you remember everything else and forget this,
then you will have done nothing in your life.'

– Rumi

I am going to enjoy this ride with you.
And I with you.

You are a sweet, sweet Soul…
And I will reveal with you your loving form.

1
C-C-C-COURAGE

'One, two, three... he's not breathing.'
'*Keep trying. We must keep trying.*'
'But I can't. I don't know how.'
'*But you do, Jeremy. You just don't know it yet.*'

The voice inside haunted me. It held out hope, when all seemed hopeless. It believed, when I had no reason for such. It saw in me what only it could see.

I would have screamed of my own discontent, self-loathing, if it were not for the screams of another; one with much more cause indeed for screaming.

Her shrieks were defining, unnerving; piercing every veil of security for those around. Our presence gave her hope through the hopeless state of the man who lay before us.

My skills offered no reason for such.

This was not in the script—his, hers, mine. A fortnight had passed since my brother Thomas and I had set course for Kenya, ready to let go of our adult realities and live the dreams of children. We had ventured to a land filled with mystery, unknown—the Dark Continent. If there was light to be had, there were no signs for such. For only shadows loomed.

'Please! Somebody help him! He's dying! Oh, Sebastien! My poor Sebastien. Please! Someone. *Anyone!*'

I panicked. I was the wrong person to be given such duty. Life. Death. My hands were not gifted for measures as determining what may live, what may not.

Sebastien's wife clung to both his aged hand and memories nearly fifty years in the making, overcome with a fear that finds its origin in the darkest corridors of what lies beyond the known, the familiar. Thomas and I worked feverishly to save the life of a man we barely knew, and of a fate intertwined with this horrid event.

'One. Two. Three.' I felt his withered chest collapse with each thrust of my hands.

'Nothing. Jeremy, give him more air.'

His lips were dry. Mine, as reluctant as they were required. The air that breathed life into me, taken for granted time and again, was transferred into the parched mouth and empty lungs of a man we had only come to know through a serendipitous adventure through the Serengeti.

'He's still not breathing,' I exclaimed to Thomas.

'Again, Jeremy. Try again.'

I offered what air I had. His lips were cold. His mouth dry. His eyes tearing in the intensity of the midday sun that would provide no reprieve in the matter. I felt his life slipping. I could do nothing to keep this from being so. I never could.

'Oh my God! Sebastien! Please don't leave me!' Anika's screams gave way to a helpless pleading, a desperate recognition of all previous chapters in her life story being ripped from her heart in one singular moment; the collapse of an entire novel into one darkened page and memory. Her pleas were frightening. Her husband, motionless, except for the twitch of his left arm, and a set of eyes glazed over by the sudden realization of a life in retreat. His shirt, drenched in sweat as cold as the reality in its undoing, of one man's battle for one more breath.

I sat back. My brother took over.

I looked to the heavens, as if awaiting an intervention from some higher power. The wings above were not of angels, but of vultures looming. The vultures were always looming.

Thomas and I continued. Each taking turns providing what basic training we could recall from our early years. Sebastien's pulse was slowing, his eyes fading into that murky haze when form gives way to formless. His lungs straining as he battled for a breath that eluded him. We continued with the CPR, at the insistence of his beloved—

nearly twenty minutes beyond the time it took for Sebastien to leave his wife, and journey on.

Poor Sebastien. This was his dream, a vacation into the wild side of one's inner nature through nature herself. And here he lay, lifeless, having suffered a fatal stroke. In one quick stroke, as well, we were reminded of the delicate balance between life, love, and our awaiting departure.

Africa—as with life—was a contradiction. One moment I sat mesmerized by the beauty and grace of this predatory paradise for those seeking emancipation in some form. And in the very next, I was ready to pack up and never return to a hardened land that modern science had not yet fully embraced.

The sky above provided a fitting metaphor for life in its fated unfolding. One cloud, then another, all traveling, none allowed to stay in one place for too long; all against a backdrop of deep blue, hazed over by the impurities of this place. Life was in motion. In constant motion. Even when it was no longer.

I lay there in the dirt torched by a merciless sun. I lay there, in thought, sweat pouring down my forehead, hands clenching the soil of a land that claimed yet another as its own. Would it have made a difference, I queried within? If, back in the Netherlands, with updated equipment and available assistance, would it have made a difference in allowing Sebastien one more chance at life's romance?

We, of course, will never know. We are not graced with such information. Perhaps, we are simply undeserving. I knew I was.

One thing remained painfully clear, as Anika lay collapsed over the carcass that was once her husband, weeping...

Life as she knew it was no longer.

'Please! Somebody help him! He's dying!'

The body lay there, motionless, face down in the earth beneath. I rolled it over, the form barely distinguishable. The clouds above made their way across the sky as if in a hurry to dismiss this day for another. The trees chatted among themselves in their own sacred language. They seemed to pay little attention to what was occurring under their watch. The body began to disintegrate, each particle of the person evaporating into the nothingness.

'Wait! I can fix this! Just give me a moment...'

And the moment was...

Gone! He was—I was—gone!

I jumped up, drenched in a cold sweat. I was dreaming. It was just a dream, a very disturbing dream. The face was not that of Sebastien, but my own. It was my body that lay helpless. It was my life held in the balance.

The stillness of Sebastien's body played curse upon my mind. I lay there, shaken, within the netted sanctuary of my earthly bed, as if in some manner protected from the world surrounding by a thin veneer that only served in reminding me of our inevitable vulnerability. I lay there, troubled, not by the pretense of a death, but by the life that preceded. Was it a good death, a painless death? More important, was it a good life?

The crescent moon provided little in the way of illumination through the rustic windows framed by years of co-witnessing the events on either side. On the tree branch just beyond the window, a spotted owl presided over the darkness. What he spotted was me. What I saw was the vastness of nothingness. Darkness was the winner this evening, casting a grand shadow over the safari. I feared the darkness. I always have.

I knew not what lay beyond the boundaries of the known, the familiar. Does darkness loom just beyond the corridors of our comfort levels? How can one find comfort when what we see we do not like, and what we cannot see is what awaits us in the shadows? So many questions invaded my inner sanctuary as I tried to erase the events of earlier.

Within earshot of a cast of mosquitoes who sought to pierce my skin with a thirst for something more basic than the answers that elude, I looked over at my brother. He was off on his own inner travels amid a periodic snore that served as a deafening anchor to this world. Thomas was a good man, a good father, a good brother.

I was none of these.

As the elder, I had the unique privilege of being the first to everything. And Thomas was always second. What a tortured life conceived merely by order of conception—and thus the contrived pecking order. This I thought, as I gazed upon my little brother, my only brother, curled up as if to protect the innocence that remained of the boy we can neither escape from nor so easily recapture.

Destiny or merely life as a series of unfolding events through choices made, it mattered not.

One is graced, another cursed, and that is that.

———

'Boys, we go now. We go... and see what she has in store for us today.'

She was nature. Wilson was our guide. Wilson was his Christian name. He was as short on words as he was tall in stature. Six foot four, a mountain of a man, a mystery in most measures of matter, his size spoke volumes. His words —his few simple words—only what mattered in the moment.

Wilson looked over at Anika, who sat in silence in the passenger seat of the nearby Range Rover. She sat with two policemen who would escort her back to Nairobi. Her own destiny further unveiled through that of her husband's. What awaited her was a series of interviews—more like interrogations—with government officials. This would be accompanied with bribes of sorts to expedite the process of simply getting Sebastien's remains back to the Netherlands. They were his remains. They were hers to deal with. This was not their country.

Wilson turned to me. 'Her life will go on. Life goes on.

It is the way.'

Wilson was right. Anika's life would go on. For each of us, the journey would continue. It had to.

As we watched Anika being driven away, her face aged a year in one night, I was reminded of a man by the name of Paracelsus that once dared to mix the medicine of his time with a mysticism that included the understanding of the role that astrology and alchemy play on illness and the treatment thereof. He was quite the controversial figure during the rather dark period of the Middle Ages, often emphasizing the importance of our dream state in providing clues as to our purpose—and possibility.

'*Dreams must be heeded and accepted. For a great many of them come true,*' Paracelsus once declared.

With Sebastien, he was tempted by something inside that beckoned him to follow his heart to this most distant land, and live in an awakened version of himself. One could question whether Sebastien chose an earlier death by coming here. Perhaps he chose a greater life by having the courage to do the same.

'It is time for us to move,' Wilson instructed.

We pulled away and continued on. The plume of dust kicked up by our tires helped to cloud any remaining visions of a recent past we all would choose to leave in the past.

The past was precisely what I did not want to include in my present. I had enough baggage to fill our van ten times over. But this type of baggage was the kind that no suitcase could hold. My life to date was a series of dates. Each chance to make "more," I found "less" as more convenient. Love came and went, returning again in another form, with a most predictable outcome. Life gave. I took, giving back far less.

I closed my eyes. The image last captured remained upon the screens of the inner. I began to drift off.

'*What choice do we have, but to go on.*'

'Well, yes, I imagine this is true,' I retorted, as a dialogue between myself and some other Self began (more like continued, if one were to admit to how often such inner discourse and debate would arise). It was the same inner voice that remained with me since my youth—source unknown.

'But what of the purpose in it all? Why continue, when so many of us have lost our way, if there is in fact a "way" at all?'

'*To fulfill a promise.*'

A promise? What promise? Whose? This was no longer simply a conversation between me and myself. I would not be able to conjure such a moment. This I knew.

'The only promises I have known were the ones made, and broken, time and again.'

'*Between you and another.*'

'Between me and *every* other.'

'*Ah, yes. There have been many that have graced the place known as Jeremy's love chest. One would think with the chest so close to the heart itself, we would find the door we seek.*'

'A door? More like a revolving door. One that always places me right back where I began.'

'*Perhaps it is in the beginning where we may find our end.*'

'Perhaps. But in the meantime, there is more to uncover. A lifetime of moments that await my senses... as senseless as this may be.' My response, a mix of sarcasm with perhaps a bit too much in truth.

'*The senses deceive from time to time...*'

'Jeremy, are you with us?' My brother broke the dialogue, as the sound in the silence gave way to the chatter of the world.

'What? Yeah. Yeah, I'm here.'

'Well, don't be here. Gaze over there.' Thomas pointed west, in the direction of the late afternoon sun.

Grace. That is the one word that captures the movement of the giraffe as it cascades across the plain, softening our troubled minds with a canvas painted by their gait and beauty.

Ease. As we play witness to the gerenuk, as it stretches upward, balancing on its hindquarters, using its long neck to nourish itself by way of the offerings of the acacia tree.

Grace. Ease. And that which moves us to more basic callings.

'Look,' Wilson pointed. 'In the brush. Two brothers. One thought.'

The party in our van peered through the dust-laden window. Barely distinguishable were two cheetahs, crouched low to the ground. They were thin. They were attentive.

They were doing what cheetahs do.

'These boys. They are in hunt.' Wilson paused for a moment, then whispered, 'And there is their prize... if God wills it.'

The gerenuk was taking in the leaves about thirty meters from the cheetah brothers. She was not taking inventory of the boys who were taking inventory of her. They moved in, slowly, each muscle in accord with the other, stopping from time to time as to go undetected. They would begin again. Slowly, with each measured step, they shortened the distance between themselves and the meal deprived them for some time now. Slowly, slowly, until such time as temperance gave way to intolerance with such.

The one brother took off, followed quickly by the other. Their movement—majestic. Their stride—measured. Each muscle put on display. They flowed with a rhythm and symmetry that could only be found between two brothers. The gerenuk saw none of this at first; then moved on instinct alone. It appeared to have shed its would-be suitors, making one gallant leap over a small bush. The first brother met her in midair. His jaws found her neck. The second helped wrestle her to the ground. It was over. In seconds.

One would live. The other would sacrifice so that it would be so.

'They did not heed the warnings,' Wilson offered. 'The taller ones let the little ones know. But they did not heed, so they must go. It is the way.'

I sat there, both mesmerized and mortified in the same.

It was remarkable. It was horrible. It was "the way."

He had a way. Wilson had a way of looking at the world through a simple pair of lenses. Life to Wilson followed a basic set of rules—live, learn, and when it was your time, leave.

'We go now. There is more to see. There is no more to see here.'

There was so much more to see.

The following day we were on the move once again.

The rough terrain and natural displays served to both shaken and awaken. The dust kicked up from our van clung to me as if it, too, preferred to journey forward as opposed to wither in its own stillness. I faded off from time to time, exhausted more perhaps by a troublesome mind than by the wear and tear of the heat upon our bodies. Hours of travel along the rough patches of the developing world demanded from the body what it offered to the eyes in return. An occasional patch of trees would break up the monotony of the journey. The baboons along the roadside seemed to watch us with the same curiosity we held for them. The flies were impartial in their chosen hosts. The trees swayed to a light breeze that reminded each of the song that plays within the soul that is Africa. It was magical, mystical, and maniacal all in one.

I toyed again with the thought of never returning to Los Angeles, my current home. LA was filled with opportunities for the imagination to both reveal and conceal. It was my home for the moment, this was certain. But like a gypsy who moves with the prevailing winds—and promise of change that rests in the unrest of the heart—I had once again driven a stake in a ground whose soil was soft enough to ensure only a temporary commitment to the ground beneath. My feet wandered. My heart wondered. My mind left to spin tales of love while in a tailspin.

'We stop here,' Wilson informed. 'There is a tribe. Samburu. They have a rich history in dance. You will like.'

We exited the van and were immediately under siege by a parade of young entrepreneurs masquerading as children. Their smiles masked their true intentions. The good nature was genuine; the transaction, essential. They escorted us to the village center while peddling Chiclets gum and other Western goodies that had penetrated this seemingly virgin territory.

As we walked, I took notice of the women of the village. Each wore a series of beaded necklaces, their faces marked for the occasion with traditional tattoo embroidery. They sat amid the shade provided by the sparse trees, weaving baskets and threading bracelets. These were also for our benefit—and purchase.

The men were in a circle, performing a ritual dance, dressed in *shukas* made of red cloth, wrapped around like a skirt, draped with a white sash. Their faces were painted using patterns that accentuated their striking features. Their chest and ears were enhanced with colorful beaded necklaces, earrings, and bracelets. And the dance itself was a rhythmic jumping up and down, using their lungs as a sort of accordion. Like the wind section of a small orchestra, leveraging the gifts of nature in harmonic accord with one another. The symphony of sound was astounding. The composition from the lungs—breathtaking.

A large, gray cloud emerged between the midday sun and ourselves. A wrinkled woman approached me, her eyes glazed over. Covered with the same traditional bead bracelets and necklaces, she was moving with both an awkwardness and purpose. She studied me from arm's length then moved closer. I was taken aback by the clarity of her character that shot forth through her decayed outer form. The strange visitor proceeded to grab me by the face with both hands, pulled my eyes open, gazing deep into my windows...

'This boy—he is on a journey. Where you are going, *nooo* one else can go.'

She pulled back, eyes remaining transfixed on my own. The old women studied them further; then laughed.

'Don't forget to take the little boy *with* you.'

She moved away, glancing back several times in her retreat.

'"Don't forget to take the little boy with you"?' I stood there, eyes attempting to refocus through the series of purple spots that were disrupting my view. What could the woman have possibly meant? "Little boy"? I had no children—and preferred to keep it as such. At twenty-seven,

I was hardly what one would consider a suitable candidate.

My brother asked me what was up. I hadn't a clue so had little to offer. Wilson informed me she was a tribal witch doctor, highly respected by the Samburu people.

'Her visions,' he said, 'always come true.'

Africa was an escape. At least that was the plan. Problem was we brought our minds along with us.

We sat there in silence, my brother and I. The Kilaguni Serena Lodge along the Tsavo River provided the latest setting for reflection. The sturdy teak wood chairs afforded the only real sense of stability. The wooden railing that played footrest for the weary offered little protection from the wild life just beyond and in plain view. It was the end of the dry season, so there wasn't much of a waterhole at all; just parched earth to go with our parched palate. The motivation to resolve my thirst was met with a lingering contemplation of the tragedy which consumed my mind. Thomas was equally quiet, an untouched glass of Kenya Gold liquor awaited his senses, and the perfect moment for its consumption—one that had yet to arrive.

I stared up at the wood beams that held the thatch roof in place. My brother gazed beyond the stone walls and toward the horizon. Neither had a word for the other. I had plenty for me. I usually did.

My mind was restless. My heart cursed. My life could not possibly have been mine in its design. Blessed with a life that was anything but a blessing, I could make sense of relationships of the professional kind, solving problems, "building bridges" along the way. What I was not so good at were those of a more personal nature. Each valve of my heart a mere turnstile. So many women. So many moments. So many lusts forward; steps backward. I loved them. I loved them all. I loved them in all ways. I did not know love.

I felt imprisoned by my own actions, my nature. Perhaps an adventure in Africa might free me of whatever it was that felt so eviscerating, so incarcerating, and allow me to know myself better. This was what I thought. This was what I hoped for, the intention for a new direction. This I did know...

My mind would torment me while I did. My heart until I did.

'What did you make of what Wilson said to you yesterday?' my brother broke the silence.

'What? You mean about the old woman?'

'Yeah. "Her visions always come true." Kind of spooky, don't you think?'

'Especially if there's a child in my future.'

Thomas laughed. I did, as well. Yet within me, there was no laughter to be found.

I took a sip of my drink, closed my eyes, hoping to erase from my memory a life that had ceased to excite; the image of Sebastien in his final breath; and of the old woman that haunted me still.

That woman...

Her eyes. Clouds of gray with streaks of purplish blue. Eerie. Like gazing into the haze of some protected secret. Revealing as they were piercing.

Her hands. Dry as the earth itself. But vibrating. Transferring.

And her words. What was she seeing? How did she know? What was the source of her information?

"Where you are going, no one else can go."

"Don't forget to take the little boy with you."

A faint chirping noise captured my attention. It was as if a handful of crickets began their melody in symphonic harmony within my ear. It was early evening, a setting not unusual for such natural performance. But the source of the sound was not out in the world.

The wind kicked up, scattering the parched earth, providing a drape across the landscape, and a reentry into the world external.

'Jeremy,' my brother began, 'I can't get Sebastien out of my mind.'

'Me neither.'

'Do you think he was happy? I mean, with his life?'

'I don't know. Are you? Am I? I'm not quite certain what happiness looks like.' This was for certain.

'Different. For different people, I suppose.'

Well, I was certainly different, I thought, while taking in the herd of wildebeest along the edge of the river—or what was left of it. So perhaps happiness was not so elusive after all.

'I know he had the courage to follow his dreams.' I said. 'Coming to Africa was a childhood dream of his, one he never gave up on. He shared this with me.'

'We all have dreams like this.'

'Yes, but with Sebastien, he worked his whole life to give himself this one dream. And even at his age, he still believed.'

'And had the courage to follow it.'

Thomas was perhaps reflecting on his own life, as he spoke these words. My brother was also fidgeting. He had this habit of grooming his nails with his teeth, as if unnerved by life's moments that seem to beckon us to go deeper. Thomas was more comfortable with the shallow end of the pool. Not happier, just more comfortable. Or so it seemed. He was a typical man in that fashion. One could not argue with the comforts of such, even when tempted by wave after wave of possibility to delve into the depths of the unknown.

We had moved back into silence. Deafening in its prolonged state, as each awaits the other; words frozen in time and an opportune moment that ceases to exist. My eyes readjusted to the diminishing light as day gave way to night. Looking up, I saw the vastness. Looking down, the grounding of my own reality. A growing restlessness in the revelation. The simple truth that I was not what I could be.

I disturbed the silence. I had to.

'It is time.'

'Time for what?' Thomas asked.

I took a sip of my drink.

'Time to make something more of my life.'

'Your life seems pretty good from here, brother. What could you possibly want for?'

'I have no idea, and that's the point. Something's missing. I watched Sebastien's eyes give way to lifelessness. Did he know before he went? Did he find the answers to his questions?'

'What questions?'

'The questions. *Our* questions. We all have them. They're not the same questions, but we all have these un-answered questions that stand between our lives and what we came here to know—to do even. I don't want to die without knowing.'

'Knowing what?'

I moved the glass to my lips, but did not drink. I sat there quietly for a moment. The pause was perhaps longer than I may have known. The air was stifling. The land wanting. Mount Kilimanjaro offering only the melt waters to quench the thirst for something more. The words that followed escaped my lips before they could be vetted by the limited mind.

'Knowing love.'

Thomas chuckled. 'Jeremy, you have studied this subject enough for us all. I imagine you have earned a PhD by now.'

'No. I'm talking about a different kind of love, not the

many lusts that masquerade as something more. I want to know. I want to know what awaits me... with this thing called *love*.'

Thomas raised his glass. It met with my own. The clang of two gave way to the sound of silence, one that echoed through the airwaves and into the chambers of a longing heart. It also served to shift the moment, if for but a moment.

Out of the darkness of an African evening, within the peaceful stillness of the wild, one flicker, then another, from the fireflies that emerged played timely reminder to the light that was available, if for but a fleeting moment. And perhaps of an awaiting illumination within the darkened consciousness of a man in search.

There was nothing more to be said.

It was time—to do.

The stars made their presence felt as we made our way to the airport. The crescent moon was in full tilt, beckoning one and all to elevate and enjoy the world from a better-seated vantage point. The ghostly trees that lined the road pointed the way—to where I did not know. The streetlights acted as flashlights through the corridors of the unknown; dusty houses and makeshift shops merely markers for the traveler. The shadows lurked just beyond the incandescence, the same shadows that seemed to haunt me wherever my body and mind would take me—the heart left to follow.

I glanced over at Thomas, set adrift upon a sea of thoughts. The adventure nearly over, the reality of my own life once again was upon me. There was simply no avoiding the shadows.

Through my windowed view, I watched a group of children playing along the roadside. Filled with laughter and oblivious to the conditions that would make their lives challenging in many ways to come, they were in the moment, with five minutes before and five minutes to come the only span of time worthy of any real consideration. They were young, free in spirit, full of life, energy and possibility. Impossible had not yet entered their vocabulary. They were simply being who they were. And they were filled to the brim—with Him.

I felt envious.

God knows I seek the truth.
God is Truth... and so are you.
Seek not what already is.

2
THE CITY OF ANGEL

'I saw the angel in the marble and carved until I set him free.'
– Michelangelo

I gazed. The distant horizon offered hope. The spectrum of colors remained unaltered by man's deeds on earth. The scenic array as we descended on Los Angeles ushered in an emotion that stirred my inner being, and beckoned me to tears. These were not tears of joy and appreciation for yet another example of nature's limitless capacity to upstage herself. Rather, through the fullness of this moment, I was again reacquainted with an emptiness, a loneliness, that breached the walls of my own security, and found an unwelcome home within me.

My throat tightened. My eyes welled further. I could not speak what I wanted to say. I could not see what lay before me. I was lost. I was alone. But I was intent on not being lonely. And there were others, many others, who were intent on the same.

The whitecaps across the turbulent waters below seemed to echo the sentiments of a man adrift upon the sea of my own humanity—and vulnerability.

Too far offshore to cast a line back to what was known, familiar. Too immersed within my own fears to see with clarity what awaited me.

> An ocean of possibility
> And a boat with but one oar to traverse it

Africa's momentary emancipation was met with the reality of my life. Kenya provided a wakeup call; a much-needed wakeup call. It gave me perspective, a better life to be conceived. It provided a blueprint—or at least the beginnings of such—through the imprint left from the final footprint of a fellow traveler. Yet what to do with this was all mine in choice.

My choice...

I awakened to the crow outside my window that found it necessary each day to ensure that I did just that—awaken and begin. I awakened, as well, to the familiar sound of yet another companion, and incarcerating pattern.

'Mmm, mornin'.'

'Yes. It is. Another one of those mornings. The sun seems to make certain of it.'

I wanted to provide something more for the attendant who allowed me to take flight for yet another night. I wanted to, but there was nothing more to offer when wading in such shallow waters. Claudette was one of three flight attendants who made convenient entrances—and exits—in my life chronicles. United Airlines provided Rachel. British Airways, Rebecca. And now, thanks to KLM and my recent journey to Kenya, Claudette had found a home in between my sheets and my shorts.

'Fancy a bit of breakfast?' she queried.

'I would, but I can't. I have things to get done today.'

And this was true, all of it. I would, out of a sense of comfort. I couldn't, out of a desire to escape. Not from Claudette, as she was a most delightful woman in both sight and sound. But rather from the reality of my remit to satisfying the needs of another through my own needs. As for having things to get done, I always had something to do. Keeping busy was the perfect remedy to the sobering reality I found easier to avoid than acknowledge.

'Well, then, Mr. Braddock, I shall be off. If you would be so kind as to provide me with my panties...'

'These?' I queried, as I waved the lace lingerie through the air, like the flag of some lame conqueror. The scent that emanated was entirely familiar to the man who lay siege on the territory of its origin throughout the evening prior (although it remained vague as to precisely who was conqueror and who the conquered).

'I will let you know when I am back in town again.'

And with that, another magical night gave way to the requisite vanishing act. Now you see me; now you don't (if one ever had). Claudette and I knew the game. We played each other masterfully. There were no illusions as to what it was and was not. It was, and that was that.

Claudette vanished. The crow remained, head cocked. He was just as confused as I, with the actions of me.

———

'Jeremy. Are you ready yet? Don't want to be late. It's a unique exhibit of Monet's early work.'

'Well, we wouldn't want to keep him waiting.'

Not that Claude would care. Probably more disturbed with his masterpieces being parceled off as postcards.

Georgia Hamada was a masterpiece herself. Japanese by father, Peruvian by mother, she embodied the peace and passion befitting of such bloodlines. Her nature was nurture. Her time spent as curator at the Getty Museum a means of nurturing one's appreciation for Renoir, Monet, Picasso and the rest of the artistic dream team of human time. She honored their gifts to us all, the curator of their craft, conveyor of their brilliance, and modern display of the humility that often accompanied the masterful nature of these talents well before their time. She was also my latest attempt at avoiding contempt—with myself, my life.

The evening waited patiently. Georgia did, as well. I promised Georgia I'd be right with her. The question was whether I was ever really *with* her—present that is. I returned. I usually did.

'Jeremy, I think if we take the side streets we may find it a bit easier this evening.'

I heard her. But I didn't listen, to either the words or the instruction. As a representative of the male population, I had almost a duty to be dialed out. I was with Georgia, in some manner, this evening as with times before. Our moments together had already taken a predictable path, starting strong, filled with passion for passion and choice discoveries befitting of a glance at new romance, only to run the course of one who was far from certain of his own destiny, better yet one shared with another. At least my relationship with Georgia had managed to avoid the train wreck of those before, ones that moved from sex to ex in familiar fashion.

We pulled onto the 405 freeway and proceeded—to "park."

'Damn traffic. Look!'

'I see,' Georgia responded.

'Everyone is flying solo. No consideration for anything. Planet. People around them. All rushing to nowhere in particular. A highway to hell perhaps.'

'Perhaps. It could just be a sea of cars navigated by men who also did not listen to the information provided them.'

Georgia was being facetious. I was not. My impatience found a great test track among the freeways of LA that were anything but free. Granted you didn't pay a fee, but it certainly exacted its toll. So, too, the case with life; when one is caught between the life we live and the life we love—that is, the one we covet. Or so I allowed myself to believe.

'Honey, turn here.'

Was it my turn yet?

'Jeremy, our exit...'

Time to exit this place. I was unhappy. Not quite certain as to why. Just was.

'Jeremy...'

I mean, there had to be something more. This could not have been the life I was born to live; the one I chose...

'JEREMY!!!'

I hit the brakes. The car slid, but managed to avoid making an unplanned acquaintance with the Mercedes in front of us.

People stared. Georgia stared, in disbelief. I just sat there, staring out into the vastness one moment provides through the context of eternity. Flashes of opportunity made their way across my screen. I could choose to listen. I could choose to awaken. I could choose in, choose up. I could choose so many directions that would prove worthy of a man who had something to prove. Unfortunately, there was only one choice once the male mind took over. I unbuckled my seatbelt, opened the car door, and stepped out.

'Jeremy, what are you *doing?*'

I didn't respond. I began walking. Whether to or from was not so easy to discern. In between the parking lot of stationary vehicles on the freeway, for certain. I was finished: with the moment, the traffic; my life. My heart had no real say in the matter. There was no higher nature that was going to trump the lower order.

The rambling within was the voice of choice.

Everywhere I turned, there were castles. Made of sand or stone, it did not matter. There were castles, erected by one, to keep the other in or out. My own constructs were a mile high and a feather deep. I wanted someone in, badly so. But I created the illusion that the walls would be insurmountable, the challenge too much, the reward maybe less so. Georgia was trying. She was not perfect herself— however perfect in my eyes. She was good, maybe too good. Her light, maybe too bright.

What was not so bright was this man claiming to be Jeremy Braddock, paving a trail between onlookers as I made my way down the 405—on foot. This continued until the gaze of a small girl from the safety of her backseat shook me into reality, and to the idiocy of my current journey. I looked up at the stars as they made a rare appearance upon the LA stage. They were not there to guide me. That would have been convenient. They were there to shed a bit more light on the moment. And they served their purpose.

I returned to the car (where, presumably, I still belonged) and found Georgia on the driver's side. I had no issue with this; none at all. We were both better off when she was "driving."

'What? Where *are* you, honey?' Georgia asked, visibly

shaken by my crazed performance.

'Sorry. I'm right here. I'm fine. Just fine. Fine really.'

'Jeremy Braddock, you just told me you are "fine" three times in five seconds. You are clearly not fine.'

Clearly, I was not.

Georgia dismissed my latest act as we arrived at the museum. The private event was filled with the glitter and glamour any celebration of the masters would duly demand. Too often these brilliant beings were rarely seen in such favor during their time here on Earth. Humans have always been a bit slow in our awakening to a greater expression and messaging. This I determined while downing another glass of sparkling wine—the poor cousin of champagne. I sat there, half-cocked and in full contemplation—perhaps just another word for digression. My mind wandered. It often found the need to do just that.

Such radical ideas, those introduced by the multitude of masters who have graced history. Christ, Mohammed; even the likes of da Vinci and Descartes. Many more. *So* many more. As many as were needed. Each requiring their proper gestation period, along with a captive community. Enter organized religion. Enter periods known later as Renaissance or Enlightenment. Enter those whose message through pen or brush finds a more receptive audience in today's venue than in earlier settings. Enter...

'Okay, honey. We can go now.'

'What? Already? I was just beginning to warm up to the high brows who could not possibly have taken in and understood the brilliant works in display from such a lofty perch (nor without the aid of their PA, stylist, and therapist).'

'Oh, really now, Jeremy. I know you have more in your heart than that. These people are trying their best just like everyone else. Looking down at those who are looking down at others just has us all looking the same direction in the end anyway, right?'

'Yes, I suppose we can all go down together. A *Titanic* moment.' I clearly had had too much to drink.

'That, too, was a love story.' Georgia clearly had the capacity to absorb more than I.

Love. A story indeed. A tale told by—and to—many. Georgia believed in love. I believed she believed. It was easier for her. She was a good person. She had to know this. I was not so good. I knew this too well. I had little patience for others. I had less for myself. How would I know love? How would I know love, when I could not even recognize it in me?

Georgia looked into my eyes—what she called my baby blues—then grabbed a hold of my arm. 'Jeremy Braddock, if you were not so charming...'

'Let's just leave it at that. Jeremy Braddock... "charming,"' I responded, as she placed her head upon my shoulder. 'If I have you fooled, I see no reason to enlighten.'

We made our way to the car. I opened her door—on the driver's side, once again.

'Charming *and* a gentleman.'

'You can thank my father for that one,' I added, as I closed the door and made my way to the other side.

'Where to now, sweetheart?'

'Well,' Georgia replied. 'If I know you, you have our next destination already mapped out... and it includes a rendezvous with Ben & Jerry.'

'Always willing to reconnect with old friends, you know that.'

Georgia knew me well, better perhaps than I did myself at this stage of my life. For the little boy in me, my most basic self, would have to be satisfied in some form that was pleasing to the palate, after a parade through "adult land." Not that I didn't enjoy hobnobbing with the humans; just had more of a taste for Chunky Monkey ice cream than for the many simians caged within the context of what it meant to be "grown up." How I ended up getting ice cream this evening, this I wasn't about to explore further. I had been less than the model escort.

We made our way from the Getty—using only the side streets this time—and into Santa Monica. We parked along Main Street, and set a path for the ice cream parlor. The universe provided the detour.

A disheveled man was sifting through the garbage, in search of whatever remains of the day would soon become the spoils of his night. As we approached him, the menagerie of my own make-believe gave momentary authority to my mind.

Is he safe? Clean? Diseased? Does he want money?

'Hey there, what's your name?'

Leave it to Georgia to go right to the heart of the matter—and to the matter's heart.

The strange fellow cast a strange look in our direction. He straightened himself, adjusted his weathered cocktail jacket, as if to honor a lady through the faint memory of manners past.

'Good evening, young lady. Sir.'

His hair was mangy. His dark features hidden by layers of dirt and decay. His eyes tired, yet absent of any signs of alcohol as an inducing agent to suppress such distressed life. His soiled clothing gave off an unpleasant odor. His smile provided a most pleasant addition to the moment.

'Name's Robert,' the man continued, while squinting as if to get a better measure of what stood before him.

'Well hello, Robert. Pleased to meet you. I'm Georgia. This is Jeremy.'

Robert smiled at Georgia. He looked at me with more suspicion.

'You know, no one ever really speaks to me,' he offered, with a mix of shame and deference.

'Well, they should,' Georgia replied. 'Everyone is worth the time. Even Jeremy.'

'She's right. I am quite the project,' I added, as if acknowledging it made it any more palatable.

Robert glanced my way again; this time smiling. He resumed his assessment of humanity.

'They shy away. Think I am lesser, I suppose. That all I want is a free handout.' His head began to migrate to the ground, his eyes no longer playing equal with our own. He pulled his coat a bit tighter to adjust for the unusual chill this evening.

'"*Do unto others as you would have them do unto you,*" right? That is what *He* once said.' Robert, of course, was reciting the words of the master Jesus, the Christ.

'Are you Christians?' he asked.

'Not really,' I answered. 'Have a hard time buying into the whole religion thing. I've never been one to be boxed in.'

Georgia laughed. 'Yeah, Jeremy Braddock is a hard one to pin down. Trust me, I've tried.'

Robert smiled again. 'Why choose one item on the menu when you can have a bit of it all. I have seen plenty on these streets that would not be looked at too well by "the Big Guy."'

'I don't imagine so,' I added. I could only imagine.

'Yeah. He tells me so.'

'Who?'

'God. He talks to me all the time. Says I have to be more understanding.'

'Of whom?' I was now more engaged in the discussion.

'Of people like yourself. People who walk the streets thinking people like me are crazy. I listen. I hear all the back and forth that goes on between everyone... couples, parents with their kids, friends who are not very friendly. I

tell you, I've seen crazy. This world is filled with crazy.
Everyone unhappy. Everyone lost. And He says, "Robert,
you have to be understanding. They are just children.
Children finding their way home."'

Robert paused for a moment. Georgia and I just looked
at one another. Class was in session.

'They have no idea,' he continued.

'No idea of what?' Georgia asked.

'That there is no bottom. You can fall and fall in this
world... all the way to having nothing at all. Nothing, that
is, except God.'

There was a whole lot more to this man, his life story,
than we would ever know.

'How does God talk to you?' I had to ask.

'God talks to all of us. Just no one's listening. I listen,'
Robert chuckled. 'I have nothing better to do than listen.'

He pointed at another homeless man, rummaging
through a nearby garbage bin, mumbling to himself. 'He's
not listening. Chatters all the time. God can't get a word
in.'

Georgia and I laughed. This guy Robert was a good
guy—funny, too.

'I like you, Robert,' Georgia said.

'Yeah. Best time I've had all night.' And this was no
exaggeration, given my evening with the glitz and glamour
of the Getty crowd.

'You know, I would give anyone on this street my time.
Hell, my money, if I had any,' Robert added.

'Well, we've got something better than money,' Georgia responded. 'Come with us as we pay a visit to Jeremy's two best friends.'

Robert stared at Georgia and me as if we were just another addition to the world of crazy.

'She's talking ice cream, Robert,' I offered, to diffuse the confused. 'I happen to love ice cream, in particular Ben & Jerry's.'

Robert smiled again. Missing teeth but not the moment, his eyes glistened as if powered by a source from within. Of course, it could have been merely the idea of ice cream. It certainly had that effect on me. Regardless of the source, I felt my heart fill with a warmth I had known on but few occasions. My ears with that sweet chirping sound—its origin still unknown.

'Well, then, let's not keep your friends waiting!'

'Always willing to share.'

I glanced in Georgia's direction and smiled. She was beaming. Her smile raised my awareness of her most en-dearing quality, given life by way of a simple feature. There were a number of features possessed by Georgia that would have provided many an artist with the inspiration to capture divinity in the flesh. Yet, the one that revealed everything one ever needed to know about Georgia Hamada could be found upon her face, just above her cheekbones—an array of subtle freckles against the backdrop of her natural browned hue. These freckles represented the delightful balance of a woman with a greater truth revealed through such childlike essence and means of embracing the world. I loved this about Georgia. I loved this and much more.

We spent nearly two hours sharing with Robert, over ice cream and a Johnny Rocket's burger and fries. And I was present, the entire time. My mind neither wandered nor wavered. It was by far the most fascinating exchange of the evening, and served as an awakening to a part of me that I rather enjoyed, a better side that could not help but find some union in everything and everyone. I even felt a little bad about the way I handled the crowd at the Getty—a little. After all, they had everything, but missed the point. Robert had nothing, but got the picture.

Where I fell in the spectrum, I didn't know. It was easy to see where others were off track. Our propensity as humanity to see ourselves above it all would provide such a distorted view. I was looking down on the high brows of the world, when perhaps I should have been looking *over*. Robert had "nothing," but had everything on me. He was listening. I was just another one of the many, mumbling away.

But for one moment, one evening—this evening—under the guiding light of a captivating night, I was listening. I found a common brother in the most uncommon of places; a transforming moment, if for but a moment. I knew myself better, through the eyes of another; in this case a man without a home, who was anything but homeless. Robert was just another one of us, as welcomed as the rest...

Better prepared, perhaps, than most.
Certainly than me.

My time with Georgia continued to serve as both guide and teacher in my awakening to something inside me. She played an unwitting example, a mirror of sorts. I knew little of what lay beneath the superficial, nor how to crack the code beyond the accidental visit through my inner pursuits. I only knew that with Georgia around, and the nature of her kindness to others as a model, new things began to unfold before me. And in the months that followed, I was given ample opportunity through such a compass for compassion. Sadly, her higher reality just made my lower state too much for me to play daily witness to. She reflected back to me a loving unconditional in nature. I had little capacity to gaze at such a view. She messaged. I was not a willing correspondent.

My penchant for self-indulgence and frequent vanishing acts eventually wore on our relationship—and those that followed—all playing second to the one I wrestled with, the one within me. I was straddling the wall between the "me" I wanted to be, and the "me" I was. I remained determined to find the answers to the questions that escaped me still; so much so that I was willing to sacrifice even the comfort of Georgia to appease a growing discomfort with myself, and of a life that taunted me in mystery.

The distance grew longer ever still.

It was cold. It was rainy. It was the perfect day for such an imperfect ending.

'There was a master once by the name of Saint Francis of Assisi who, in a prayer that is as timeless and as pertinent as with all great messengers, captured the essence of such divine constructs as Georgia Hamada in action.'

I sat there. Alone. Staring at the casket from a safe distance. The flowers were beautiful. The purpose, anything but.

As with all masters past and present, and in the words of Gandhi himself, Georgia used "her life as her message." It was a life of meaning. It was a life of service, one of loving. It was a life cut short by a rare tumor of the pancreas that took this particular angel home, and away from the city that bears such name.

My bloodshot eyes moved to the cross above the casket; to the man upon the cross; to the scars upon the man. He was a prophet to some; the Son of God to others; a good man to many. He was crucified for loving. Was this the destiny of all who seek love?

The pastor continued...

'Lord, make me an instrument of your peace...'

My attention shifted to a small child in the pew to my left. He was humming to himself, while moving his head from left to right, as if connected to a world—an inner world—beyond the grief of those around him. What did he know that we did not know? What could he see that we could not see? Our discontent was his pure content. Our darkness: his light. Our sadness: his joy.

'...*For it is in the giving that we receive*;

'*It is in the pardoning that we are pardoned*;

'*And it is in the dying that we are born to eternal life.*'

The pastor finished. My thoughts continued.

"*For it is in the giving that we receive...*" These words were foreign to me. They were foreign to me; native to her. Georgia lived these words. Her acts of service, through the unselfish gift to another, served in forging a better relationship with herself. Does the same reward await me? Would I be the beneficiary of the very love I give, when wise enough to let it flow—flow, that is, without conditions? How would I know? I thought to myself, as the service finished. How could one ever know of such gift if I were predisposed to giving only when it served me? Georgia showered me with loving. I offered her an empty cup in return.

The service ended. I departed. The rain tapped upon the roof of the car, as I sat there in the parking lot of the church for what seemed like hours. I sat there, alone in my thoughts—alone in the world. I sat there, with only myself as my company. It was not good company I kept. I sought better company in the most unlikely of places.

'Hey. I remember you,' Robert declared. 'Where's that lovely lady you were with?'

'She's gone... passed away... recently.' Tears formed in my eyes. They mixed with the rain as it made its way down from the crown of my head.

'Aw, I'm sorry. She was a good person.'

'The best.'

'She'd been by here. Many times, in fact. To help out. Give me food. Sometimes just to talk.'

I, of course, knew none of this. How could I? Self-absorbed and out of contact; with Georgia, with myself.

'She was a good soul,' Robert continued. 'An angel.'

What followed was an awkward moment of silence. Neither Robert nor I knew what to say to one another next. The onus was on me. After all, I originated the moment.

'Robert, is there anything I can do for you. Anything at all?'

'What do you mean?'

'I mean, do you need anything? Money? A place to stay? Anything?'

Robert chuckled, 'Not at all. Have everything I need.'

'Well, I just figured...'

'Hey, man. I chose this life. I like my life. I like it here... on the streets... the freedom. No one to answer to. No race to run. Nowhere to be. Just be.'

My head migrated to the ground. I felt ashamed. What was I doing here? Trying to make up for the loss of an angel by some last-minute act of desperation? Of course he didn't need anything from me. I was the one in need. I was the one who was lost.

'You are lost, brother,' Robert offered. Or was it God talking; through one who was listening, to another who was not—but needed to be?

'You are lost, man. But only because you think you are.'

My eyes remained fixed on the ground beneath. There would be no answers to be found there. I was looking in the wrong direction—*still*.

The rain descended. I looked up, at Robert. I thanked him with my eyes, and my hand upon his shoulder. I thanked him, and walked away.

I could only hope I was also walking *toward*.

The following day, I was back at my apartment, continuing with another common ritual beyond the one of unceremoniously degrading myself. I was packing for a move—this time to San Francisco, and the chance to begin anew, once again. Running to or from I wasn't quite sure. Just away, perhaps, from the shadows, the darker sides of me.

I proceeded to box up everything required to remain in motion. Everything was in its proper order. I had mastered this exercise if nothing else, through countless resets on my life. Ironic, really, how one who would pride himself on never being "boxed in" found himself boxed up time and again. This I thought as I continued.

Numbered, with descriptions, the contents of each box were fully disclosed. There were no surprises. There was an order about things, a structure. There was a logical explanation for the source and use of everything. I could account for the contents and the destination was clear.

There was nothing abstract about it. Something I could control. When *I* was in control, it all made sense. *Everything!* The discord came when I had to rely on another.

I was better off alone. After all, what lies in waiting for those who find goodness—love even? They are stripped from us, taken somewhere else as some just reward for their good work in this world. What was left were the leftovers; those of us who were in struggle to simply be, better yet be good.

It made no sense, none of it.

I made no difference, none of me.

I was insignificant in the universe.

The thought made me angry. I reached over, grabbed the closest object to me, and flung it against the wall. It was the glass statuette Georgia and I had bought together while in Sonoma. It shattered. I shattered with it. I dropped to the floor, then feverishly attempted to pick up the fragments of glass.

'I can fix this. Wait! Just give me a moment...*please, God!*'

A rush of emotion followed. My body shook un-controllably. I began to weep.

'Georgia. I'm sorry... I'm so sorry.'

There, on my knees, I begged her forgiveness. It was the desperate plea from a boy, caring little of my status as a man. The tears streamed down my face, a river of remorse for my many failed attempts at simply being better.

I gathered myself for a moment, realizing amid an ocean

of tears that this man needed a lifeline or I would surely drown. I sat down, broken glass surrounding. I saw my reflection in one of the many pieces. I held such disdain for myself that I could no longer even gaze at my own image when faced with a mirror in any form. I closed my eyes.

'God help me!' I pleaded.

I waited. I waited for a response that did not come.

'God, please!'

It was a prayer; the prayer of a man in need.

My eyes remained closed. I thought of never opening them again. I did not have the luxury for such a thought.

A flash of purple and what felt like a thud on my forehead—just between my eyes—shook me from my downward spiral.

'*When you're sick and tired of being tired and sick, that's when change happens.*'

The words—origin unknown—graced my mind and awakened my heart. I knew the words were not my own, yet I *owned* these words. They were *mine*. They were for *me*.

I opened my eyes, looked around. There was no one. I checked my forehead. There was no mark, no sign of any impact. There was nothing. Nothing, that is, except the tingle of my body—every cell—and of the resonating tone that accompanied the words.

'*When you're sick and tired of being tired and sick, that's when change happens.*'

'Where to next, Jeremy?' Arena queried.

'San Francisco. I figure it's time for a change.'

Arena just nodded. She knew my life. She knew a change was in order.

Arena Arcova was my friend and confidante. We met while in Colombia—Medellín—over scotch and a few failed attempts at salsa. A bottle of merlot sat between us. Neither the spirit nor setting on the deck of Moonshadows in Malibu could provide respite for an unnerved spirit within.

'I was sorry to hear about Georgia. When had you seen her last?'

Tears began to well up inside. My heart hurt. My throat choked; sore from many failed attempts to swallow my own pain in some attempt at maintaining a manhood that had its basis in false bravado, and no business showing itself in the moment. I felt guilt—incredible guilt—for having cast aside such a gift through a patterned reckoning that had yet to avail something greater to me.

My eyes remained fixed on the ocean. I could not bear to give them to Arena.

'Six months, I think. She looked fine. Typical of Georgia. She never let on. Preserving my peace... even through her own pain.'

'She was special. I know you loved her.'

Arena knew more than that. She knew pretty much everything and everyone that had made their way into my heart over the years. She knew, as well, of my misguided ways. Arena and I had a special connection. We knew each other in ways not so easily understood by even us. It allowed us to understand each other better, without judgment. Everyone has their "go-to person" in times of emotional upheaval. Arena was mine.

The sea spray cleansed my face and played reminder to my reality.

'I had better get going. I have a flight to catch. And a life that awaits my arrival.'

'You know, Jeremy, my father used to say a chicken with his head cut off can still cover a lot of ground.'

'What's your point, Arena?' I knew her point—on some level at least.

'Whether you're running from or toward, keep moving. It is in the moving that we get our next step. The universe rewards action. Even if you don't know where you are heading—or why—just keep moving, my love. The answer will come when it does.'

She was right. I didn't know where I was heading next, or why for that matter. San Francisco, yes. But to what end? I felt lost—like a headless chicken. Lost, but aware enough to know I was.

What I did not know—could not possibly know—was the true purpose for the next entry into my life story. I could only hope that the steps to follow would provide another clue, and perhaps a greater understanding as to the purpose of my presence here. For I was certain of one thing: there was a growing discontent for the content of my life. More like a disgust with my disguise.

The surf exaggerated the moment. The beach stood firm as each wave attempted to move the immovable. Force. Power. Power. Force. The battle continued. Which would triumph? Was there a moment where both could co-exist? For one to win would the other have to concede? What would the heavens allow—demand, even?

I looked out across the ocean, once again, and toward the horizon. The birds in the distance were en route. Their journey was clear.

'What territory awaits me?' I considered within.

'*A kingdom for the King in you, Jeremy,*' the voice of reason responded, without need of hesitation.

'God, I am not worthy of such. I am not worthy even of your attention.'

His attention? I was not sure of His existence. Could not possibly know. I could only hope at this point. Hope would have to do.

'I could use a hand, though,' my thoughts continued. 'Just a hand.'

Across the sky that was giving way to eve, an image appeared as the sun bid adieu. A cast of what looked like five fingers of light emerged from the horizon, and graced the sky before me. I was aware of my ability to imagine. But for the moment, I allowed it so.

He was offering His hand.

Can love divine be known with another?
Yes... if you are... then it is so.
Regardless of the other... words... actions...
It is so as it is so.

3
I LEFT MY HEART...

'Home...
Is where the heart is.'

Homeless...
Is where *I* could be found.

S an Francisco was chilling to the feel, warming to
the eye. The soul could find amusement in such a
place. The mind could find diversions.

'Where to, sir?' the cab driver inquired.

'Sausalito.'

'Nice place. Are you visiting?'

Visiting? What, Earth? More like moved in for good.

'Moved here a couple months ago. Just returning from

Europe.'

'Well, then, I wish you well in your return.'

Probably the last words spoken by whoever granted me access to this body—this life.

The diversion came by way of a pair of legs that somehow I was convinced would create the distance I needed from the despair I felt from my failed attempts at simply being better. These were not my legs, however. And in this, I should have known where they would take me.

Stunning, alluring, breath *taking*, and oh-too-familiar, Tessa Milonas had a trance-like effect on one seeking deeper waters but moving with the precision of a trawler engulfed in Bay Area fog. Her body came with a warning, signaled by the thick wave of auburn that embraced her face. Those sounds that could be heard off in the distance were a call to a higher order—the desperate cries of a hopeless romantic—still floundering upon the sea of the unseen, craving for a place to lay dock and call home.

Truly hopeless, I thought.

'Hopeful is not hopeless, Jeremy,' retorted the one within.

'Yes, but the dance of romance has left me both weary and leery.'

'Perhaps you are simply dancing with the wrong partner.'

This time, I could take that one literally. For Tessa was just that—a dancer. And I was in tango once again.

I met Tessa shortly after I decided I was no longer available to the female gender. She was a pole dancer at a night-club in the city—San Francisco. Well, not really, but she might as well have been. Tessa danced for the local profess-sional football team. These women were talented. Dance was their passion. But they had other lives. Some were teachers. Others, managers. One was even a commercial pilot. On Sundays, however, they flew into the hearts of every man who coveted sex and sport—and there are a lot of them. In the latest attempt to sabotage my own life, I joined in these circles.

'Here you go, sir,' the taxi driver said. 'You have a lovely home.'

If it were only *my* home. Tessa was not only my latest affair, but also a permanent housemate. She was also Greek. So on Saturday evenings, on the weekends of home games for the Forty Niners ball club, all were welcome.

I opened the door. And entered.

'Honey, welcome back! The girls and I are in the midst of real mischief. We're trying to solve Ashley's problem.'

I knew Ashley. I knew this was no easy task.

The foyer gave way to a sunken living room. The living room offered a captivating view of the city across the bay. It also housed ten to fifteen cheerleaders whenever the team was in town. The girls were in from around the state and beyond, some from as far off as Texas—Tokyo even. The passion for performance provided for an incredibly committed group of girls. And I was left committed as bed-and-breakfast operator by way of affiliation with a filly.

Tessa was the poster child for wild. I should have known what lay before me the day I walked into her dance studio–

–and walked out with her phone number. Her red hair was a red flag. This woman was mercury. Too close to the sun to safely land upon without getting torched. Coming off the heels of my failed time with Georgia—and those who followed—I was in the frame for some self-inflicted pain. Tessa was the perfect companion in this sense.

'Honey, come join us. We need a male perspective.'

I needed some perspective, I thought to myself, as I set down my bags and descended to the living room.

'Hi, Jeremy.'

'Hey, cutie.'

'Why hello, Mr. Braddock!'

The girls provided their own version of a salutation. I was already in need of salvation.

'Red? Or red with gold? Which do you think is sexier?' Tessa was talking about fingernail polish. I was not about to.

'Hey Tess, did you hear Diya's got a new plaything?' The girls caw over that piece of news.

'Now *this* is what *I'm* talking about,' another girl named Channel exclaimed while holding up what appeared to be a magazine shot of someone named Justin.

I saw where all this was going. I made my escape to the bedroom upstairs. The bedroom had an outdoor deck. The deck graced the tops of the surrounding trees. The scent of fresh pine welcomed me home. I was traveling quite a bit these days. I could take Tessa, but only in doses—increasingly smaller doses. It was not her, really. More of a case of trying to lose my self entirely in another, with the inevitable discovery there was simply nowhere to run. I had run out of places to hide.

The phone rang. It was Nick.

'Hey, brother.'

'Jeremy. What's new in your world?'

'Let's see. Just arrived back from Brussels. Cab ride over was fairly uneventful. Walked in the house. Did I mention a dozen cheerleaders in my living room, in nighties and pj's?'

Laughter from the other end.

'Man, you died and went straight to heaven, bro.'

'You call it heaven. Hell is not quite that glamorous.'

Nick Garcia had been my good friend since university. I admired him. His days on the surf, in harmony with the waves and his board, helped chisel away at the parts of him that were rough on the edges. The result was a man who was *chill to the world*, kicked back while those of us continued to tempt fate on yet another ride on the rollercoaster.

'Jeremy, man, what's up? You sound lost.'

'Lost would be a good description. Georgia's death hit me hard. And love in general has been nothing more than a series of disappointments.'

I paused for a moment, surveying the city off in the distance, clouded over by the incoming marine layer. The chill in the air made its way to the bones—as did the revelation.

'I understand it's a result of my own doing, my own

choices, but I feel like I've made four left turns and am right back where I started.'

'You started with a dozen hot cheerleaders in your living room?' Nick was good at bringing me back in the moment, and finding the humor in it. It was not, after all, *his* life, so it could be enjoyed like a reality TV show—*my* living reality from the safe distance of *his* home.

'Yeah. Can you believe it? One moment I'm in heaven with an angel. And the next, I'm dancing with the devil himself.'

'Brother, if the devil is this hot, we're all screwed.'

I laughed. Nick had a way of making me laugh, even when my life was no laughing matter. He was also another witness to my many attempts at love over the years.

'And with Georgia... just wasn't meant to be, brother.'

'What does that mean anyway... "wasn't meant to be"? I keep living the *not meant to be*s. They keep showing up. I keep living them out. Only to be left with pieces of me scattered around the planet. Brother, I'm tired of dealing with this.'

'Well you know what they say..."when you're sick and tired of being sick and tired, that's when change happens"...or something like that.'

'Yeah, something like that.'

'Can't run from your karma, brother.'

I laughed, 'Well, I certainly have given it my best shot. I suppose it's time to turn and face the damn thing.'

The door opened. Tessa entered. 'Honey, why are you

hiding up here?'

'Speaking of karma, gotta run, brother.'

'Just take a picture at least, will ya? If you're leaving this all behind someday, we'll need the memories.'

I laughed and signed off.

'Honey! Why are you hiding out?'

'What you should be asking is why I am here in the first place.'

'You're here, silly, because this is your home.'

'That's the problem, Tess. It doesn't feel like home. *Nothing* feels like home. I feel empty inside.'

Tessa stood there for a moment. Only for a moment. 'Well, if you need me, I'll be downstairs.' And she was off.

Tessa and I had this sort of unspoken arrangement. I promised never to swim in the deep end of my thoughts around her. She promised to always meet me in the shallow end. Role reversals when compared to the world itself. It was the only way things could work with us. Trouble was it didn't work for *me*—if it ever had.

I joined the girls downstairs. I joined them for no other reason than the living room where they were camped out stood between me and the kitchen—my true destination.

'He has returned!' Tessa proclaimed, adorned in a tight T-shirt and lounge pants. Her long legs were cast over the arm of the couch. Her head rested upon the shoulder of Ashley, while another worked on her toenails. Queen of Sheba was reborn.

I was in need of a rebirth myself.

'Jeremy, join us...if you dare.' This warning came from Emma. She was the wise one of the bunch. One of the youngest pilots for US Airways, Emma had a different flight path than the others.

'Nice read, Ems,' I said as I entered the lair. She was reading *The Odyssey*, by Homer; the story of one man's journey home after the fall of Troy, and of the greater price paid in earn of such a journey.

I took a seat near the fireplace, and took in the many forms that accentuated my living space. Each girl represented a slice of American pie as seen through American eyes, carefully selected to assure all male tastes were met. From blonde to brunette, red hair to black; tall and trim to mid height and busty; freckles; cheekbones; dark; light; Asian, Indian, and *South Beachin'*. These girls had the legs, bodies, busts, and beauty that would serve as appropriate entrée to the main meal of muscle and mass that made for American football. All that was missing was...

'Jeremy, wanna beer?' Tiffany offered.

'Sure.' It seemed to fit with the intoxicating scent of hair spray, nail polish, and perfumes on display in the palace of this adorned harem.

'Okay. Honey, get over here,' Tessa insisted. 'We need your thoughts on something.'

I moved from the fireplace—and "into the fire."

'Why are men such sissies when it comes to being sick?'

'Yeah, what's with that whole *man flu* thing?' Channel chimed.

'Man flu?' I asked, knowing I was heading into territory I would regret on so many levels.

'Yeah, man flu. You never heard of it? Tiffany, tell him what man flu is.'

'Man flu is when a guy gets a little cold... and acts like he's on the verge of death.'

'Yeah,' Ashley jumped in, 'the symptoms are a sniffle— maybe two—followed by a pleading... '

'Honey! Please! I'm dying! Call the doctor!'

'Better yet, call my mom!' Channel, of course, had to provide the appropriate amount of real-time acting to go with the words.

'Oh, that mother thing! "That's not how *mom* does it. My mother would..." uh, makes you wanna...'

'Hit him with a bat!' Tessa finished.

'Yeah! How you feelin' now, honey?'

The girls all laughed. Then, all became quiet. They just stared at me—every one of them—as if I represented all of mankind with the next words uttered from my apprehensive lips. All of mankind. This one deciding moment. And I, their unsolicited spokesperson.

'Yeah, I can't imagine what they could be sick from. You are all so... '

I stopped to take heed of the next word to roll from tongue to lip. For many a man had cast his last line in the water in moments such as these, only to be flung from the vessel, lost at sea, never to be seen nor heard from again.

'...so *divine*.'

My words were met by a shower of socks, used paper towels, and scrunchies. At least it wasn't the barrel of a bat.

I made my way back upstairs, closed the door behind me, and found my choice spot on the deck once again. I had forgotten why I had ventured downstairs in the first place. I was corralled before I ever made it to the kitchen. Seemed only fitting, as my medicine for what ailed me— my own *man flu*—would not be found downstairs. Not this evening. Of this I was certain.

The winds swirled through the gulch that was Sausalito to the south. The chimes from the neighboring porch could be heard attempting a melody. Each thrust of wind composed a sonnet of supper bells, and not the original score of its intention. The clanging was an awakening. It was time to eat. The hunger within me was growing once again. This was not a hunger that could be satisfied with another attempt at the kitchen. This was a hunger for something much more indeed. It was a longing for a feast fit for kings (and queens). A kingdom awaited me. But the road paved that would allow for such arrival was as long, as trying, as treacherous, as I chose to lay myself. This I could see. This, perhaps, was all my senses could sense.

Off in the distance, I could hear the faint chorus of sea lions. They, as well, were hungry for something that would serve in satisfying their emptiness. The crows above cawed from their perch, laying claim to a branch as their home, satisfied with their view for the moment. They knew. They *all* knew. There was something more that was required, to fulfill what each desired—longed for even.

I sat there in a temporary solace. The wind provided the appropriate blanket upon my ears. I smiled as I considered my life in its current form. I dreamt of angels, dared consider myself destined for immortality through some new portal to a more serene, more divine existence. But as with all dreams, however real in their possibility, they require a partnership, an anchoring, through the actions made by mortal men here on Earth. The gods live through us, the God perhaps within us. This celestial union requires we have one hand in the heavens, and one foot firmly in this realm. It is the way.

Where these thoughts originated I hadn't a clue. I would catch myself at times, wandering off in what seemed a more enchanted place, carrying on as if I were no longer there in form, but rather as witness to something greater than my mind could wrap its thoughts around. It was during these brief glimpses that I became more and more certain of one thing, if nothing more:

There was more to know that remained in the un-knowing.

A small bird landed on the weathered fencing that bordered the deck. It made a series of deliberate movements, checking out all that surrounded it, as if in constant record of each new possibility—and possible threat. It calculated every characteristic it encountered, processing through its small mind, small thoughts. The little bird began chanting in my direction, as if carrying a very important message, one that I must hear. Its little mind capable perhaps of but a single thought in each singular moment. My sophisticated brain with the capacity to overwhelm every moment with a surge of needless chatter. The little bird, one message. My superior mind, with no capacity to embrace it. It flew off, perhaps in frustration that I did not hear its call. I remained, wondering how many other callings I had missed.

"When you're sick and tired of being tired and sick, that's when change happens."

Nick was simply repeating my words. I was simply repeating wisdom provided me back in LA one desperate, despair-filled day. Chirping a song back and forth. Until one was actually ready to do something with the words, words that may point the way.

Four left turns. No right direction.

I looked up. It was the only direction left to look. At least, this is what I thought. This is what my mind thought...

While my heart waited.

Patiently.

For the next direction.

'Ladies and gentlemen, I direct your attention to the south end of the stadium, where our Gold Rush girls are now performing.'

There's nothing quite like watching your girlfriend

dance around in essentially a bikini, in front of sixty-thousand people—and a whole lot more via television. The amount of testosterone and accompanying sexual energy generated during a three-hour game could power a small city—and provide enough raw data to occupy any clinical psychologist for years. It's an overdose of everything that keeps man swimming in the shallow end of the gene pool. Thank God I had the good sense to wear my swim trunks, and avoid the humility of my humanity, standing exposed--butt naked—in knee-deep waters of my own making.

'*Your humor is a good tool. Keep it handy. Easier when we find the amusement in it all,*' the voice within provided.

'Oh, amusing I can do. I could keep myself entertained for lifetimes.'

'*True. In fact…*'

'I know. I know. No need to tell me.' This I replied—aloud it appeared. For the man to my left gave me a look as if I were distracting him from his view, of *my* girlfriend and her mates. Shallow end indeed, the deeds of men.

I was drowning. This I knew. The awareness of such was comforting in some manner. My humor, a necessity for my sanity.

'*The senses deceive from time to time, and it is prudent never to trust wholly those who have deceived us even once.*'

These were the words of René Descartes. The origin of the voice was less clear.

'Enough. I'm watching the game.'

'*No. You are the game.*'

The crowd roared as Garcia—the quarterback—made a brilliant pass down the field.

'I *am* the game? What kind of nonsense is that?'

Boos filled the stadium as Owens dropped what would have been an easy catch.

'*No sense at all. For it is not to be known by the senses, what sense you are to make of this world,*' the voice continued, again with René's words.

The crowd roared in approval.

'Are you saying that what it is I seek I cannot find in a manner that I would be able to identify through my own senses?' This was becoming altogether uninviting, the thought as with the messenger.

'*The senses deceive from time to time, and it is prudent never to trust wholly those who have deceived us even once.*'

'"...*those who have deceived us even once*"? I cannot place the blame on anything or anyone else but myself for the choices I have made,' I retorted within. 'Reliance on the senses is one thing. Overindulgence in them, something else altogether. It would seem pointless at some point—sense-less even.'

'Touchdown!' the voice over the stadium loudspeakers shouted. The crowd roared, hitting a decibel level that was off the charts.

'*Good conclusion. Very empowering,*' the voice continued. '*Perhaps by "those," we are speaking not of others, but rather of that part of you that continues to seek refuge in the same home of your impending discomfort, as opposed to trusting in the heart that sees what the mind and senses fail to comprehend.'*

Made sense. This inner guide really had a beat on me, like it had been along for the journey for quite some time. I bid adieu to the voice within, to René, and eventually to Tessa. There was nothing in her that would warrant such. Tessa seemed happy enough with who she was. She would also take little notice of my absence. As life would have it, we were simply a temporary tonic for what ailed us.

Of course, saying goodbye to her took much longer than planned. It's a slippery slope indeed, when love is meshed with need. I was in need of knowing that I could love and be loved in the same. It took another year before I could break free from it completely.

It took even longer for me to trust that I had.

Days followed days. Weeks followed weeks. With me attempting to follow something altogether unfamiliar.

'...and follow your heart into the inner realms.' This after an invocation that sounded more like I was calling forward the all-powerful Oz himself.

I was on a new kick. This new kick required no sidekick (which was a good start). That is, unless one were to consider his meditation teacher as such. I certainly needed a kick in the backside. And Reshma had just the spirit required by Spirit.

'Jeremy, focus! One must be clear on their intention, vigilant in their effort... to obtain what is rightfully ours.'

Reshma Patel was from India. She was a meditation teacher. She was also an expert in Hindu Vedic Astrology. Her reading of my own chart was hauntingly accurate. She knew things that no one could possibly know, from my past that gave legitimacy to her presence. It was as eerie as it was intriguing.

'Jeremy,' Reshma shared. 'You will meet a man. A man who will give you what no other could give you... what you are seeking. It is your destiny.'

At the time, I wasn't sure quite what I was seeking. It was clearly not in the form of a man. Reshma should have predicted my plight with Cassandra. That would be far easier to predict.

Cassandra Taylor and I met at a conference. This connection would lead me to Reshma. Reshma would guide me into the inner worlds through meditation. Outer forms strung together to get to the inner kingdom. Another form of "string theory"—threaded masterfully.

My time with Cassandra began as all things do, with a conversation. She proved hauntingly familiar, giving more credence to this past life thing I was gathering data on as the scientist in my own spiritual laboratory. It appeared the universe was providing reunion after reunion, in some form or another. Perhaps it was merely the re-*union* of what I was with what I was destined to face. In this case, it came in the form of yet another pretty face, one that tempted the lower parts of man. Such gifts only served in providing another nail in the coffin, securing the contents of a man's hollow remains.

I was hooked by the beauty and sensual nature of women. This was obvious to anyone who was paying notice. Spirit knew it. I knew it. Reshma knew it. Hooked by beauty and skewered by a teacher who was intent on aligning me with something greater. What would be served up was, presumably, up to me.

Reshma was a woman of striking features. I was drawn to her, however, not by any primal directive, but through an odd familiarity, as well. I trusted her without really knowing her. She spoke of divine wisdom, and of a will greater than my own. She spoke of many things, things that made sense even if I did not understand why. And I was open to awakening to what she described as another set of senses, a higher set that was available to me, to us all. She called it "the library of the all-knowing." And I was into knowing all I could at this time.

My journey through the outer forms of meditation had me questioning whether the inner worlds were, in fact, even open for business. There I was, in a room lit only by the incandescent flame of a white candle (it had to be white, I was told), the smoke and adjoining scent of sandalwood looming in the air. I was to recant an invocation, then pierce into the flame, "stilling the mind and awakening the inner chambers of my being."

'Jeremy Braddock? Still his mind?' Cassandra giggled at that one.

This evening, I was determined to knock on a new door.

I only hoped there was someone there to answer.

My focus intensely on the candle before me, the flame began to grow. It flickered emphatically, as if calling me forward. The movement of the flame slowed to a hypnotic dance, beckoning me to leave behind my own form. Within the white light emerged a rainbow of colors, with one most prominent. I focused intently on the violet flame within the flame. Then blurred to my outer sight, I entered. I followed the purple flame as if guided by some force to a place within places, by way of a light within light. I watched myself as some other form of me, observing myself from above.

Then, I was off.

First, I was a tiger. Sprinting. Through a tunnel. The tunnel became a jungle. Running, toward an opening. The opening gave way to a cliff. The tiger to an eagle. I found myself traversing the skies, the planet even. Whisked away. Toward. And into a smoke-filled room.

I hovered above, undetected. The floors were covered with Turkish rugs, dark in color, burgundy. As with the thick drapes that outlined the window frames with such majesty. The cabinetry, old and dusty, acted as watch guard to the room and its inhabitants. Below me: a group of men with cigars. A liquor in their hands, the candlelight illuminating its golden color.

Then thrust through another portal. Through a beam of light once again, a construct of other light forms disguising themselves as separation. The light dispersed; with I left underneath a starlit sky, on a couch, with a strange man, surrounded by a language I did not understand.

Another portal. Another place. A park bench. Sitting there, chilled, warmed by...

And that was it. Back into the room I had never left. The candle reappearing. The flame united into one gentle burn, illuminating the four walls of my study.

Four walls never felt so emancipating.

Romance. The great dance. It appears to require of us that we master all its forms. Learn to tap around sensitive issues. Both lead and follow as we salsa together. Engage in a waltz at first, a tango eventually, until courageous enough to break free; so that we may someday move with the grace and ease of a ballerina across the floor of present life. At least this was the theory.

'Well you sure tapped around that one.' Arena was in a playful mood.

'Cute, dear. Yeah, not sure what I was thinking.'

'Thinking. Yes. There might have been some of that going on. I saw the pictures. I think I know what you were thinking.'

She smiled, as we continued our walk together along Crissy Field in the Presidio. Arena was in town for an art showing. Her work was coming along. She managed to avoid any serious distractions of a more romantic nature, choosing authenticity as her recipe. There was no clouding her judgment; no altering her course, her direction. She was clear, and steered clear of the minefields masked as romance.

I admired her, while mired in my own mischief.

'Romance has but many forms as it seeks to satisfy our appetite for existence,' I offered.

'This city certainly provides a romance of a different nature,' Arena responded, as she and I took in the majesty of man's creativity, arm in arm—armed with a friendship anchored in experiences together.

The fog severed the Golden Gate Bridge, creating two worlds within range of one another. The image played reminder to the dichotomy of the life here and the one promised us by so many, in so many forms. For when one tries to bring heaven to earth, it seems this world cannot give proper homage to it. As well, to take our humanness and rise above such seems to require a means to perfection that is beyond the reason of the mind.

'Are we trapped between two worlds?' I asked. 'Trapped between worlds, or are we like the bridge itself, a means to traverse the two worlds and transcend it all?'

'I like you when you're like this.'

'Like what? Alone and taking notice of it?'

'At *one*, and in peace with it.'

'Arena, dear. I am anything but peaceful.'

'How do you know? How do you know you're not full of it? Peace, that is,' she shared, smiling.

'Oh, I'm full of it. Piled higher than those kites, the

many pieces of me. A human puzzle...puzzled by being human. *Very* human.'

Arena laughed. I smiled. We let the conversation go for the moment. We watched the kites kiss the sky with but a string connecting them to the land below. Such a thin thread, the difference between anchoring here on Earth and venturing off into the ether. Such a frail connection between the lower realm and those above. With but a whisper so faint that the sound would vanish if one would lose attention for but a moment.

I broke the silence. 'How long do you think we have...I mean, to get it right?'

'How long? I think we have as much time as it takes.'

'Well, good thing. For I am certainly taking my time with this... whatever *this* is.'

I smiled. Arena joined me. She was always there to join me, when I needed adjoining.

The eucalyptus trees in the Presidio cast a tall shadow over all that existed beneath it. The wind carried with it a promise, allowing no one permanent stay in this temporary fixture. It was time for me to leave. It was time for many things to take form, take flight.

I was done taking my time. At least this was my thinking.

'Where are you heading?' the cab driver asked as I later made my way to SFO airport.

'Russia. I have some unfinished business there.'

I had unfinished business *period*.

What would you like from me?
*Partnership... a commitment... to Yourself
through knowing me better.*

4
RUSSIAN TO NOWHERE SPECIAL

'No matter where you go,
There you are.'
– Confucius

'Please ensure your seat belts are firmly fastened, as we'll be experiencing some turbulence.'

The voice was faint, barely discernible through the maze of my imagination, and the corridors of my unconscious.

I wonder if my seat belt was firmly fastened when I entered this world? I thought to myself.

The plane shook from the wind currents that were not entirely aligned with our current course and direction.

Turbulence, indeed! If only I had been inclined to take a

higher trajectory, an altitude that would allow me a smoother flight path this lifetime.

'We will be touching down shortly in Helsinki. For those of you who will continue with us to Saint Petersburg, please remain in the boarding area, as we have a short stopover for refueling, then will be on our way.'

The pain came without warning. It pierced my veiled heart, shooting through me as if releasing from bondage something lifetimes in the making. I was shaken, awakened, not by any turbulence caused by shifting winds or other outer forces, but by a longing unfamiliar that made my heart scream, my chest collapse in an unidentifiable anguish. And it apparently had something to do with the land beneath. Helsinki.

I closed my eyes. An image appeared. It was a woman. Her eyes, an ice blue. Her hair, golden. Her face, as if chiseled by Michelangelo himself. The setting was un-familiar. Clouds on earth. Earth in sky. Everything ap-peared upside down. It was Earth, but not an Earth familiar. And the woman... was my wife.

The image disappeared—the image, but not the pain.

What was this vision? This pain? Why here, now? The inquisition of the mind gave way to an overwhelming feeling that invaded my body. My stomach muscles tensed, as if preparing for a gut wrenching punch. A surge of energy emanated from my inner chambers, as if the cries of joy and sorrow collided within every cell of my construct. I struggled to find my next breath. I struggled further for an explanation. Was there something sacred to this land beneath? Maybe I was merely experiencing an understandable anxiety as I loomed ever closer to my destination, and to the destiny of living up to the expectations of another—mainly my father.

Shaken again. This time, it was accompanied by the movement of the plane itself as we descended, wheels extended, with every intention of landing, safely. I could feel each vibratory note, each sensation within my body. I closed my eyes, but not my mind nor my memory. I began the inner chant I had learned from Reshma. Calling forth whatever light was available, I moved into what was either a deep contemplation or a momentary sleep (sometimes the difference was hardly discernible).

The pain would remain until we created distance between Helsinki and ourselves. My heart returned to old form.

Perhaps an older form than one lifetime could explain.

We arrived in Saint Petersburg. I made my way through the terminal and into the baggage claim area. Pulkovo Airport was run-down, in need of new paint and perhaps a new image. Yet beyond the need for a facelift, there was an air of promise, one nearly a century in the making. There was also the lingering memory of the pain experienced back in Helsinki.

Three men, wise in the methods and customs of their

land, awaited me. While there was no star that guided them—at least none I was aware of—we all knew of the inherent nativity of this first encounter, and of the ensuing trust that would be required. There was always the matter of trust.

Arkady was the first to speak. A slender man of perhaps six feet and change, his silver hair and Hollywood looks were captivating, and his demeanor effective. His gestures were those of optimism, a fellow bridge builder who understood the opportunity associated with change itself. Behind him were those who would pale in comparison both in sight and insight. Vladimir and Viktor struggled to keep pace with their colleague since their early days together at the Russian Academy of Sciences.

'Welcome, Mr. Braddock. It is an honor to have you here in our country,' Arkady offered.

'Thank you. I'm happy to be here.'

'We look forward to our joint collaboration,' Arkady responded. He took notice of my features. 'You know, you look just like your father. He was a good man. He would be happy to know you came here to finish what he started.'

I just smiled, in part to conceal the ordeal going on within the mind. Why was I here precisely? And what role was I to play? Perhaps a bridge. To where, none of us knew for certain. I could only hope that the universe in its infinite wisdom had set the table properly.

I was put up at the Hotel Astoria. The glamour and alluring nature of this historic building sat in stark contrast to the many sights experienced on the ride over. *Glasnost* had arrived. Poverty was readily apparent. The lines were a hundred deep for what Arkady explained was a mere loaf of stale bread. The roads were laced with potholes, an aged aftereffect of an arms race that left everyone "out in the cold."

As we entered the hotel, the windows of the revolving door provided a weathered reflection of an elder woman in devastation, while playing grand divider for two worlds whose fates were inescapable for those caught between what was, is and what was yet to be. The door spun, as if capturing the movement of a society in flux. My feelings of guilt as we entered the lavish lobby of the hotel were displaced by the vision of a most godly creation—perhaps another test and testament to my search for love amid the oscillating definition that plagued me so.

From the moment I first lay eyes upon her, I was in trouble. Activating the memories of lust camouflaged perhaps as love once again, I found in Natasha that same draw that has apparently played me like a finely-tuned instrument for my systematic return to this world. The latest folly came in the form of a woman whose natural features were the link to my most natural disaster. For I was forever in love with the idea of love, and any opportunity to taste the pleasures of such would lure me in as with a baited fish fixated on its next meal, and the consuming fate that awaited.

'May I help you, sir?' Natasha asked as though sensing

my inner needs to be fulfilled. Of course, she was working the reception desk at the hotel, with her query being nothing more than the appropriate gesture required of her employment. My imagination made certain to ignore such inconvenient details.

'Yes, I'm checking in.' (More like checking *out*.)

Natasha was a model representation of those women whose beauty is only trumped by the genuine modesty of such exquisite nature. Her eyes were velvet brown. Her face, a perfect balance of fullness and definition, tempered with a softness that spoke to the gentle nature of a mother's loving amid this hardened land and times. She was beautiful, yes. Yet, it was the perceived manner and quite humble nature by which she saw and thus carried herself that made Natasha most attractive. This I picked up immediately.

Natasha meticulously took care of the details of my room. I took notice of the details of her, conspiring from within on just how to move this "relationship" along.

'Will there be anything else?'

Yes, of course. Candlelight, romance, a gentle unveiling in accordance with the movement of two, as one. There is so much more.

'No, thank you.'

Coward, I thought, as I planned my exit. My next thought was of Sebastien. My next action…

'Sorry. One more thing… have dinner with me.' The words came forward before my mind had time to react.

She just smiled.

The pause was only for an eternity.

'Okay. Meet me at Palkin at eight o'clock. I will make the arrangements.'

I agreed, and made my exit before she had a chance to reconsider. The elevator took my body up to my floor. There, we met up with my heart which had leapt ahead ten stories. My heart was in dance—a familiar dance. It was the dance of opportunity, accompanied by a melody; a melody that spoke to possibility. The other sound was merely the knock at the door.

'Mr. Braddock. You have message.'

I opened the door to find a young bellman dressed in a uniform that more closely resembled the outfit donned by the flying monkeys in *The Wizard of Oz*. He handed me an envelope. I reached into my pocket while my mind struggled to regain control. A proper tip? Unable to do the math in my head, I settled on overtipping (likely by some insane amount). After all, it was the least I could do for the hotel staff that had offered me so much in return already.

The porter left, smiling. I opened the correspondence and read:

"Mr. Braddock. Your attendance is requested by Dr. Petrovsky at the State Institute tomorrow morning at ten o'clock. We will meet you in the lobby at 9:15. Dr. Petrovsky looks forward to your visit."

The message was basic. My feelings that followed, unexpected.

I walked over to the window, pulled back the curtains, looked out upon the dampened street, and felt a nervous anxiety. The source of this feeling was clear. The shadow of my father was vast, one that consumed my sisters, my brother, and I, along with pretty much everyone else within his net of influence. I had felt inadequate when in the presence of my father, and this feeling usually was displaced by anger, frustration. I accepted this project as not simply a promise made to a father—that would have been noble—but as an opportunity to prove my value to myself, a rapidly decreasing value as I entertained the possibility that I may actually fail, and thus have failed him in some manner. The basis for this fear was not rooted in anything tangible. I had succeeded in my career, at least to date. Yet nevertheless, the fear of failure waited just beyond the corridor of my comfort zone.

There was only one way to handle this feeling. One way for me, that was.

'Another beverage, sir?'

Natasha and I enjoyed the ritual unveiling of one another over dinner, and the appropriate concoction for stirring the mind, and stilling the memory.

'Another Standard, please, for the lady and me. Straight up.'

The waiter obliged, one of many servicing the table. Palkin was an old, Russian-style restaurant with a Bohemian feel to it. The setting was a perfect complement to the feeling that was emerging from my loins with each dip into the vodka pool.

The conversation was limited by language, but the meaning was captured through the gestures of body, and through a language of the heart available to each. Natasha spoke of her life. I listened. I spoke of my journey. She smiled. Our higher selves were locked in a continuation of what seemed an ageless knowing. Our conscious selves stumbling through the barriers of mind and language. Our most basic selves holding hands, twirling around like two lovesick teenagers. All conversations blending into one. She reached over and caressed my hand with her own, extending her long, thin fingers in invitation. The many levels of me met with her own, awakened to the connection that was her intention—mine, as well. Or perhaps this was simply another version of the story I would tell myself when graced with such beauty, and limited by the nature of my own free choice.

'Shall we walk?' Natasha offered.

A casual walk to follow a *causal* dinner. Not only good for the digestion, but even better for the continued ingestion of another. We gathered our belongings and were off.

Taking little notice of the chilling details, Natasha and I left the creature comforts offered from within and stepped out into the frigid Russian night. We walked with pace and eventually found our way to Alexander Garden. The park was blanketed by a recent snowfall, leaving all but the reflective streetlights hidden from view. A brief glimpse into the reality of our rather dangerous saunter—given the mafia and its early control over this freshly-christened marketplace—gave way to my lust for *lust*. Lust by any other name would be merely concealing such for love itself. And at this stage, love was an elusive prize indeed.

We can leave that 'til tomorrow, I thought, without remorse.

Natasha and I proceeded along the hidden path, feet crunching amid the fresh snow pack, invigorated by the chilled air and warming company. I was taken in by the feel of her arm within my own. I enjoyed knowing that I could play guide and support for another; that she would trust me so; that I was of some value to someone. It made me feel good. It made me feel needed. It made me feel...

Lighter!

Lighter than my 180-pound frame would first suggest, as in one swift action I was planted on an unassuming park bench by my determined companion.

Natasha moved with the precision of a drunken sailor, as she navigated my winter wear. She proceeded to loosen my tie, unbuttoned my shirt, and run her chilled hands up my chest before I could catch my next breath. I provided the same in return, assuming her intention for a mutual reward.

In one fluid motion, Natasha straddled me, undressed me, exposed herself, and thrust me inside her. I was swallowed whole by this Russian princess, as if universe upon universe collapsed within this singular moment. Our heated exchange gave way to a steamy escapade that lasted for hours within minutes, the kindling of a flame set ablaze at first gaze. Head cocked back, I was offered a glimpse of heaven while taking in the crisp April air; the skies lit with a million stars; my view distorted by our joint exhale into the night.

Was I dreaming? Did the near liter of vodka shared finally make its way through the capillaries and into the container that housed my brain? Would I awaken to a truth not nearly as tantalizing as the woman here before me (actually, *above* me)?

She was real. I was real. It was real. All of it. Her creamy breasts, hardened nipples, concealing a heartbeat raised by our joint discovery. I moved beyond her outer beauty and into her pure essence, a rhythm and pace that would yield but a moment of ecstasy amid a frigid backdrop, and most public place.

Through a brief glance at love in the raw, Natasha and I entered the realm where thought gives way to form, transformed into another time and place through an odd familiarity. It felt neither wrong nor entirely right—a duality of fullness and emptiness. Joining perhaps in the spirit of Catherine the Great as yet another member of the league of lonesome lovers, the scene disrobed both my divinity and humanity, playing worthy backdrop to the most opportune of occasions for a rather chilling revelation. The euphoria experienced served as a temporary tonic for a more permanent pain. I gazed beyond the beauty before me and into the starry eyes of the universe, twinkling in such fashion as if to say with a wink and a smile:

'*Still looking for love in all the wrong places, dearest Jeremy.*'

My victory served as yet another defeat.

'You are sad. Was I not good?' Natasha was left confused by a face that could not conceal the ordeal within.

'No. No. No. I mean, yes. *Da.* You were amazing. *It* was amazing,' I stumbled through the most basic of English vernacular, when words fall short of their intended end. 'Perhaps I am just a bit more affected by the alcohol than I thought.'

My eyes could not conceal a deeper sorrow. It was not Natasha. It was never the "Natashas." It was me. It was my irreconcilable thirst for whatever was driving me, while leaving me empty. I did not understand the nature of this emptiness. Natasha offered more than enough to satisfy the cravings of both body and mind. I could feel this in her. She was warm, loving, passionate. Her eyes were caring, giving, embracing. There was simply no room for such within the heart of the distracted, the disenchanted. My disenchantment was with me. It always was.

Natasha did not pursue further what was going on inside me. Perhaps it was her limited vocabulary that kept her from delving deeper into the moment. Or possibly it is that part in each of us that finds it easier to live within our own fantasies than through another's realities.

She offered me everything. I gave in return, but had nothing really to offer.

Cool was the air. Chilling, the reality. I wanted for love.

She wanted for love. We settled for this.

After sharing in the silence post-event that often reveals to us our more naked form, I escorted Natasha back to her place via taxi. I was joined as well by the many thoughts that invaded the palace of a more preferred, more contented state. With her head upon my shoulder, her eyes bidding adieu to our evening's affair, I wrestled with a dichotomy of dialogue within.

'Okay, Jeremy, what's the point? So we scored another beauty only to find the beast within growing ever stronger. Longing for something, we are clearly something else indeed!'

'Oh, stop all this self-judgment,' the lesser side of me commanded. 'Are we not having fun? Is this not life being lived? Lighten up!'

'Lighten up. A good direction, if we would choose such a course. I mean, do we even know where we are? We've been driving for what seems like an eternity, with the lights of the city no longer available to us. Another foolish folly. Another brush with the bonfire.'

We arrived. I swung around to her side of the taxi, opened the door, and walked her to her flat. As Natasha and I said our goodbyes, intoxicated with the aftereffects of an all-consuming evening void of the finer qualities that might otherwise accompany such expression, I could not help but notice the modesty of her surroundings. The apartment building was pre-modern, built for efficiency, an amalgamation of concrete with a spattering of windows so as to provide a distinction between a housing complex and a military bunker. Aesthetic beauty was an unnecessary evil during the old days.

Natasha had shared with me the story of her mother's hardship, and a father's early exit through one too many visits to the bottom of a bottle. Her brother was lost in the Soviet Afghan campaign—along with a part of the country's soul— leaving her to support what remained as the duty of a daughter who had been graced with the courage of a mother throughout her upbringing. Natasha, unlike so many who were enticed to use their beauty as means through prostitution, chose instead a life of hardship in maintaining a dignity, an integrity, founded in the actions of a mother who sacrificed for the simple yet unconditional love of a daughter.

It was not fair. The life conceived by birth left each of us to our own. Natasha was left to struggle. In me, perhaps, she saw a way out. Little did she know of my own struggles. I was looking for a way out, as well. Perhaps the difference was she could see her way through, while I was still scrambling for the flashlight.

And the moment we shared, under the illumination of a few scattered streetlamps that reflected truth amid the blanket of white? Yes, it was love in some distorted form, but not the love I sought. I doubt, as well, it was the one she sought. Perhaps the only difference lay in the language spoken, and in the meaning which escaped me still.

Whatever it was I was searching for, clearly I was no

closer to the truth.

I stared out the frosted window of the taxi, confused and conflicted, filled with a fleeting gratitude and a ghostly presence of pervading ignorance. Understanding. Misunderstanding. Another missed opportunity for a greater under-standing of the person before me; the person that was me; and of a world suited for more questions than answers.

I drifted off.

I was simply too tired to look any further.

'Jeremy, today we will go to Institute, and have lunch with the good doctor. Then we will take train to Gus-Khrustalny, where the factory is,' Arkady shared as we traveled by way of a black sedan I suspected was a former KGB car, reassigned to spy on the new enemy: the Western capitalist.

'Good. I've heard much about Dr. Petrovsky. I look forward to our visit.'

Arkady just smiled. A peculiar smile indeed. Like the one offered when they know much more than you would ever care to know—and likely ever will. I would have pursued this further, but I was battling a hangover that came with the requisite absolutions that often follow an evening like the last. I stopped short of promising never again to put myself in the situation of landing on a park bench with a beautiful Russian woman. I knew my limitations as well as my weaknesses—more like addictions. More important, I knew that *They* knew.

I gazed out the window, feeling a bit like James Bond. The setting, the girl, the mysterious scientist that awaited, as we dashed across the city in our KGB transport. Perhaps it was all a grand set up, and I was "the mark." Perhaps this was true of my life in general.

I had stopped by the desk to say goodbye to Natasha, but she was off today. What was the point anyway? I knew that nothing whole could come from the piecing together of broken parts. I did not know, could not possibly know, if she was broken. But I knew I was, and that was all I needed to know.

I could fool the world, and I did. I could not fool myself, and I did try.

Withholding any further self-judgments for the moment, we arrived at our destination. I spent the morning meeting with several scientists—and future capitalists—none more prominent than Dr. Petrovsky. He was the head of research for the State Institute for Fine Mechanics and Optics. As first impressions go, he also moonlighted as a character out of a *Rocky and Bullwinkle* episode.

Petrovsky's eyebrows had not seen the sharp end of a pair of shears in years. His body was built like a Stalin tank. His demeanor was rough, with a gait and purpose that covered decades of committed service without question of authority. His hands were thick, calloused by a hardened life like many a fellow comrade. A throwback to the old way, he would pierce your eyes with guarded suspicion, calculating your every word and action.

Yet the defining characteristic of Dr. Petrovsky came from the most unlikely of sources—his laugh. Petrovsky had a booming howl that filled the room and adjacent hallways, often followed with but two words—as he would have you believe, the *only* two words he understood in the English language.

'So good. So good.'

Precisely what was "so good" was a mystery to me, as he would offer up this appreciation at any moment, under any circumstance, without notice or pre-empting of any kind. It was as if Petrovsky was viewing life through his own choice kaleidoscope, measuring the colors and relative circumference of each shape and image, without a hint of relativity to the conversation of the moment. It was his show, after all, and he could applaud whenever he felt compelled to do so.

Of course, we would all join in. Something to do with the mix of new company, new possibilities, and an age-old cognac whose own mission was to conceal the bottom of the glass.

'You like?' Dr. Petrovsky inquired, as I consumed black caviar on a slice of stale bread, with a thick slab of butter in between.

'It's good, thank you.'

Actually, I despised it, especially the butter that conjured up haunting memories of my sister and her freakish habit of eating it by the bar.

'Ah, good. So good!'

'So later we will take train to Moscow; then on to factory,' Arkady said. 'Dr. Petrovsky will join us, along with Vladimir and Izabella.'

Izabella was our translator. Fresh out of university, she had a degree in economics, which, of course, qualified her to be a translator at minimum pay under this new era of prosperity through austerity in Russia.

'It is short trip,' Vladimir added.

Izabella just smiled. She knew what was meant by a "short trip" in Russian terms. She was young. She had a sweet smile. And I was clearly screwed up. My attention to such details was an addiction to love in some manner. But not the love I sought. This was certain. How to tame it was not.

The server came up to our table, leaned over and asked Arkady a question. He responded in a firm but understanding manner. She quickly walked away.

'Arkady, what was that woman discussing with you?'

'She has a brother. Her brother needs work. She said he is a good worker, an educated man. I told her I have nothing for him.'

'It must have taken a lot for her to come up to you like that, during our meal.'

'People are swallowing their pride here every day.'

'At least then they have *something* to eat,' Vladimir chimed in.

It was this sort of black humor—along with inexpensive vodka to wash it down—that served in tempering the mind and stilling the heart which yearned for greater days for this in transition nation.

After lunch, we boarded the train. It would take until the following morning to arrive at our destination—a "short trip" by some measures. Gus-Khrustalny was located about sixty kilometers southeast of Vladimir, one of the ancient capitals of Russia. Founded in the mid-eighteenth century, the town carried the honor of being one of the first centers for the glass industry in the country, once serving the Tsar's Court and the Shah of Iran with fine crystal. We disembarked and made our way straight to the factory.

The plant manager met us at the door. He was of average size, weathered beyond his years, with forearms like a sailor. His grip was as with so many others I met in Russia—firm as a vice, crushing to any whom came ill prepared.

The plant manager escorted us throughout the building, going through every detail of production through our hired translator. His words faded as I took notice of those taking notice of me. The men handling the raw material, and machinery. The women, the finished product, the detailing. I watched as one woman was blowing raw glass into the most stunning arrangement, working the shapes like a fine craftsman, polishing up any rough edges. The symbolism did not escape me. Raw material. Finished product. And the level of detail required in making it so.

The warmth that was offered through the weathered eyes of the workers bridged any doubt that may have existed as to our kinship. I was a foreigner, but so were they. Displaced from a system and philosophy that was life here for nearly a century, they were foreign to this new world that was to become their own, in some form or another. Separated only by the sight of our own breath as it made contact with sub-freezing conditions *inside* the plant, we were to begin a journey together in bridging two worlds with one common goal. All involved were counting on all involved to make it so. The toothless smile granted by an aged woman with a tattered broom in her hands gave me hope.

That evening at dinner, I sat with Petrovsky and the others, enjoying the celebration that followed the joint agreement signed earlier, while challenged within to solve the puzzle of a man who was layers deeper than what he revealed. I thought of my father. His business here finished. And here I was, still living the life in some form that was his to live. I came to Russia for one reason—his reason—yet was uncovering a few gems that were solely for me.

Arkady reached over to catch my ear in the moment.

'*Time stays long enough for anyone who will use it,*' recanting in near-perfect English the words once spoken by the "Renaissance Man" himself, the master Leonardo da Vinci.

Arkady went on to share how da Vinci was correct. Time so often proves either ally or foe, due to our own use of it, and the willingness to accept the change that accompanies it. For within the change lies the opportunity, he added, and we get as many chances as we need to awaken to the greater understanding that is available to us all.

Understanding. Arkady understood. He could see the moment before us.

'We have sat in silence for nearly seventy years, awaiting the chance to see the world in a different light,' he confided. 'We are a proud people. It will take some time.' Arkady glanced in Dr. Petrovsky's direction. 'Some of us only want to know one way, some a better way. Whether today or tomorrow, we will all get there... in time.'

I might as well have been breaking bread with Leonardo himself. For this is what perhaps he was offering us nearly five hundred years ago; a glimpse, into not only ideas and concepts that were centuries ahead of his time, but into a greater knowing that some divine presence is available to us anytime, anywhere. The idea was attractive enough. Now, how to go about proving its validity?

Clearly, I had spent a few too many hours with the scientists, I thought, as I sat there at the table—in silence—taking in all, setting and people alike, as the observer. Here I was, sharing cognac and conversation with my new Russian colleagues, in an antiquated parlor house. The thick curtains were stained and musty. The meal, a grand gesture in its modesty. The inquiry of eyes a sign of new—if not yet trusted—times.

The curtains. They looked familiar. The setting, like I

had been here before. The rugs were typical of what you would expect, the last remnants of excessiveness—likely from Turkey.

That's it! The Turkish rugs. The thick burgundy drapes. The men. The cognac. The cigar smoke. I had seen this before. *All* of this. Back in Sausalito, the night of that meditation. I was hovering above, but clearly remembered the details. But how could this be?

The group carried on. So did I—inside myself.

'Okay, universe, explain. A clue... something. A glance, at least, at what is going on. And give it to me like I was a man of the mind. Logic works best here.'

The clanging of glasses. The laughter. The joy in the room, deafening. If there were a voice inside, wisdom to be shared, it was certainly drowned out by the chorus of the crowd surrounding me. There was little difference in the manner of men, choice of conversation, and general character of these new comrades of mine. All were one in the moment, leaving behind generations of germination, a systematic poisoning of the minds that left us all sick and tired. Sick and tired.

"When you're sick and tired of being tired and sick, that's when change happens."

I recalled the words that blazed a path across my consciousness back in Los Angeles. I wanted answers. I wanted answers but was unsure still of the questions themselves.

'So good. So good, is it not?' Petrovsky intervened,

followed by his booming laugh that captured the moment, and attention of all around the table.

So good. Okay, I give. What precisely is "so good?" I thought as I looked around the room. Everyone was laughing. None of them had anything but a hard life, yet everyone was laughing. They weren't consumed by their self-misery. They weren't floored by their own fears, doubts or uncertainties. They weren't plagued by their current poverty. They were drunk, but not *that* drunk. No denial here; just acceptance. Through decades of deprivation, over nearly a century of service to a State in a not so pleasant state, the Russian people had adapted and evolved; accepting their lives; finding ways of seeing their destitution as "so good."

It wasn't good. It wasn't even fair. But it was accepted.

Then, it clicked. When Dr. Petrovsky would utter his magic words, "So good. So good," he was really saying, "It is what it is." Total surrender to the situation, to the moment. Total acceptance. It was more than just a technique to survive. It was a pathway to thrive.

"Let go, and let God," Reshma would say. It was easy for one to say it. The words themselves were easy. The *doing* was more difficult—more difficult indeed.

I turned to Dr. Petrovsky, who was just looking at me as if I had awakened to an answer.

'Dr. Petrovsky, you are a man of few words... but with great meaning.'

The good doctor smiled. He may have even understood.

Again, he offered his glass to my own. I toasted him as I toasted whatever higher power was directing this moment, rehearsed by the light of one candled evening's past, to be played out upon the physical through the main character that is me. It had to be so.

So good.

So good indeed.

———

I made my way to the airport once again. Images flashed over the car window fogged over by my breath. The white birch trees that lined the street provided a flicker across the screen of my mind, like an old motion picture exposing each new frame and reference.

The mix of Byzantine and Neoclassical architecture of old Russia playing backdrop to a new Nike ad in bold display.

A street musician strumming Stravinsky, unbeknownst to the kid with the new Walkman strapped soundly to his ears.

Young men on their way to work, passing young ladies on their way home, an evening's wages in their purse for deeds done, what had to be done.

An aged woman and timeless wisdom, being aided across the street by a young, well-dressed banker in a bit of a hurry, yet not too much so to lend a hand to a generation that gave so much more.

Change. A reality for every living creature on this

planet; and the target of the great resistance itself.

Accompanied by hope. For a new way, a better way.

My fellow comrades here in Russia had hope. They knew not of what the future had in store for them, but the past was past, and that was certain. I could only hope the same was true for me.

I took to the skies yet again, reminded by our purser to 'make sure all handheld devices remained in the switched-off position until we arrived safely at our next destination.'

Our next destination.

As with Arkady, Petrovsky, and the rest, I had little insight as to my next destination. I sat there wondering as I made eye contact with a little girl of maybe seven years, studying my every feature before shifting her attention to the family of Russian nesting dolls on her lap. Did it really matter, our next destination? For hidden within our mapped-out version of our life as we saw it—or wished it to be—was life as it was.

The little girl was meticulous, as she uncovered each new doll within the one before. Her facial expression revealed a clear determination to get to that which lay within. Doll after doll, she uncovered the gift within the gift. Until all that was left was the one inside.

I was unraveling my own mystery, step by step, given plenty of clues yet still clueless as to where this was taking me—or when I might arrive at *my* destination. I was on a treasure hunt for the elusive, be it love or some other concoction that must be satisfied through a thirst years in the making—lifetimes maybe.

I drifted off. My mind drifted on.

I found myself in a hospital room—my father's hospital room. The room was cold; the walls painted with a sterile off-white color that was altogether off-putting for one who felt imprisoned within the inevitability of my own mortality.

I stirred within the confines of my seat, and from the more disturbing elements of this defining memory.

My father, the rock of the family (my mother was "the glue"), was dying. I was at his bedside. The rest of the family had retreated for the moment. My father was also in retreat, a mere whisper of the man I had come to respect as well as fear. There, within the confines of his room, with no prospect for the impossible, was just he, and I. There were few words at first, with a mere ocean of feelings awaiting the opportunity to pour through. The words that followed took me by surprise.

'Kid, I'm afraid,' my father whispered, fragile in form, cloaked in a thin gown and ever-thinning waistline. 'I no longer have the strength to fight this, but am so scared of what lies ahead. I want to believe, in something… *anything*. I just don't know.'

My father, afraid? A moment that shook me to the core, the pillar of the indestructible showing its cracks, revealing his own humanity, his vulnerability. I was calculating with my response.

'Dad, you have nothing to fear.'

This I wanted to believe. For whatever the truth was, I hoped the rewards would be just, especially for those who have given so that others may know a better life. And my father was such a man, even through his own humanity.

I looked into his eyes, and gave him what he was looking for. 'Dad, it's okay. It's okay to leave... it's okay. I understand.'

He smiled, took my hand. I held it tightly. And with this, I transferred a lifetime of gratitude to his awaiting heart.

The following week I sat once again by his bedside—at his home, this time—witnessing the humility we must endure as we give back what we have accrued, and give over to this "unknown." This time, what I saw in my father was a peace; a peace that had eluded him until this moment. He reached over to attend to me through another whispered message.

'I've seen the signs. All of them. Like road signs along the highway... pointing... home.'

I sat there, disturbed by his objectivity, in awe of his clarity. He continued.

'Like pieces of a puzzle. I picked them up, all of them. One by one. They formed a matrix. And the picture... beautiful. More than beautiful.'

I knew that he knew what I did not.

It was only on the day of his passing that I had come to know another great discovery about my father. His favorite song was "Somewhere over the Rainbow." On the day of his passing a blue bird foreign to the region sat upon the windowsill that provided the final portraits for my father's fading eyes. If that were not enough to reveal the true power of the universe to create in concert with its own creation, two days after his funeral a double rainbow with a vividness of color that could only have found its origin within the celestial studio of the universe itself sat majestically over the property of my parents—this, on Thanksgiving Day.

Our plane broke through the clouds and into the space where the light could no longer be denied. It is a new world when the kingdom of clouds is below us, the power of the possible before us.

A faint rainbow formed as it danced with the moisture on the window beside me.

A warming reminder of what remained before me.

Somewhere.

I find sadness in not knowing.
There is joy within all sadness… like sunshine beyond all clouds.

5
HEAVEN IN HELSINKI

Hell...
Is but Heaven in waiting

I had been tortured for quite some time with the thought of returning to Helsinki. My life, satisfying in some manner, lacked in ways undetectable to my mind and outer senses. Clearly there was something amiss. Clearly there was more to be unveiled. Clearly I had no idea what that may possibly be. But Helsinki held the answer. This I did know on some level where knowing found a proper home.

I knew, as well, that what fueled my fancy and fed my past love interests no longer served me—if it ever had. My search was now for the answers, the answers to my questions. I knew not where these answers may take me, but I was certain a more awakened version of me was at the other end of my journey, my rainbow.

One day, I awakened with the courage to know what I did not.

'I'm going to Finland,' I blurted, as if the words were governed by some secret pact made between my higher self and basic me, bypassing the mind completely.

'You're going where?'

'Finland. Helsinki.'

'Finland? What's in Finland?' Nick was confused, if not entirely captivated.

'I'm... I'm not sure. But I have to go.'

Something was lined up inside. There were answers there, clues at least, to what it was I was searching for. I had continued to replay the experience I had while on my way to Russia. It had set in motion what my mind could neither understand nor circumvent. It was a gut feeling, one I had no choice but to follow.

'Want some company?' he asked, sensing a pending adventure.

I thought about it for a moment. It would be nice to have a good friend along. And Nick certainly fit the criteria. He would be an asset on any journey to the more familiar.

I paused further.

I had no idea what was on the other side of such an impulsive decision. Yet, this particular journey had a quality about it that spoke to a place of calm inside me.

'No. No, this one I have to do on my own.'

The answer seemed to settle in with Nick with little room for discussion. He tipped his glass in my direction.

'Well, then, off you go. To whatever it is you seek, may you find it or something greater.'

I would be happy with simply something else.

The airplane was a transport. It took my body where my mind wanted to go. My meditations and deeper contemplations transported me to a place where my mind could travel but was no longer in charge. My mind did not enjoy this. It had no choice in the matter—except in how to experience it. It came along for the journey. It came along, kicking and screaming.

Thoughts began to pass across the screen of my consciousness—faces, too—like clouds across an otherwise clear sky.

There was Confucius. Then Buddha. Sir Isaac Newton. And a lady, on a horse, leading men, her armor glistening in the sunlight, stained by the blood from the shadows of man's lesser deeds.

My thoughts shifted to the journey itself, to Finland, to chase a feeling. Madness, really. The image of my father appeared. Strong in point, undeterred. Ruthless, impeccable—a nightmare to those who were not. A fine line drawn between creative brilliance and madness itself.

'*Duly noted. For I must concede, I can calculate the motions of the heavenly bodies, but not the madness of people.'*

Reappearing on the screen of my inner consciousness was the face of Newton, and a symphony of words repeated.

'I can calculate the motions of the heavenly bodies, but not the madness of people.'

Good to know even the most brilliant were left confused with the interactions of us all, once God placed flesh around something so heavenly as soul. Is it possible Newton's principles of mathematics carried far beyond certain relativities, and into the realities of the true human dilemma? This I thought as I gazed out the window of an airplane that defied gravity in its own. I suppose the laws of gravity apply to people, civilizations as well, that have run their course and no longer serve the higher end and intention. What goes up must come down, eventually. Right, Sir Isaac?

'It is the Law for all things in nature.'

Our plane descended.

I wasn't quite certain precisely who or what was speaking with me as I opened this channel through meditation. Madness with a voice, perhaps. The only thing I knew was it was wiser than I, and seemingly worthy of my attention. And the appearance of these timely masters through a myriad of media did not go unnoticed. The fact that I was somewhat of a "closet historian" helped in my recognition of the source of the words, if not the source of the voice.

I opened my eyes to find a Finnish woman of maybe forty standing next to me, staring. Did she hear the voice? Perhaps she was just interested in *me* in some manner. I had heard Finns have difficulty expressing their true feelings.

'Sir!' Spoken in English with a hardened accent, the lady continued, 'I would like to leave, sir.'

I looked around. There was no one to be found. The plane was empty. And I was blocking her exit. Clearly I had been "out" for much longer than I thought. I apologized in English, as there were no words I was aware of for such in the Finnish language.

We deplaned. As I made my way across the parquet floor of the terminal, I felt the deafening sound of—silence. A hint in the form of a piercing anxiety that left me breathless during my last brush with this country still remained in the archives of my mind. It was accompanied by a faint tremor in my awakening heart. There was something new going on inside me, something stirring from within. It was as if each cell was being ignited, reminded perhaps.

It was different. It was re-sounding. It was *in* me but not entirely *of* me.

I knew very little of what was going on, yet knew this: I was no longer moved by the pedestrian nature of life. My soul—or what I thought to be such—had been shaken if not awakened by the nature of a "Dark Continent" that had projected light, if for but a moment; an illumination of a life filled yet unfulfilled; and of a promise of something greater.

And the pursuit of something greater had taken me from an African adventure, on a journey through Russia (after a slight detour on life's dance floor), and brought me here, to Helsinki; to the singular moment of now.

The airport was eerily quiet given the number of people moving about, most in rectangular spectacles as if in geometric solidarity with the triangulation of dark winters, passion for literature, and genetic commonality. The silence was piercing to one accustomed to the decibel level of a society where one speaks merely to avoid the awkward moment where no words may be found. Finland offered the gift of peace from the outset. And there were more presents awaiting this lad who finally set foot upon the soil that Finns take pride in as shared space with *Santa* himself. At least I hoped there were.

I made my way to the Hotel Kämp. Situated along Esplanadi Park in the center of the city, the hotel provided a blend of storied history with modern times. It was regal. It was refined. It was everything I was not. I swung open the tall windows of my suite, inviting in the fresh breeze and mid-summer light. The room overlooked a park filled with Finns enjoying the brief reprieve from the long, dark winters of the region. Most were enjoying a bit of ice cream, as well; the only food proper to eat while on the move. I moved to Market Square. I feasted on a selection of organic berries sourced from the Finnish countryside, as well as on the city in all its splendor.

Awakened. From the Great White Church at Senate

Square to its gothic brother of Russian Orthodox origin, Helsinki awakened me to a more peaceful side of myself. I ventured out along the sea toward Kaivopuisto Park. The sea was turbulent. The skies moved at a pace most frantic. Yet within me was a calm unfamiliar as it was inviting.

I nestled in at Café Ursula, set along the embankment built to keep the gulf waters at bay. I tuned out the world around me. The land was new, unfamiliar. The people were strange, unexpected. The sounds, undetected. I found sanctuary amid the sounds my mind could not attach itself to, a secret language I did not understand. With nothing to preoccupy it, my mind had no choice but to take a break. And in this moment—a rare moment indeed—my heart was given access to the stage. I took in all that surrounded me, as if it were one with me.

The scent of smoked salmon as it teased the nostrils, and tantalized the taste buds.

The dress and manner of an elder woman who paid attention to the details of common dignity.

A young couple attending to their younger daughter, adorned in a reindeer hat (odd for this time of year); fresh chocolate painted across her angelic face.

The seagulls engaged in a battle to remain in place amid a strong breeze that danced with the surf below.

The peace was a perfect remedy for a man who was seeking such. The stillness, received with gratitude for whatever orchestrates such defining moments.

I felt at home with the heavens.

The following morning, I agreed to meet up with an old acquaintance. It was a warm summer's day—not by any means a given in Finland. With the exception of a few scattered clouds, the skies were defined by a deep shade of blue. The weather divas provided the perfect backdrop for gathering with good friends.

I had met Mikko a few years back, during a seminar we attended in Geneva. Mikko was not your average Finn. His parents by their own nature provided a unique combination of Finnish and Greek upbringing, a sort of meeting of stoicism with the festival of hearts. Bold, brash and begging for adventure, he was a rather odd fit for the reserved ways of a people whose history was wrought with subservience to both Swede and Russian domination. We shared a passion for history, philosophy—and for women. Mikko embraced me from the start as a brother.

'Hey, brother. I told Katariina to bring some of her girlfriends along,' Mikko shared, followed by his boyish grin that usually indicated he was up to something.

Katariina was his wife. I had the good fortune of meeting her during Mikko and my destined union in Geneva. She was as generous by nature as she was gentle to the eye. She was also a brilliant young doctor.

11:11 on the watch. Everything was pointing up. Good sign, as shared once by Arena. The angels were near.

'Ah, here they come now.'

The mid-morning sun concealed the contents, the details of our new arrivals. Her silhouette joined with Katariina's. I squinted in an attempt to separate the elements of light that both held and withheld in the same the object of my fascination. A faint violet hue graced her entrance. There was an attitude with her walk, a way with her; a confidence in who she was. There was also a familiarity that only my heart could understand. The separation evaporated. I was offered a better view of *her*.

Her eyes, concealed by a pair of shades, left me in wait. Her hair, a dirty blonde, served as the only detail that could be described in a manner as not cleansed by the heavens themselves. Her legs, long, thin, inviting, were exposed through a conspiracy of the nature gods by way of a sultry Finnish morning.

It was her lips, however, that demanded my attention in the moment. She took great care in ensuring such. Lush, plumped to perfection by the gods each evening, these lips would smack the air in gratitude as the artist performed her masterpiece to her reflection. Edges "penciled" as if sketching the work to be created, she would complete the performance with a touch of gloss, as the spider does the last weavings of her web to lure and procure her prey.

One could only pray for such a moment.

'Jeremy, this is *Miia*. Miia... Jeremy,' Katariina politely provided.

'Sorry we are late. Trains and all,' Miia offered. Miia

was her pet name, the one her friends would know her as. Her full name was Maaria Elisabeth Saario. I would know her as *kultani*.

She withdrew her sunglasses. I gazed upon her face.

Her face. The perfect composition of structure and softness, Miia's face was one of God's single greatest creations. Unless, of course, one were to delve into her eyes. An arctic blue graced with such transparency, one was willingly swept away into an ocean of essence. They were piercing, revealing, as one would imagine the sun piercing the Nordic ice, revealing the life form that dwells just below but within reach. They were concealing, the strength of her a shield withholding a secret vulnerability just beyond their protective walls. As riveting concerto, her eyes would release a smile, and with it hope that today would be a better day for awakening the soul within.

My mind returned from its storybook state.

My heart knew of a different tale—one told over lifetimes.

Miia stood before me. Destiny was knocking. Divinity was at my doorstep.

We shared the cheek-to-cheek salutation and standard pleasantries; then boarded the ferry to our destined island picnic. The trip to Suomenlinna Island was a quick one, merely 960 seconds—each spent transfixed on her. I listened, as the rough intonations of the Finnish tongue seemed to roll with a symphony of sounds across her freshly dewed lips. My mind had no idea what the three of them were discussing. My heart ventured it had something to do with me, this day, and what was amounting to a set up between two eligible people from starkly different worlds. It mattered not what was being entertained by the others. For the anxiety that had invaded my heart awhile back when en route to Russia was displaced—cell by precious cell—by an awakening to the most familiar notion of loving emotion I had ever known.

Of course, there was the matter of another anxiety; the emotional rollercoaster as concocted from my mind throughout the course of the picnic itself. Simply details.

'What is it with Americans? Selling the virtues of freedom to anyone who has the resources to buy it. Do you not have enough buyers at home?' Miia was an attorney, and she was on the attack. All of this while meticulously ensuring my plate remained full and that my efforts during this island feast were minimal. The litany continued throughout the afternoon, along with Miia's great care in servicing my appetite.

'Miia! Why so rude?' Katariina queried her in Finnish. 'This is not like you.'

Mikko just sat there and smiled, translating from time to time only the details that mattered. Back behind those Ray Bans, there was a plan in play. And as far as he was concerned, it was being carried out to perfection. Today, he was playing instrument to a higher plan than even he was aware. I was aware of the growing uneasiness inside me.

Does she like me? Does she even notice me; that is, in

the manner I wish to be noticed? Am I merely on display for the day? My mind was on the move, escorted by emotions. There was something at stake here—*everything* at stake. I suddenly felt quite inadequate.

I pulled Mikko aside.

'Hey, buddy, what's going on here? I feel like I'm on trial for the crime of a country.'

'She likes you,' he replied, grinning.

'She likes me? How do you know?'

'She's behaving like she doesn't. That's how I know. Trust me. She likes you.'

Trust. Well, why not? Was it not trust that delivered me to this moment in the first place, letting go of that which was not serving me? Fate had its hand in it, too, but without trust I would not have done my part in creating this moment, this I knew.

The day gave way to evening as we moved our gathering from the blanket to a bar known to most as Kaivo. The setting, which once housed an old, Russian spa, would play perfect host to lengthy conversation that would serve in undressing the ego—leaving us with the naked truth. Destiny had delivered to the unsuspecting doorsteps of our minds the sacred longing of our hearts. We would just have to wait a bit for the minds to catch up.

Kaivohuone was the scene on a Saturday night. The Swedish Finns in particular would make this the stage for their "coming out party"; accomplished through fine dress, fine music, and alcohol—massive amounts of alcohol. It served in bringing the Finn to the surface.

The bar itself was a swank indoor-outdoor set up located in the middle of Kaivopuisto Park that provided ample corners and comfortable couches for exploring the shallow or deeper aspects of another—usually in reverse order— with the pool of participants and content of conversation becoming shallower as the evening progressed. Miia and I had somehow discovered a more secluded area indoors where an actual conversation could be had. The tall, red velvet booth proved more appropriate than first imagined, for the discourse to follow.

'So, Jeremy. What is it that you want with me? I mean, if you had a chance?' Miia delivered, to point. 'You are a handsome man. Mikko told me you have had many admirers. Well, you have had many. Whether they admired you or not, we would have to ask *them*. But really... what do you want from me?'

She licked her lips, not on purpose, but as a habit for one who craved moisture at all times in that region of her body. She licked her lips and caressed her champagne flute. On purpose or not, it served the purpose of arousing in me the carnal nature of sheer obsession. I wanted her. In every way imaginable. Most important, I wanted her in ways eternal.

I paused. The champagne we had been drinking since the afternoon was clearly staking its claim with each of us. Miia was more forward than ever. I was more reserved than normal. Until words, which seemingly had no business in this moment, made their way from heart to lips, and from my mouth to her ears.

'I will marry you, or I will marry no one.'

Miia sat there; just sat there. Her eyes moved away. Her lips moved as if they were between the thought of a kiss and a word—escape perhaps. And I was mortified by what I had just said. Mortified not by its content—for the content was all real—but by the ease in which I opened that portal, on this, our first night together. Marry her? The thought had not crossed my mind *ever*, with anyone.

'Well, I believe you believe that,' Miia responded, smiling. 'Let's just hope you are right, for your sake... and perhaps for mine.'

Right. Yes. Let's hope.

The evening drew to a close. Miia was engaged in what seemed an intense discussion with a good-looking man on the steps of the club. I waited, patiently. Of course I waited. I had been waiting all my life for this woman, this moment. Waiting was what one did when faced with the possibility for such divinity.

She walked over to me, the man still standing a few feet away—waiting perhaps, as well.

'Jeremy, if I go home with you, what will we do?'

Silence. Was this a trick question? Should I be cute in my response? Direct? I chose honest.

'Probably stop for a quick bite. Go back to my hotel. The rest is up to you. I just don't want this to end, not tonight, not tomorrow.'

Miia glanced over at the man in waiting. She returned

her attention to me. Her expression was a mix of concoctions consumed, with an assuming state.

'That man... he is my ex-boyfriend. He thinks he's still the one I covet.'

She paused for a brief moment.

'He is mistaken. Let's go.'

The remainder of the evening was something out of a Woody Allen film. There was the taxi queue that lasted an eternity—all the while with a growing concern that the decision to come home with me might wane with each precious minute in wait. Then, the obligatory stop at McDonalds (her idea). The mad dash downstairs at the hotel in search of a condom "just in case." The internal struggle between want and wisdom, especially when in discovery of "the one." And the morning after, with its necessary dose of awkwardness no matter how proper the behavior.

For Miia was a person of great integrity. She was honest, forthright, a woman of morals; of principles. She knew this was no ordinary evening. We both did. But we would leave the extraordinary for another day.

Even so, Miia's account of the evening proved a source of shock for Katariina the following morning as she divulged the series of uncharacteristic choices and events which unfolded. We crossed the threshold, yet left enough to the imagination for the future to hold in significance. Katariina may have been surprised by what Miia had done. I was amazed by what we had not. Given the opportunity to consummate fully, we chose to wait. It was, after all, the beginning of a union that had its origin in the heavens themselves, a symphony in its timed unveiling…

A note within a sound that beckoned one closer.

———

'What do you do with these?'

'Oh, they're birch leaves,' Mikko responded, as he threw a ladle of water on the red-hot stones resting on the wood stove.

'You hit yourself with the branches. Good for the circulation.' Another ladle of water.

'And the sausage?' I asked. 'You're not planning to cook that in here with us?'

'Why not?' offering his boyish grin—and more water.

We each took a swig of our Lapin Kulta beer. The setting at Katariina's summer cottage was altogether spec-tacular. The lake was placid, pure, perfect in its posturing. The forest, a sacred surrounding of birch trees; wickers of a white, winter-like wonderland. The flowers were wild in their fancy, sharing space with the berries accented for the season. The setting, the scents, the sounds were surreal. For the moment, our view was merely of one another—two naked men, a couple beers, and some roasted sausage, both planned and unplanned.

Another ladle of water and the test of manhood began. My ears started to tingle—then burn. I took another drink of my beer, as if cooling the insides would somehow balance the roasting effect on my hair, ears, and body as the searing temperatures began to scorch my most precious parts.

Another ladle of water...

And another...

And...

'Okay. Let's go...' the words trailed behind as Mikko dashed from the wooden sauna house.

I followed quickly, the cool air a welcomed friend upon my torched skin. We sprinted up the dock, and, without a moment's hesitation, cast our bodies—our *naked* bodies—into the air and lake below. The frigid, ice-cold, *man-should-never-attempt-this-ever* lake.

As we stood there, chest deep, mud seeping between our toes, the aftereffects of such a shock to the system became apparent. For what was earned in manhood while roasting inside the sauna was stripped away in a cruel, humbling emasculation of the man, inch by precious inch. As one good mate would put it, "our boys" were nowhere to be found. Good thing Miia was nowhere to be found when we took the obligatory *walk of shame* back to the cabin, our "manhood" barely distinguishable to the world around us.

Evening arrived. The many stars above played witness to it. A romantic dinner on the deck of the summer cottage followed. The girls had spent the entire afternoon preparing for our feast. The meal of fresh salmon and other Finnish delicacies was touched off by an assortment of berries picked from the nearby woods, with its complement of homemade cream. The view from the deck was alive with birch trees whose white bark provided their own form of illumination. White and purple lilies surrounded us. The lake was so serene you could skate across its placid surface within the confines of a mind equal in stillness. The sound of the crickets in the background reminded me of a similar symphony that played at times upon my inner ear—times when all seemed perfectly aligned. The evening and company were as close to such as this planet could provide.

Miia walked up behind me, placed her hand upon my shoulder, reached over, and kissed my left cheek.

I was happy beyond possibility.

I could remain here for eternity.

Miia and I were engaged four months later. The following summer, we were married at the Great White Church at Senate Square in Helsinki. It was a regal ceremony, from the classical quartet and harpist, to the flower arrangements and Bentley that escorted us to the shoreline. There we were picked up by a boat that shuttled us over the NJK Yacht Club on Valkosaari Island within view of the city. It was a stunning day, filled with sunshine and the greater presence of light that comes to bless such occasions in varied settings, with one singular note in common.

Love.

I was thirty-five; Miia twenty-five. We had our whole lives ahead of us. Finland would be our occasional home;

San Francisco a more permanent one. Whether here or there, no matter where we were, we would be together.

Marriage.

Two people coming together under the same roof—together as one.

For love? Maybe.

So that we may know ourselves better? Most certainly.

Miia and I married not so much for what we saw in each other, but what we wished to see in ourselves through the other. Each was incomplete and seeking greater union with our self. She was facing real physical concerns related to such. Mine were of a more emotional nature; a yearning for belonging—and desire to be loved. Neither was complete as we came into union. And no marriage certificate would serve as the diploma for the "College of Greater Emancipation" that all here on Earth appear to be attending, as either willing or unwilling members of the student body.

San Francisco. Boston. Washington DC. No change in locale could alter that which is everlasting. And the everlasting can only last while love is present.

Two summers later, I was walking the beach of our summerhouse in Avalon, New Jersey.

Alone.

'*A friend loveth at all times, and a brother is born for adversity.*'

I awakened, startled by what appeared to have been an

uninvited guest in my room. I looked around. There was nothing, no one. Just the wind battering against the window of the beach house; lightening streaming over the ocean. Was I dreaming? I lay my head back down, closed my eyes.

'A friend loveth at all times, and a brother is born for adversity.'

The words were repeated by the source, familiar as it was unknown. I knew these words.

'A friend loveth at all times, and a brother is born for adversity.'

The words were the fainted whisper from a faded king in memory—King Solomon.

'A friend loveth at all times, and a brother is born for adversity.'

The words grew in intensity, as did the ringing in my ears.

'Who is the *"friend"*?' I thought.

'God is,' the voice answered.

I was startled by the speed of the response. I was surprised I was not startled by the response itself.

'Then who is the *"brother"*... the one *"born for adversity"*?' I queried.

'Why, you are.'

'Me? Why would I want to play adversary to myself?'

'A good question. With only one good answer... to know yourself better. To know Him better.'

Admittedly, I was like many, at a loss for precisely what

or who was governing us. God, Spirit, Universe, Cosmic Consciousness, the Great Oz Himself. I knew something was at the helm, breathing me this gift of life, a "present" even when I wasn't. Knew it? Well, maybe believed it. Hoped, for certain. Precisely what we called it probably mattering little to the some*one* or some*thing* itself. Non-intrusive, but conducive, through my head, heart, or another it did not matter. Whatever the source, it was a voice of reason. It was a voice of knowing. It was not my voice.

I looked out across a sea of darkness. I was at a cross-roads—this was certain. I was also my own worst enemy—this I understood. I hated who I was. I was whom I hated.

A flash of light across the sky illuminated my view for but a moment.

I lay my head down, once again. Hoping to fall back to sleep. Hoping the mind would still whatever was moving me to awaken.

I wanted never to awaken again.

Miia had returned to Finland, our fated union unable to live up to the hype stirred by the soul, but to be lived out through the imperfect nature of our lower nature—the ego itself. And, while the love of our souls did inevitably give way to the frailties of our humanness—and, more accurately, our own personal journeys—she would remain an ever-lasting marker for what love in this world may offer, if for but a fleeting moment. I realized with this thought I was once again cursing the mortal with immortality.

'Your marriage or her life. It was thankfully an easy decision for her.'

Once again, Arena was playing counselor. My life's ventures into love would have been a story of amusement to her if it weren't for the devastation I was enduring at every turn.

'Failure. At only the most important time in my life.'

'Jeremy, you are not the keeper of love, of marriage, as if you were in some way better wired to handle it all. The planet is flawed... on purpose. Just like the rest of us, you are a human being.'

'I am tired of being, Arena. I am tired of a world that rewards your loving with anything but.'

'You don't mean that... '

'But I do. Love only exists to torment me more. The greater the prize, the more painful the surprise. It awaits me. Taunts me. Then haunts me.'

'Jeremy... '

'I mean, look at me. I'm a wreck. There is nothing left for me to give. I have given all I know... to all I've known. There is no more.'

'*A great part of courage is the courage of having done the thing before.*'

Arena was quoting Emerson.

'I think he was speaking of a new vantage point that allows us to venture into a similar situation with the courage to foresee, and then manifest, a new and better outcome.'

'A better outcome?' I responded. 'A better outcome? How can there be a better outcome? She was everything! Everything I wanted...had been waiting for! Everything I knew love to be in this world.'

'Go higher.'

'What?'

'A teacher once shared with me, "*We are never given more than we can handle.*"'

'He hasn't seen my life.'

Arena giggled. She tried not to, but it was an amusing notion.

'Arena, I don't think I can get through this one.' My throat tightened. My eyes filled. Tears began streaming down my face, tears I had become quite familiar with—too familiar with.

Arena put her arm around me. 'Perhaps it is not in love where you are falling short... but in how you love and who you are turning to for such, hun.'

'But, I don't get it. Miia was perfect. Perfect!'

She stepped back. 'Jeremy, quit it! She is not perfect. You are not perfect. Your insistence on seeing others as more than they are is leaving you as less than you are... less than you can be... less than *you*.'

It made sense, although admittedly I wasn't seeking sense while wallowing in my nonsense. I could see a pattern emerging. We all have them. This was certainly one of mine, the tendency to deify the women in my life. But identifying the pattern and actually doing something about it—clearly there is a great distance between recognition, cognition, and ignition.

I became silent. Arena became silent. What else could be said?

I left the house and headed down the beach. Alone. Once again, I felt utterly and entirely alone. Arena was, of course, a godsend. But gratitude for such would have to come later. God and I had some unfinished business.

There was the matter of me.

Maybe Arena was right. Perhaps I am flawed in my perception. Perhaps I am not seeing the whole picture, of me, of those I loved, of love itself. This I thought to myself as I paced the sands, a ritual I had perfected over several weeks now. I had lost fifteen pounds in under a month. Those around me feared I had lost much more than that.

'I am screwed, cursed, damned to everlasting hell. This is clear.'

'*Jeremy. Forgive.*' The voice within managed to get a word of its own in amid my defamation of self.

'I *have* forgiven her.'

'*No. Forgive yourself.*'

'But, I could not...' I paused for a moment, in an attempt to hold back another wave of tears. 'I couldn't... couldn't fix it.'

'*It is not yours to fix. It never was.*'

I sat there in the moment, in the words. I was grateful for the company of the voice. I watched the waves as they continued to crash upon sands that had known an eternity of these moments. A small boy determined to feed the entire flock of seagulls encircling him reminded me of another small boy, at another time, in a similar setting. I made this beach my sanctuary since I was five. It provided both a destination and an escape. I dissected every major love I had known this lifetime, on this beach. My mind found peace with that. My heart remained restless.

A couple walked by, hand in hand, laughing as the fresh spray kicked up in their face, my focus on their laughter. A weekend fisherman cast his line once again into the sea, in the hope of perhaps landing "the big one" in this, his next attempt.

Tears found their way to my face, once again, as I witnessed the rays from the early evening sun in salsa with the incoming waves. Pink hues painted the skies above. Violet shades shimmied across the scattering waves, the rhythmic sound of each against the shore. Grains of sand journeyed between my fingers, toes; then vanished into the vastness of itself.

Well, at least I can hear. I can see. I can feel. That's something, I thought to myself.

'It's more than something. It's the difference between this world and the others. Here... here in this world... here on this planet... we get to feel, hear, and see. We get to be... all levels at all times.'

All levels at all times. It was a pretty special place, this place. And the voice within me was a welcomed friend indeed.

I felt better. Not great, just better. Small steps were also a part of this grand journey. This I was beginning to understand. I wanted the big leap, but my life was shaping up to be a series of small steps, stepping stones, to get me from here to there—wherever *there* was.

But forgive myself? Perhaps another day.

I picked myself up, dusted off the sand that had formed a connection with one who felt anything but connected to anyone or anything. One in a world of many, many within the confines of one confining form, I began the journey back to the house—step by step. The music blaring from a nearby beach house moved from their deck to my ear, and right through to my awaiting heart. With an unlimited track of melodies, a universe of possibilities, that same universe provided me with the only song befitting of the message worthy of my receiving.

"One."

By U2.

What territory awaits me going forward?
A kingdom for the King in you, Jeremy...
With the rewards most suited for the throne of the Highest.

6
A TIGER BY THE *TALE*

Some do more with less
Others, less with more

It is in the doing where we may know goodness better

'Where are you off to, sir?'
'To India.' For some spiritual cleansing, I thought to myself. Given my life choices, a karmic bath would be more in line.

'It is very funny. I am Indian. What are you in need of?'
Peace. Some direction. And apparently, a bit of forgiveness.

'Need of?' I responded. 'Nothing. Everything. I have no idea.'

'Oh, this I see. I see many things. I see things that one cannot see. My auntie used to tell me it is a gift. There are

127

many such gifts. I see without my eyes. And I see an Indian in you.'

'An Indian in me?'

'Yes, oh yes. You are a seeker. And an entrepreneur in spirit. You build things. You are building something now. But where you are building from; this is different. Oh yes, different.'

The driver paused for a moment. He adjusted his mirror, presumably to get a better view of me; then continued.

'It requires many pieces. And you have only a few.' He laughed. 'No. You have more than a few… pieces, that is. But you are standing on some, so you cannot see them. Keep moving. That is what my auntie used to say. Keep moving, and you might just see what otherwise you would not.'

I found myself both disturbed and charged by what this man had to say. He was tiny in stature, but spoke as if extending across realms of meaning. I wanted to see what he could see, know what he knew. I found this invigorating and vexing in the same. The driver found our way to the airport.

'Okay, we are here. I hope you find what you are seeking. I think you will.'

'If not, I'm sure your auntie will let me know of it.'

He laughed. 'Yes, auntie knows. And she is watching. She is always watching.'

I hoped she wasn't watching too closely.

I cleared security. The airport was abuzz. Fellow

travelers moved about, all in transition. Some were arriving. Others departing. With a range of emotions in tow. And baggage. Lots and lots of baggage.

We boarded the plane. My phone rang. "Unknown." Hmmm. Why not? It fit the moment.

'Hello?'

'Jeremy!'

'Ah, yes?'

'It's Reshma. Reshma Patel.'

I hadn't seen her since my time with Cassandra in San Francisco.

'Reshma. It's been years. What compelled you to... '

'Jeremy. You're about to embark on a wild ride, my friend. One that will take... through... choices... conse...'

'Reshma? Hello? Are you there?'

And she was gone. I went to ring her back; only the call was "unknown." Her number was one of many that I had lost while losing myself with Miia. I sat there on the plane, waiting, hiding my phone beneath my leg in the hopes it would buzz before takeoff.

What was it she was trying to tell me? What did she see, read, that compelled her to call me after so many years? The plane began moving. I had no choice but to let it go.

'Sit back. Relax. And let one of the flight attendants know if you are in need of any assistance.'

Easy for her, I thought. It was not her life held in the balance.

And while I appreciated the offer, it was not *her* assistance I required.

Traveling the world in the pursuit of the unknown is one thing. But twenty-nine hours to visit an ashram void of any civilized measures just to "find myself"? Jeremy, we are trying to silence the mind, not lose it completely. This I thought, as we descended once again to the earth below.

'Ladies and gentlemen, please make sure you take all of your personal belongings with you.'

Actually, I kind of had it in mind to leave all of my "belongings" *behind* me.

The airport in Mumbai belonged to no one—and everyone. The noise was deafening. People shouting. Horns blasting. Beggars surrounding, young and old. *This* was to be my place of awakening? It only served in awakening an angry man within. I forced my way through the crowd. I was saved by my driver who somehow found me in the mass of humanity just beyond the customs exit. We made our way to the parking area, navigating a sea of solicitation, with barely a word spoken to one another. I felt alone and suddenly quite vulnerable. I knew neither this man, this place, nor where I was heading. And no one else knew enough to know where to claim even my remains if something were to happen to me.

Fear was present. Trust was nowhere to be found. What I found, discovered, was a concern for what came next, and the desire for control. The uncertainty of the moment was entirely uncomfortable for a mind that wanted answers, not to the questions of the universe, but to those more basic for survival. Where are we? Who is driving me? Where are we heading? How long will it take? How do I contact someone if I am in trouble? Fortunately, the chaos in my head was met with one rather carnal reality—I was exhausted and craved sleep. And for this reason, my mind and its delusions would have to wait. I closed my eyes under such noted condition. I closed my eyes, but there would be no rest.

Filled with dreams and fears, an anticipating heart and somewhat reluctant mind, there I was—in India—reclined against a rather unforgiving back seat of a jeep that had seen better days. The stars remained our only source of light. They were magnificent, entirely present if not aligned in my favor. I certainly was banking on the fact they were.

I stirred from time to time, just long enough to see there was nothing to see. It was dark, dusty, and desolate. Not even a tree to tease us with the possibility of perhaps a bit more oxygen for my struggling lungs. The driver seemed nice enough. My suspicions calculated his kindness as just a polite gesture to yet another of the many "seekers" on the road to some degree of self-discovery—or in my case, some sense of recovery.

Our jeep rumbled along the dirt roads to Ahmednagar. I lay there, immobilized by a back seat suited for sleep in only fetal form. Silence prevailed, except for the humming of my driver, who appeared to be in some state of nirvana, oblivious to my pain. Who was this man anyway? What was *his* story?

'Where are you from?' the driver broke the silence. His name was Dileep.

'I'm from the US. Traveled quite a distance to get here,' hoping he would get the hint.

'You have come here to find something. I think you will.'

Dileep continued humming. I continued in disbelief. How could these people possibly know this? I'm not even sure why I am here. Perhaps Dileep felt inclined to share such encouragement with all seekers. But the taxi driver back in the States?

'I will take you to the cave of Sai Baba one day, if you like,' Dileep offered. 'He experienced enlightenment there.'

I wonder if enlightenment can only be found in that particular cave, I thought to myself. No wonder so many of us have missed the moment. I smiled. I had to.

Dileep spoke to me in moments throughout our drive, few words, rich in meaning, as if orchestrated by some higher conductor that knew just which notes to hit in harmony with the now. Exhaustion aside, the experience was quite peaceful, once I allowed it to be. My mind attempted to convince me that such peace was but a momentary fixture within the permanent frame of each unfolding tale. When did this begin, I wondered, a sense that anything extraordinary was but temporary? Perhaps, when as a child filled with possibility—with my soul so close to surface one could barely distinguish it from the ego itself—someone found it necessary to pierce the veil for the sake of bridging my bliss with their reality. Like painting an illusion across the landscape of truth. What exists in the real? Our dreams and imaginations as children, or the tempering of such through a lifetime lived in perhaps a more false self. Beyond the "reality" as provided us through adult lenses, is the possibility as seen through the looking glass of our youthful selves. One is governed by the mind; the other, from the heart.

'A chief event of life is the day in which we have encountered a mind that startled us.'

These were the words of Emerson, emerging into my consciousness as timely recollect. He likely had his share of "run-ins" with enough heads that lacked greater heart, purpose and direction, I thought, as I gazed upon the stars that have proven most faithful companions on many an occasion past. I have been "startled" by many things in life, not the least of which a mind that could conjure up fears, doubts, worry where none was required.

The jeep took a right turn, then a left, then another right. We could not possibly be there already, I thought. Fear emerged once again from the shadows of my own distrust.

The jeep came to a stop. I sat up and peered through the dusty window, squinting, as if that would in some way improve my view. My eyes eventually focused on a dilapidated shack. Dileep invited me from the vehicle, along with my most untrusting companion—fear.

I stepped from the vehicle. The stars above were all that was familiar. There were four men—rather shady-looking characters—all standing around two metal vats about the size of a small water heater. One was filled with water, the other with an elixir that more closely resembled the earth than anything remotely consumable. The man to my left, shirt unbuttoned, belly in full view, dipped a smeared glass into the water, then into the muddy concoction. He handed it to Dileep. My glass had its origin with the man to my right, his defining odor sourced from his stained armpits. Our server took the glass, gave it a brief bath in the murky water, dipped the cup into the mystery potion, then found its way into my hands.

'Drink up, my friend,' Dileep encouraged. 'Have you ever had *chai?* I suppose this is your first experience with *real* chai tea. I hope you enjoy it. I believe you will.'

I smiled, an uneasy smile. One that came with a thousand warnings: about the water in India, general cleanliness, especially when men were charged with such duty. I drank from the "community cup," passed on any further opportunity to tempt fate, and prayed to whoever was listening that my attempt at courtesy would not be met with two days of incessant vomiting, and a death by diarrhea. The men around the kettle paid little attention to me or my inner dealings. They spoke in a tongue that did not require me to participate. They spoke in a manner weighted in hardship, a hardship I could not possibly comprehend. They spoke. I drifted.

A mangy dog kept our company. His hair matted, twisted from months of deprivation from a decent bath. His stench filled my nostrils. I turned from sight—and perhaps higher insight—as if my lack of gaze would reduce my role and responsibility. Dileep noticed my apprehension for both conversation and current company.

'My son, Alok, he is not much older than three,' Dileep began. 'He asked me today, "Father, where does God sleep?" I told him, "He sleeps with the stars." He then asked me, "Father, where does God work?" I told him, "He works here on Earth." My son then sat there for a very long moment, no sound, just thinking, then says to me, "I will help Him. I think he is too busy to do everything. I will help Him, so that he can sleep at night."'

Dileep paused for a second himself, then continued. 'There is an old saying in the Hindi proverbs that goes something like this:

'If one is good, then the whole world is good.'

'I believe it speaks to our choice in how we choose to live and what is returned to us in kind.' He chuckled. 'Maybe, when the whole world is good, that is when God gets to sleep.'

I felt ashamed.

We arrived in Ahmednagar. The ashram was located just outside of town. It was modest by any standard—a couple of bungalows, a dining hall, a communal area, and a few more buildings scattered about the compound. It was worn, dusty and not very pleasing to the eye. Two weeks. I was to spend two weeks here. This will be interesting, I thought, as I gathered my belongings and made my way to the reception hall, and eventually to my room.

Of course, my room was not *my* room at all. I was to bunk with the rest of the male seekers. The women had their own quarters. I would have preferred bunking with them. Men have a nasty habit of making portable their nasty habits. And amazingly, these go unnoticed by men themselves. But not by me. Not on this trip.

The scratching. The picking. The clearing. The symphony of sounds in the nighttime air, many of which would rival the bush region in Kenya. Animals. All of them!

I lay one evening on a most uncomfortable mattress, staring up at the bottom of another, somewhat bemused by the manner of men. It was clear the universe had spent more time in the construct of woman than that of her lesser partner. As with all in the lower kingdom, however, men had their place, their role. Tonight it was in providing a concerto of odd flesh-based "instruments," playing in the most inharmonious fashion with one another. It would have been beautiful, if in the eyes of a more benevolent beholder. It was not, for I was not.

I eventually succeeded in silencing the sounds, thanks to a pair of highly-effective ear plugs, and a tone of my own that had a much more pleasing result; that is, when I bothered to chant it. I bothered this evening.

I followed my breathing. In... Out. In... Out.

I chanted my tone.

The light energy surged.

The mind quieted (as best it could).

The heart opened.

The sound appeared.

At first, it seemed an echo of the tone I was chanting. But the chorus of sounds that followed had another source entirely. The light that was available seemed to pull me from myself. I remained a part of me, yet there were more parts than my mind was privy to. The purple light seemed to beckon me forward. To move toward required that I move away. It required that I trust. I did. I did for but a brief moment. The brief moment gave me a glimpse of the universe of universes. The return was earth shaking.

I opened my eyes, still feeling the effects of the reuniting with myself. It could not have been more than a few minutes, my travels in the inner realms. My watch told me otherwise. I had been "gone" for over an hour.

I wanted to return...

Return to wherever it was.

It felt like I had been gone for way too long.

The time I spent at the ashram was two of the most eye-opening, self-deprecating, and exposing weeks of my life. There was bliss, as well. But first I had to move through the unavoidable process of awareness, to understanding, to some sense of responsibility, and finally to action. One could call this building a new "*aura*" around myself. I had a slightly less sexy name for it: gut-wrenching, foot-stomping, fit-throwing, complete and utter exfoliation of the personality. For through this process:

I learned to shave with one cup of lukewarm water.

I learned to share my quarters with a sonnet of snorers that seemed to play the role of instigator for my insufferable self with precision.

I learned to eat foods without complement (nor compliment).

I learned to sit by myself, walk with myself, talk with myself, and pretty much come to despise myself.

In short, I learned to be ordinary, and leave the "extra" behind.

I learned, but not without pain. For there was nothing more painful than looking honestly at my own reflection. And this ashram was no sanctuary. This ashram was a purgatory, armed with judge and jury self-contrived. I judged myself. I judged others. I judged the whole damned experience. My personality that seemed to serve me so well for nearly forty years had become my arch enemy, standing before me, between the *me* I thought I was and the *Me* I always was. Imposing, yes. And also the imposter.

'Good morning,' Madame B would offer. Madame B was the caretaker of the property. Her silver hair and bright eyes spoke of a lifetime of service to Meher Baba and his ashram. She was such a pleasant person, so full of life. I came to despise Madame B.

'Good morning,' I begrudgingly returned.

For this had been anything but a good series of mornings. The people were so nice. Everyone was so joyous, so happy. It was so annoying. And that guy that played folk songs on the porch each afternoon? God really had quite the sense of humor, and mistakenly assumed I did as well. Some spoke of visions. The only vision I could muster was one of wrapping that guitar around the guy's neck. I would, of course, apologize afterward, with a look on my face befitting of one who was as confused with my own emotional upheaval as I truly was. These types of thoughts actually crossed my mind, and only served in feeding the self-contempt that was growing with each new day in the wasteland paradise.

I spent hours upon hours, for days, contemplating everything and everyone—mainly myself. What was the purpose? Of my life? My loves? The many characters of me? I posed many questions; received no answers. It was apparent whomever was in charge of "this" was not in the mood to indulge the self-indulgent. The silent treatment I received made me question whether there was even someone at the helm. I was lost, and apparently the Great Dispatcher was, as well.

I never considered the possibility that God, Spirit, Universe may be of the non-intrusive kind. That It may allow us to go through whatever we had to, to steer clear of our own devise—our karma. This would be an inconvenient truth, for certain. And my mind was not interested in such inconveniences. In fact, it would use the absence of any answers as some proof that perhaps there were no answers at all. That there was nothing more than me, than us, than *this* in the most contracting sense. No emancipation. No salvation. No higher world or worlds. Just the stuff made up in this world by those of us who managed to create, promote or allow all of this. It was a deflating thought indeed.

I was in need of another thought. It would arrive only when I was ready to let go of the one before, and any one to follow.

I awaited the day of reckoning. I knew it was coming. There was no way the higher powers were going to leave me walking away empty handed. I came here for illumination, and found myself basking in the shadows beyond the fringes of the light itself. While I understood one could not stay in the shade forever, the presumed illumination that would come with any entry into the light had not yet summoned the will to do just that. Perhaps today, this day, would be the day.

I awakened, avoided any connection with myself through mirrored reflection, and others by way of the iPod. I shaved, showered (barely), and ate a bit of something. I walked across the grounds and took refuge in a small building, which provided a quiet space to meditate. I assumed my half lotus position and began. After about twenty minutes to still the mind and open the heart, I was prompted to awaken. I was prompted not by some divine message, but by the sound of construction workers hammering away nearby.

I unraveled my legs, allowing the blood to circulate, my mind to percolate. I was frustrated. This retreat was anything but a treat. I couldn't even capture a moment of peace in a peace village. I set course toward Baba's tomb. A brief pilgrimage to where the avatar had been lay to rest would be better than experiencing any further dissection of what was left of my patience by the "local surgeons and their blunt instruments."

I had yet to actually enter the hallowed area as seemingly all other retreaters had done. I was still harboring judgment on the ritualistic practices surrounding this product of earth and stone. I was harboring judgment on my life, as well.

It was sweltering, the temperature. Beads of sweat made their way from hairline to eye line. The dust was stifling to the breath. The trees, painted by the earth, offered little by way of comfort for creature, big and small. My pants clung to my legs, absorbing every bit of moisture generated by the torrid conditions. It was hot. I was hot. And I was in no mood for any mood other than my own.

I found temporary solace in the shade of a *neem* tree, opposite the tomb. An inviting rock wall just out of harm's way provided a suitable post and resting place. Safe from the sun, with no demands of its own lest I chose to find its edginess a bit hard on the body, here I could lie, in observation, taking in all that I wished of the entourage just up the hill, without any risk of actually being seen with these people.

The invocation in song made its way to my ears through the kind assistance of a slight yet growing breeze. The wind was a new entry. There had been little of *her* presence. Lady Breeze began kicking up quite a fuss, making it a bit more challenging for me to execute on my planned participation through non-compliance. But I was strong in ego, a trait that had yielded me much success in this world—at least how many defined success.

The wind blew in more than merely the dust from the parched earth. Eyes closed, balancing my broad shoulders on the narrowest of stone walls, I lay there in a somewhat meditative state, my eyelids barely shielding the intensity of the sun that danced between the branches. The occasional shadow provided by my benefactor played havoc with the images of nothingness as projected against the inside of my lids.

A form emerged. It was violet in color—the silhouette of a man's face. Defining (and a bit frightening), I quickly opened my eyes. As they readjusted to the light, the image disappeared. I would have spent more time on this freakish occurrence if it weren't for the fact I was now under attack. An army of tiny ants swarmed my body. Apparently, the colony had a similar idea of how to cope with the heat. Or perhaps I merely stood between them and the journey they were on. These ants were fierce, unrelenting, devoted to their cause. Great qualities for anyone on a purposeful path, I thought. I brushed the petty tyrants aside with the loosely bound copy of the *Bhagavad-Gita* I had borrowed from my room. The wind kicked up again, flipping the book open. My eyes transfixed upon the words before me.

'*The mind is restless, turbulent, powerful, violent… trying to control it is like trying to control the wind.*'

The symbolism was difficult to ignore. The wording perfectly timed. The contrived conspiracy was on. The hammers hammered. The ants awakened. The wind blew. The face emerged—for *whatever* reason. And the book revealed.

'*The mind is restless, turbulent, powerful, violent… trying to control it is like trying to control the wind.*'

I remembered the words of a spiritual teacher introduced to me by Arena. He shared that "*control is the master addiction.*" He taught that it was not the lack of courage that kept us from moving forward, but the fear of losing control.

The wind yielded. The ants retreated. And I was left with nothing but a thought, and a choice.

What was it I feared? What was it that kept me from stepping forward, stepping out? The unknown? The comfort with what is? I could try to control that which I feared, the factors which surround it. Or I could simply let go, and allow whatever was there for me to be there—*for* me.

I sat in silence. I sat in silence, but not in ignorance. What was comfortable, known, familiar, was certainly not working. This I knew. With this knowing, however, I was still laden with the freedom of choice.

My choice. It was, is, and always will be *my* choice.

This stream of consciousness gave way to a cascade of another kind. My heart squeezed. My throat tightened. Tears poured down my cheeks from the wells above. I began seeing the many loves I had known, faces, faceless in the greater meaning, a meaning that eluded, yet haunted me as if some part of me knew what the other did not.

The flow of emotion was interrupted—perhaps simply displaced. Across the barren courtyard, a young woman glanced my way. She smiled, then continued up the hill. Her smile, a welcoming kind. A kind welcome.

I picked myself up off the wall that both protected and denied. I looked up to the tree, with gratitude. Down to the ants, with due reverence. And over to the tomb of an avatar, with determination. Determination to do it differently—along with a pair of legs—took me up the hill. I was greeted by inviting faces, embracing smiles, but no words. There were few words shared at the center. It was a place where words held little meaning; where the sound of silence was deafening.

I waited, in line, to step, into the tomb, to pay homage. I waited. It felt awkward. I stepped inside, alongside another. He knelt. I knelt. He bowed. I followed. He left. I remained. After all, I had just waited nearly a half hour for this moment—and more time still. I wasn't about to give up the stage so easily. Where was my awareness, my moment of awakening? Where was my celestial seasoning, the wisdom from above?

A few more minutes passed. It became apparent I was not going to receive any gift of profound discourse from the divine. Perhaps I had not yet paid my dues. Maybe I missed the slot machine on the way in. If the connection was severed, at least my humor was in working order.

I exited the tomb. I wanted to scream out for the answers that eluded me still. I chose instead to make my way down the hill and find a quiet place for retrospective thought. I remained unmoved by the rituals themselves, and frustrated by the silence from wherever the answers were sourced.

Yet I understood better the reason for my being here, at the ashram; for the timely conversation with a friend who knew of this place; for the thousands of miles I had traveled; for enduring the seeming hardships of the retreat experience itself. Baba was not the destination, nor the answer. Rather each served as another guiding light, another sign, piece of the puzzle, allowing me to take one of the most difficult yet presumably rewarding journeys of all. Beyond the fortress of mind, of thought, piercing the veil of self-judgment and that of others, the early steps upon the pyramid of forgiveness, happiness, and dare I hope loving in a manner more inviting served as stepping stones. Perhaps as with the pharaohs who lay at the base of such structures, the tomb of an avatar was the resting place for one, a place to bury that which no longer served for others.

If I could, I would bury my mind and be done with it, I thought. At the very least, wrap my mouth in duct tape so the mind had no vehicle to express its limiting nature. Neither would be the way. The only way to deal with the mind was to not deal with it at all. Let it be. Pay little attention to it. Move beyond the matters of the mind that the master Krishna had alluded to, and to the heart of the matter.

'*The mind is restless, turbulent, powerful, violent... trying to control it is like trying to control the wind.*'

> The "wind"
> Not to be controlled
> *Ever*

Perhaps I received more than I thought...
From a wind blowing my direction.

A new day. A brand new me. Or at least a version of myself I was warming to—a warmer, more trusting (slightly), more liberated me. This was a special day, as well, as I was to meet up with Reshma, at the Elura Caves. We had managed to connect by phone. She insisted we meet up. Why she chose this particular venue for our reunion after such a long draught between visits I didn't know. She had her reasons, this I did know. And I trusted her instincts, her insight; sourced from an intelligence I was just beginning to see in myself.

The trip to the caves would take the entire day, requiring I forego yet another fear, one of entrapment, within the confines of what amounted to a guided tour bus. The thought of such means of transport triggered anxieties that still found a welcomed home within my mind. Confinement, constriction, limitation, disempowerment as my own author and authority. Not to mention traffic, uncomfortable bus seats, and the possibility of engagement in frivolous discussion by a committee of time-killers. But this was the new me, enlightened, well-armed with the weapons of courage, compassion, and understanding picked up along the way, my journey. I was ready.

Not quite.

I mean, come on, God! Could you not have at least placed *one* of your more inspiring creations on board? The bus was filled with Western women; draped in makeshift saris and other local wear; hats abounded; perfumed to the hilt; all seeking some greater meaning in life; none successful in convincing their husbands to join the trek to this far-off land.

'*Still playing in the shallow end of the pool, are we?*' The wiser within felt compelled to contribute.

Shallow. The shame. My own to own—long-term rent, at least. After apparently gifted with a chance learning just the day before, here he was again, Mr. Ego, showing his superficial face. The constant need for stimulation, still mired in illusion, he provided the perfect weapon for the "loyal forces of the opposition," testing me at every turn, luring me back into the game of *the return* itself.

I simply couldn't shake him.

'Reshma!'

'Jeremy, sweetheart. You've grown, I see.'

'Grown? I am slightly larger than my Facebook picture. That is true.'

'No, silly. Your eyes. They are beaming. Quite the journey you are on. Have you found the answers to your questions?'

My questions. The same questions I knew little of back in Kenya, other than that I must face the very questions I came here to answer. It was no longer simply about love, this I knew. At least, it was no longer about the search for love alone. I left the "beaming eyes" comment be. If she saw it, I would not correct it.

'No answers. More questions. I don't know. Perhaps. Who knows?'

Reshma smiled. She knew more of my journey, at times, than would seem possible. The information she accessed through her chart readings was uncannily accurate. She knew of the plight to be experienced in San Francisco; my impending discovery, journey and tragedy with Miia; even my inevitable encounter here on Indian soil. Perhaps it is written somewhere in the universe our destiny of a single lifetime. This I thought, as we made our climb up the mountain together.

Each new step required enough attention to safely arrive at the next new step. We would occasionally stop to take in the view around us, yet in order to arrive at our destination we would have to at some point give up the role of spectator and continue onward. It was my awareness in the moment. It was a metaphor for a lifetime.

'This was the home of Sai Baba for nearly thirty years,' Reshma shared, as we arrived at the entrance of the cave where it is said he found enlightenment. Overlooking the valley that stood between one man's lone journey with God and the three-hundred-year collaboration of men over generations to chisel out thirty of the more amazing amalgamations of man and nature to be marveled, I was *lessoned* once again.

It came in the form of an aged woman native to the region who had ventured to join Reshma and me on the excursion. She was dressed in a predominantly purple-colored sari, her third eye covered in Hindi tradition by a *tilaka*. She was slightly heavy-set, but had little difficulty keeping up with us. In fact, she set the pace. There was a youthfulness to her, a radiance about her. Her eyes were lit as if an eternal flame was placed just behind the cornea, a lantern of sorts that would light the passageway in concert with the words that soon followed.

As we sat there together on a rock that overlooked the valley in all its glory, the elder woman spoke:

'Man can love and live in the world while remaining apart from it.

'Man can love and live in the world by relating to it.

'Man can love and live in the world by co-creating with

149

it.

'But man can only choose loving, if one is to truly live.'

Reshma took a deep breath. The old woman seemed to hold the skies with her hand, palm extended outward. I closed my eyes and opened my heart to the words, the meaning. I could feel my breath moving in and out in accord with the surrounding nature. There was nothing to disturb the stillness. No worries. No fears. No doubts. No judgments. Nothing...

Except about a million crickets.

'Do you hear that?' I whispered.

'Hear what?' Reshma responded.

'Those crickets. You must hear those crickets, right?'

She just smiled, while the wise woman turned and offered me the light from her eyes. The sound intensified. It blended with what seemed like a symphony of other tones that produced one singular, calming note. This note flowed throughout my body. My feet felt as if they had grown roots in the ground below. I experienced a movement of energy from the crown of my head to the earth beneath. It was alarming. It was disarming. It was peaceful. It stirred my soul.

'You are awakening,' the old lady offered. 'Fear not. Let go, and allow *It* to take you home.' The woman paused, rolled her fingers together to form a fist; then continued. 'You must be a warrior to the way. Arm yourself. For it is a battle worth fighting. And a deserving paradise that awaits you. A kingdom.'

This was all she said. There was nothing more to be said. Her words fell upon my awaiting ears as if they were the only words I came here to know. All of my travels, the journey to India, to the ashram, to this mountaintop—all so that I might hear the whisper of one. The wisdom of many.

I knew of an eternal peace in this moment. I wanted to remain on the mountaintop for my remaining years. But this was not to be. This was not my story. There was more.

We descended. Reshma and I settled in for some tea at a small café in the nearby village. She seemed a bit reticent, which was not her usual way.

'What is it?'

'It's unclear to share.'

'Reshma, sharing has not been an issue for you before.'

'I know. It's not that I do not feel comfortable in sharing what I see. It's that... it is unclear. Your path, your road, it runs so smoothly, until this point where it splits. Neither direction clearly defined.'

'Well, that's not unusual, right? We do have choices. We make them all the time.'

'Yes, but in this case, one leads to freedom... the other, to... to servitude.'

'You mean I'm destined to become someone's slave?' I could not help but infuse a bit of humor in what was becoming a heavy—and somewhat disturbing—conversation.

'No. It's complicated. It has something to do with what you're seeking... as the key itself.'

'The key to my freedom?'

'The key to the kingdom.'

'Well, I would just take a little less drama. I don't need an entire kingdom. One room of sanity would do fine.'

Reshma hesitated, then continued.

'You had a life. A past life. One where you were given the keys. But there was another involved. A woman. You loved her. Dearly so. So much so you renounced your faith in God, scorned Him even, when the woman—your wife— was pried from your hands. You felt betrayed, as your prayers went unanswered.'

'And the servitude?'

'In that life, you were enslaved. Not by another, but by your own actions. Given much insight by the divine powers, you were to lead. You made mistakes. Your love was stripped from you. You gave it all up, your beliefs, your God. You gave Him up. And cast yourself into a dark place for quite some time.'

'Well, perhaps thousands of years, and presumably more than a few lifetimes later, I got over whatever problem I had with the Big Guy.' I was now desperately attempting to diffuse the situation.

Reshma looked distraught. Intense even.

'What is it?'

'It is not over yet. The karma. You will be tested again. Soon.'

'Nothing new there,' I responded, unnerved by the thought.

I paused for a moment, then continued. 'Well, then, let's hope I've been a good student, these past few, uh, centuries.'

Reshma just smiled. An uneasy smile.

I felt uneasy myself.

"There is no bottom."

These were the words spoken by Robert during our evening together, years back in Los Angeles. He, of course, was speaking of the reality that one could fall all the way to a miserable life—and early death. He had spent time in India when he was younger. At the time we met him, Robert was comparing it to his current state.

India, as with many places on this planet, has no bottom. This was true. I was convinced after my time here in this haven of higher pursuits that India also has no *ceiling*.

India's gift to the planet lay in the delicate message offered when one chooses to cast aside the material importance to experience the more material gain. This was not to say there was anything unloving or non-spiritual about manifestation, or abundance. On the contrary, the many prophets and masters that walked the same earth, breathed the same air, drank the same water as each of us today, offered us a direction, a means to a higher and more loving experience. It was not in the abstinence of the material that this enlightened way would be ours, but rather in keeping our focus in the right place, enjoying but not attaching greater meaning to the world and its possessions than what is due. To awe, to respect, to share in but not to lose ourselves within, that was the message in all its simplicity. At least, that was the message to me.

Now, if I could only find my *passage*.

I made my way back to Mumbai the following day. Dileep was in his familiar role as trusted guide, with I transfixed by a landscape that no longer seemed quite so desolate. I gazed through the windowpane and into the vastness, dusty enterprise after dusty enterprise, but with greater clarity. The plight of another mangy dog caught my attention. He was limping along in some vain attempt to cross a rather dangerous intersection. And no one seemed interested in his journey.

'He's not gonna make it,' I thought, as each attempt by the determined little fellow was met with a brush back that nearly ended his already fragile existence. 'Somebody needs to help that little guy.'

We sat there awaiting the light to turn green. My attention drifted momentarily to the many that were using their heads—literally—as a transport, carrying everything from fabrics to food, to wherever it need go. No one was heeding the needs of a needless canine. My gaze was interrupted by one honk of the horn heavier than the others. The little dog yipped, scattering back to the fringe of the dirt highway.

'Someone step up! Help the poor thing!' It had yet to

dawn on me that *I* might be the one. Until…

'Dileep, be right back.'

I got out of the jeep, dodged a series of motorized rickshaws and other manmade mechanisms, and made my way to the tiny warrior.

'What you're attempting is no easy feat, my friend. This is the other side of India—too busy to take notice of the intention of one small dog.'

He just looked at me, panting away from the arid climate that offered little respite for one in need. I looked back at him. I could see his thoughts, at least mocked up through what may have been merely my imagination. He lifted his eyebrows as if to tell me, "Been waiting for you." It was an oddly familiar face.

I surveyed the intersection. It was a mess. If it had wheels, legs or other limbs, it was a transport—and it was in our way.

'Okay. Let's do this.'

I started into the intersection. At first, my canine companion was reluctant to trust in this stranger and take his first step. But, seemingly as with us all, his distrust of the unknown eventually gave way to an inner intention to get to where he wanted to be. He began to limp alongside me. Through a serenade of horns, amid a growing number of angry drivers and equally curious onlookers, together we stopped traffic as we made our way across the busy makeshift road. Step by step we paved a new road across the intersection of "What Was" and "What Can Be"—one carved not in merely good intentions, but in greater actions.

Dileep joined in, as well. He caught up with us and slowed the jeep to our pace, forming a shield of protection for the little guy and me. Once on the other side, we were received with smiles from a few of the observers, with one girl of maybe ten taking the dog over to a nearby tin of water, a just reward for his heroic effort.

I returned to the jeep. After a few minutes, Dileep broke the silence.

'I see you have found what you were looking for.'

'Why? Because I was willing to help a little dog across the road?'

'No, my friend. Because you were willing to follow your heart.'

I sat there trying to gather in all of what Dileep was telling me with those few choice words. What was it that he saw in me that I could not see so easily for myself? Certainly, I had learned plenty about myself on this sacred excursion to India. But had I really found what I was looking for?

'No worries, my friend,' Dileep continued. 'You are who you are. Whether you see it now or see it later, it remains as it is.'

Oddly, I was okay with that. I was okay with much more, now that I was armed with more that mattered. The material became less material. What I wanted more of was something else indeed. More with less. There was an ease in that peaceful notion; one interrupted by the ring from my mobile.

'Hello?'

'Jeremy. Luca Gregoria. How was your trip?'

What? In a snapshot? Won't even bother to attempt that one.

'Fine,' I responded.

'Good. Good. Hey, I spoke with the family and we are interested in working with you, to expand our line.' Luca and his family had been in the wine business for nearly a century. Their Pinot Grigio was the best in Italy.

'We need you to fly to Venice. Can you stop by on your way back to the States?'

My mind was not nearly as back in form as I thought. Words scattered like letters on a Scrabble board. I could only manage one.

'Sure.'

'Okay then. Perfect. Just get in touch with Susanna. She'll work out your itinerary, get you all the details you will need. We've been waiting for your reappearance.'

Me too, I thought.

'Well, I know it's getting late there, so we'll see you soon. Ciao.'

Three words. I spoke three words the entire conversation. I wonder if Luca even noticed. So many words, so much chatter fills the airways of our Western world, I sat there thinking. So many words. Far less meaning.

'We have arrived,' Dileep declared.

I had only just begun.

Can I but know of a divine love in this world?
Yes, Jeremy... to know Yourself is to know of this Love Divine.

What will I find when I seek this love in the world?
You will find others... seeking.

7
AMORE OR LESS IN VENICE

Running from or toward,
Keep moving.

It is in the moving that we get our next step.

T he splash of the Adriatic upon my face awakened me to my next destination. The sun glimmered off the varnish of the water taxi. The air was fresh. The sea, clear. Life was beautiful. Perhaps it always was.

Venice. It was good to be back. I had been graced by this place before—with Miia. At least the *city* remained in its splendor. The pain, unfortunately, remained as well, yet not so much that it could in any lasting measure taint the portrait of me in its unveiling.

Venezia—to those of her native soil—serves as an

amalgamation of song, poetry, and ancient aesthetics, with a relative ambivalence for what lies ahead. There exists only now when in her presence. Her décor, her ambiance speaks to the heart while attuning the ear to the rich sound of the operatic, and the inner voice of loving. Known in medieval times as *The Republic of Music*, Venice moves one through the stimulation of all five senses, across the bridge into those beyond—four-hundred-and-thirty-two times, to be exact.

There are 432 bridges in Venice. It appeared I was determined to cross every one of them the first afternoon on the island. My saunter through the narrowed streets, cobbled together as medieval marvels, was interrupted time and again by a bridge. First up, then down, and if I was attuned to the moment, the opportunity to enjoy a new view along the way. Enchanting pedestrian causeways, sprinkled with delightful cafés, boutique shops and quaint hotels. Then, another bridge—first up, then down. Even Venice dare not alter the pattern provided by this planet.

Luca had put me up at the Hotel Danieli. The Palazzo Dandolo remained as it had for six centuries; certainly since I had last visited this place with Miia, who had a taste for the regal. Her mother was convinced royalty ran in their bloodline. Any attempt to explain how unlikely the possibility would have been received with less than enthusiasm. So I simply chose silence. I should have chosen such far more often during those times.

Once my legs found their voice, I sat down at a café to

enjoy a late afternoon tea with *biscotti* (a coffee of some kind would have been more appropriate if one were to dissect the dramatics of my waiter). I took in the sights around me. Like da Vinci, I played both scientist and painter, first observing, then imagining, finally creating with my mind the illusions to match my inner desires for outer joy and expression.

To my left, a Swedish couple, inviting the sunlight upon their creamed complexions; co-witnessing life in its unfolding.

To my right, an elder Italian man, puffing away at his *Cohiba*, while canvassing the latest news from the paper in hand.

Behind me, the joyful banter of a group of students, congregating on a Friday afternoon to christen another weekend in its earned arrival.

I sat there, enjoying just that—sitting, appreciating the myriad of travels that had brought me to this very moment. I looked up, beyond the Gothic architecture of this Renaissance palace city. The sky was deep blue, in shade and meaning. The periodic cloud traversed the celestial, its movement measured, its purpose known only to itself. The clouds were quite different from the ones which haunted me that fateful day in Africa. Those too had their purpose. Their purpose was not so pure.

My eyes gravitated to earth. They took notice of a little girl of no more than five, one whom was taking notice of me. Holding her mother's hand as they darted across the piazza, she kept looking back in my direction. Her bonnet was white with lavender trimmings; her hair, a darker shade of brown; her eyes were warm; her cheeks rosy. The outfit she donned was impeccably applied, from her frilly-collared, white-and-lavender-spotted dress down to her buckle shoes, likely with a *canottiera* underneath (the under-shirt was a must for any Italian mamma with a sense of duty). The white heart-shaped fabric that graced her chest did not go unnoticed.

Those were the outer *finishings*. What moved me was in the last glance my way, and the smile she offered, a subtle little movement of her muscles that provided both a bridge and a guide to something inside. My eyes warmed to her own, then made their way to the sky above once again. One chance glance, and reminder, that what we endear was forever near, requiring merely a bridge—and the will to cross it.

There may be 432 bridges in Venice, I thought as the little girl vanished from view. But there was only one bridge to the indelible within—constructed by one small child through the power of a simple smile.

I felt blessed.

'You will enjoy this one,' Luca prepared me, as the waiter prepared our wine. And, of course, he would know. His family had been in the business of turning grapes to wine for nearly a century. His father's father learned the profession from his own father. And now Luca Gregoria worked as the sales and marketing head for the family vineyard, along with his papà and two brothers.

'You see. You can tell. Look at the way the wine grasps a hold of the glass as you move it around. And the aroma, as if a bouquet of violets was laid ever so gently upon a basket of seasoned berries. The taste? Sublime... powerful and enduring. A blessing. A true blessing from the gods.'

I enjoyed the glass with my new client. Not nearly as much as he did. For while I embraced new adventures like few others, my wines generally fell into two categories—the ones I liked and the ones I pretended to.

There was no pretending required this evening. For I was with a man who knew his wines; a man aligned with his own destiny.

'Fantastic! What is it?'

'It's a Brunello di Montalcino, from the province of Siena in Toscana. It is a powerful red, but with a nice smooth finish once you have found its inner nature—its "*David*."'

'Its David?'

'Why, yes. It is the destiny of all living things to find their inner nature, their David... their soul. Would you not agree?'

'David? As in Michelangelo's *David?*'

'Si. Is there any other one?'

Why, yes, I thought. There are many. I chose to let it go.

Luca was on a roll.

'As the great master Michelangelo once answered when asked, "What is the inspiration for your creation…?"'

'*I saw the angel in the marble and carved until I set him free.*'

'Michelangelo Buonarroti was not only Italian—which would have made him great in itself—but a living example of one who emancipated his soul through his work, sculpting in turn what only the soul can see in man, and as only God Himself could manifest through co-creation with His own.'

Luca took a taste of his wine and continued. 'We are in constant co-creation, I have no doubt. And we get to choose through which lens we shall create… through our own distorted spectacles, or through the celestial as seen from soul.' He took another drink, swished it around in his mouth, swallowed. 'Ah, yes. So good. A powerful co-creation with this one, my friend.'

'Okay, then if it is our inherent destiny to find our David, as you say—our soul—well, even David had some assistance. He had Michelangelo to guide him out of the rubble, so to speak, and into the light.'

'Si. He had help.'

'And who is here to help us… to help chisel away that which we are not, so that we may better know ourselves—our true selves—our soul?'

'Look around you, my friend. The Michelangelo you seek is all around you.' Luca laughed and took another drink from the elixir that in itself was serving as co-

conspirator to what had become an intoxicating conversation. He excused himself for the men's room. I remained, in reflection.

Look around me? My "Michelangelos?" Those who have helped to chip away at what I am not? I sat there in contemplation. There were many who had made their way onto the stage of my life. My father, a reflection of integrity, a moral compass. Georgia, Arena, Tessa (in an odd way). Miia, through the painful process of falling in, then out, of love. Robert the homeless man, and the woman at the factory in Russia, working the glass like a fine craftsman, polishing up any rough edges. All played a part, as supporting actor or simply an "extra" in the unfolding of the tale of me—the sculpting of Jeremy; my life story.

And, of course, there was my mother. I loved my mother. And she loved me. We had little in common when vetted through this particular lifetime, but she held our family together through a sense of duty, aligned with a compassionate heart. The Italian in her would have it no other way. The relationship between my mother and me was complicated for anyone who but scratched its surface. For her and me, it was simple: we let each other be, and loved one another as we were.

Luca returned and we concluded our evening with a bit of business. I would see him again in the coming weeks, as we agreed to meet in New York and set up a wine distribution venture together. The real business of the evening, however, had already been concluded.

On the water taxi back to the hotel, I marveled at the magic created when the purpose revealed for a chosen encounter rarely resembles the intention of the mind through its narrowed view. I came this evening to talk of wine. I left, wined and dined by a higher force at work— once again delivered through whatever messenger is required and available. Could it be that the answers awaited us all, sitting along the sidelines patiently until we opened a door—a window even—and invited it into our consciousness through an unbridled willingness?

After the requisite brushing, flossing and general washing (the likes of which I found more daunting with each new entry into my life), I lay there in bed, admiring the level of detail that went into the angelic figures that graced the ceiling above. Those responsible for this simple masterpiece took the time and attention to not only capture beauty, but give beauty a face, a personality of its own. The walls were rich in golden color and features. The flooring, a foundation laid proper by craftsmen, made to endure. There is an art to the craft we choose, and the manner by which we release our craft into the world. It may be in the simplicity where we may find truth, but it is in the detail that we give truth life in this world.

How many times I looked up from the comfort of a bed, and saw nothing, nothing at all. And tonight, I noticed the mastery of the inlay that bridged wall to ceiling—my ego to the very soul of me. I was entirely present with what was in its entirety.

With my heart wide open, my eyes closed…
I drifted off into the sound of silence.

———

The pigeons scattered as if to clear the way for the oncoming. The mumble of many echoed gently off the marbled structures that lined Piazza San Marco, as if in a stir over what awaited. The sky had moved from pale blue to an array of oranges, signifying perhaps the fruit to be born through such laborious learning. The scent of baked breads and various fragrances mixed with the sea air; lined the nostrils. My ears played welcome receivers to the quartet before me.

My eyes took notice of *her*.

On the fringe of the seated area of Caffè Florian sat a woman. She wore a navy blue dress, with a dash of white trimmings designed to bring the eye into focus. Her posture, a product of years of schooling in what it means to be a woman in defiance of the modern. Her white gloves provided a fitting complement to a picture most *Hepburnesque* in its unveiling. What intrigued me most, however, was what her eyes revealed as they gazed in my direction.

The gates to an eternal truth beckoned my entrance.

I approached her with every intention of melting her with my charm, entertaining her with my wit. When I arrived and she gave further notice of me, nothing came forward. Nothing, that is, from any place frequented by the mind. Her eyes paid homage to my own, as I stood there, entranced in a series of memories warming to a sacred heart. I *knew* her.

'May I sit?'

She looked up through her deep brown "windows," with a purity that could not be concealed. She smiled. It was a smile similar in nature to the one offered by a younger version of her just a few days back. It was a smile, a simple smile, with a simple message:

Come join me. Join me…and be.

Through the silence that followed, I was overwhelmed by a symphony of sound—the angelic vibration of the harp in harmonic accord with the ethereal note of the flute— ushering forward a feeling of peace in union with a pure and undeniable loving. Yet this love had a different tone to it, a different voice; different source. It came through a whisper, adjoined with a promise, one of everlasting, having never left at all. It came not from her, this beauty before me, but through her. And it arrived in this singular moment, framed by innocence as reconnaissance, a recapturing if for but a moment of what had eluded me so.

Li offered few words at first, but rather through her strength of spirit and graceful motions provided all the communication required. She gestured me to sit. The waiter prepared a second setting at her table, as planned accomplice to the impending reunion. Li moved as if in continuance of a sitting and setting lifetimes in motion. She spread the awaiting napkin upon my lap; then proceeded to move each olive to my plate with the precision of a fine craftsman. Her hands moved with the graceful flow of a bird in dance with a delicate wind. She barely looked up, but when she did, magic was made. The sorcery was in the source; two souls aligned in one romance—the kind of the reacquainted.

I had yet to find my own words, yet was filled with the creative voice and tone that has set the energy of loving in motion for lifetimes past and present. I was well aware I had been down this road before. Yet, as with all who hold out hope for love, I found whatever signs I could foster that this path would take me somewhere else, somewhere greater—wherever somewhere was.

I was being romanced once again by the allure of life's most precious offering, an endearing harvest of my heart.

Li exhibited a radiance, an elegance. Her dark hair shimmered, as if in full dance with the early evening offering from the summer sun. Her face, moist as the dew upon the vintage harvest. Her eyes, gems of dark brown with amber shavings—an indication of the jewel within the jewel itself yet to be uncovered.

It was not in the mere theater of the spectacular by way of outward appearance, however, that made the moment most engaging, and Li most beautiful. This, I'd seen before. Rather, it was the underlying, overarching energy that filled the chalice of the heart, as I was blessed with yet another moment—*the* moment—when the celestial and earthly become one; when there is no separation between what is and what is divine.

I knew *this* only once before. I thought I would never know of *this* again. And here it was. Here she was.

Li broke the silence.

'I know you. I don't know how… but I know you.'

'The past. It is something in the past—a distant past. When I first saw you, I was overcome with a familiarity, as well. It was like… '

'Coming home,' Li finished my sentence.

'Yes. Like coming home, to the known… a place that only my heart would understand.'

Li smiled, as her eyes gravitated to the stone beneath our feet, overcome with a sense of joy, humbled by the moment. Her hands remained crossed; her posture perfect. Everything, perfect.

'Do you study the masters?' she asked, as if continuing a conversation from another time, another place.

'Lately, I think they have been studying me.'

'What do you mean?'

'It seems the further I go down whatever road it is I'm traveling—the deeper even—the more timely their appearance, in some way or form.'

'You mean you have *seen* these masters?' Li's query was that of an excited young girl, and not of a cynical adult more concerned with my mental state than any master.

I laughed. 'No. No, I have not seen or met any masters, none that I'm aware of. But these timely messages— reminders, perhaps—as if orchestrated by some higher power, have been increasing with the frequency of my… '

'Frequency?' Li managed to finish my thought once again.

'Yes, I suppose the word "frequency" would work here. There is something going on, something which is moving me to...' I paused, perhaps assuming Li would finish my next thought, as well. She just sat there, her eyes twinkling, awaiting my next words as if they were her own.

'I know this sounds a bit crazy.'

'Crazy? Not in the least. I have had similar feelings, similar experiences... like with this napkin here.' Li lifted her glass, exposing a napkin with a printed flower—a rose— –on one side, and an inscription on the other.

'*Accustom yourself continually to make many acts of love, for they enkindle and melt the soul.*'

'These words,' Li shared, 'they are the words of Saint Teresa of Avila. I know them. My mother made certain of it.'

'You see. Timed to perfection. She speaks of love, and...'

'And here we are,' Li finished, once again.

I was overwhelmed. By the moment, by the woman, by the way these timeless wisdoms made their way into my life, my heart, my soul. I was beginning to believe more and more that coincidence was merely a matter of consciousness, and the greater the awareness the less coincidence played in much of anything. There were no accidents. There never were.

'I'm sorry. I did not properly introduce myself. My

name is Jeremy. Jeremy Braddock.'

'I am Li… Giordano. And, yes, you did introduce yourself properly. First, there is *you*… then, there is your name.'

I smiled. My eyes twinkled as the stars aligned.

'Li Giordano? An interesting mix of names. Chinese and Italian, I assume?'

'Yes, with the details to follow. But not now. Not in this moment.' Li sat back, chin slightly tilted to the ground. Her eyes arose to meet my own. The pierce of her eyes made my heart dance.

Li and I sat there—as one—enjoying the setting sun and rising tide of emotion that filled our near surroundings. Perhaps it was the music. Perhaps the setting. It could have even been the wine that poured freely as we took in the evening together. It could have been so many things. But it was only one thing.

Set amid the backdrop of centuries of architectural marvel, a craftsmanship that turned marble into majesty, a city of possibility built upon a sea of tranquility, love found a home once again.

The pigeons flew off in tandem. I remained. There was nowhere else to go.

Li bent over, unbuckled her shoe, removed it, revealing the gentle, defined curvature of her foot. She proceeded to pull out a piece of jewelry from the same shoe. She looked at me. We both laughed.

'Do you always keep your jewelry in your shoe?'

'No. It must have made its way there somehow. It's an anklet. You see, it goes right here.' She held the gold chain against her ankle. My eyes were held captive by the grace in which she did just that.

Li sat up. Her eyes met with my own, once again. My cells filled with the light of an eternal flame, origin unknown, destination undeniable. I was falling. *Again.* Quickly, most decidedly. Lifetimes of joy passing through every chamber of my knowing heart. The symphony of crickets emerged. From whatever the source, the purpose of their presence was now clear.

Love.

I loved her. As clear as the evening air that surrounded us, the late sun that enlightened us, the setting that unveiled us *to* us. I loved her, all of her. Even the parts I had yet to uncover, the jewel beneath, hidden only perhaps by the "shoes" we have chosen to travel in this lifetime. There was no manner of the mind that could justify a love at first sight, unless it was merely first sight on this particular flight, this life, this journey. I loved her. And that was all my awakened heart needed to know.

'Life is filled with such jewels,' Li shared. 'I awakened this morning knowing where I was, with some semblance of who I was, yet not knowing why, why here, why now. When I saw you, I had my answer. I knew that all the moments before, decisions, choices made that would allow me to be here, in this chair, in this moment, were woven with but one tapestry to be conceived—the union of two threads adjoined as one strand, once again.'

I could not have expressed it better. There was no better expression than what was being expressed in the moment. And I was happy she was seeing what I was seeing.

'I have been searching for answers myself, to the many questions that taunt me,' I shared. 'As if I am involved in some type of treasure hunt. One with no map, no guide, no sense of where I'm going... or why. Yet, when I saw you, the need to know disappeared. The need to be right here, right now, with you was all that my mind could account for.'

The shades of Saint Mark's Square took on a different hue. The mid-evening sun warmed the buildings that surrounded us. The hardened marble and stone surroundings were softened by the presence of a gentler version of the light itself. It kissed off the structures and into our awaiting eyes.

Li leaned over. Her lips neared. They found their way to my ear.

'*Wǒ xǐhuan nǐ. Wǒ hěn xǐhuan nǐ,*' Li whispered. Her breath tickled my skin, warmed my soul.

I knew not what she had spoken to me. The intention was unmistakable. For what I knew as love, she entered into with an expression more befitting of her Chinese influence. The awareness was the same. This was no ordinary encounter, but rather an extraordinary marriage of past with present, with a future as uncertain as it was anticipated.

Li and I finished our wine, stomachs giving safe passage to the last tastes of a meal surreal. We decided to stroll for a bit along one of the many canals that carved this coveted city. The sea provided a moist bath upon our skin. Her hand fit perfectly within my own, leaving little doubt the conspiracy of the universe that sets in motion these moments far in advance. The perfect fit. The perfect place. The perfect form.

'Be careful, my friend. This planet is not where perfect lives. And pedestaling others just creates greater distance between them, you, and the truth.'

I was having none of this voice tonight. It was perfect; she was perfect; and that was that.

We stopped along the canal to take in the myriad of parading partners—and one another. Everything appeared as if in slow motion, where only the breath of now remained. We played witness to each delicate cadence of the power of life itself.

The ebb and flow of the sea with the *battello* as it traversed the Grand Canal, massaging the water with its polished, wooden frame.

The caressing music of Bocelli, in rhythmic harmony with the choice gesture of the gondolier.

The spectacle of colors flowering our path; hues of yellow playing warm bedfellows to the purple violets that basked in one last breath of light before yielding to night.

The scent of fresh basil emanating from a nearby

kitchen; its destination, a rich tomato base distinguished from all others through the love by which it were made, then offered.

The music.

The moon, in its early rise.

The *maître d'* with his tenor voice.

The rhythmic motion of the sea within sight.

All elements conspired as we faced, then embraced, one another. She backed against the only man-made structure that stood between me, her heavenly form, and the water below. She moved. I moved. We moved, in harmony. Her delicate hands caressing my upper chest, weakening each muscle with but a fingertip's approach. Moving in universal rhythm with my own offering along the exposure of her lower back. Each touch giving way to a gaze, a glimpse into the soul of the other—land, time, forgotten for so long and now renewed. Her eyes arose. Her lips prepared. They embraced with my own, a subtle flow along the chasm created as Li availed herself to me through the portal of a taste so consuming. Sweetness beyond the likes of this realm, a romance with the heavens in the re-unite.

Innocent, pure, a flash of past and future wrapped in one shining present.

Present...

The gift of the present moment...

For a man who has known of romance all his life, as both captor and liberator.

Li and I stepped back. Encased within a faint purple

light as aura to her form, she allowed me deep into her window, while given access to my own. Lifetimes flashed before the screen of the *akashic*—recording only loving, receiving only joy, re-*membering* only peace.

I gazed with a sense of disbelief upon this angel before me. I was aware, present, gifted by the gods themselves. The faithful and quite "loyal forces" were also in attendance, stepping once again upon the stage of the mental. Still very much a part of me, each voice of lower reason made its case for denying the reality of the form that had made its way into my being, my heart in its unfolding.

Was this the climax of a life's journey to the highest elevation, the proverbial pinnacle of near perfection? Or was this merely another grand illusion devised by a most imaginative mind and tiresome track played far too often upon the awaiting?

Li gazed into my eyes and smiled; an acknowledgment of the man I had become, or perhaps simply the man I wished myself to be. Her approval, as offered through the spectacles of the spectacular, a view into my soul through a set of eyes as piercing as they were revealing, served as a welcomed embrace for the little boy inside me who wanted to belong, somewhere, in some way.

Through Li, had I finally uncovered the true meaning of love, or simply engaged in the dance of romance once again, playing faithful fool to a lower order of the highest good?

So many questions.

So many moments with so few answers.

For the one truth I came here to know.

Atlantis had a history. It included Li. It included me.

We were in a garden. All were gods in some lesser version. We had powers that would not be considered mortal these days. I was kissing her when the moment occurred. Over the hill of this garden paradise, chariots arrived with horses ten feet in height. The guardsmen came with orders. She was to be removed from me. I had abused the powers of the gods, mixing science with that which science had no business in. It was the last time I would kiss her lips.

Reshma appeared. "Your love was stripped from you. You gave it all up, your beliefs, your God. You gave Him up. And cast yourself into a dark place for quite some time."

My memory of Atlantis came with a reminder. I gave it all up once—gave Him up—in the name of love, of all things. And in the process, I lost my way.

'Can love divine be known with another?' I asked whoever was guardian to the dream state.

'*Yes... if you are... then it is so. Regardless of the other... words... actions... It is so as it is so.*'

I awakened, to the words; words that were not my own. And to the life that was mine for the claiming.

I awakened, uncertain as to whether I would choose a

greater course this time. Or simply play victim to my humanness once again.

I awakened.

And could only hope I was awake.

I sat along the banks of Canale di San Marco, awaiting Li's arrival, cup of fresh espresso in my hand, the aroma arousing my senses to the dawn of a new day. I imagined how Galileo would sit in marvel as to the sciences of motion and astronomy, conjuring up theory after theory to meet with the reality of his own inner knowing. Galileo in his wit once noted:

'The Sun, with all the planets revolving around it, and depending on it, can still ripen a bunch of grapes as though it had nothing else in the Universe to do.'

In all his wisdom, could it be he may have been speaking about something other than astronomy here? After all, he held a strong belief in God while enlightening many to the awe of science that surrounds us. Perhaps, just maybe, Galileo understood the intricate relationship between not only Earth and the universe, but man and God Himself.

Li arrived. She was glowing. I was happy; happy to be knowing her again; happy to be here in this moment; happy we had not allowed the evening prior to be consummated with passion played out upon the mattress. There was more to this than momentary bliss. There was also more to Li than I was privy to in the moment. She had a secret. This was clear. But it was her secret, one she would reveal to me when she was ready to do so.

For now, we had now.

'You sure I can't change your mind?' I had been proposing we extend our stay in Venice; and thus avoid the moment that was now upon us.

'Oh, Jeremy, I wish I could. I wish it were that easy... life, love... *us*.'

Li paused for a moment. Her hand made its way to mine. Her eyes followed.

'Jeremy, we have now. And in this, we have everything.'

'Then it's settled. We simply string together all of the *nows* until *then* is simply where we begin again.'

'Do you always get your way with the women you covet?'

'Yes and no. Yes, initially. And no, eventually.'

'Well, you have me now, Jeremy Braddock.'

The morning hinting to an end in sight, Li and I changed location and nestled in at La Terrazza. The canal and its activities beneath us, we continued to venture deep within the depth of our souls. We were stirred to surface by the words of wisdom from our *cameriere*.

'*All the reasonings of men are not worth one sentiment of women.*'

The waiter, of course, was honoring Li. He was also quoting Voltaire. Li and I just smiled at one another.

'An *apéritif* of some kind for the lady and you, *signore?*'

'Yes. We'll have...'

'*Due champagne, per favore*,' Li interjected.

'As you wish, *signora*.'

'Champagne?' I inquired.

'Are we not still celebrating? If it really has been lifetimes since we last met, well, I believe that is cause for many celebrations.'

'Yes, it is.' The pause that followed allowed just enough time for my mind to make its entrance, and thus its nuisance.

'Li, I don't want to ruin what has been a gift, a blessing by any definition, but you leave this afternoon, as you know…'

'Yes, I am leaving. But I will not be gone.'

'Yes. I get that on some level. But that does little for the little boy in me that wants everything now… and fears a tomorrow that does not include you.'

Li laughed, 'Oh, Jeremy, do you not trust that there is something bigger in play, something grander than our minds can possibly understand?'

'Of course. I've been feeling that way more and more. Yesterday, today, have been examples of life unfolding in a manner I could not have predicted. And the sound of the crickets is always a good sign.'

Li smiled. She could not hear the chirping, but she got the message. 'In China, a cricket singing in the home is a sign of good luck.'

'But to trust that I will see you again… '

'*Know* me again. Seeing is for this world. Knowing is for

181

all worlds.'

Li and I finished our time in the light with an embrace of our eyes under a warming sun that offered safe passage to the innermost chambers of our hearts. There were no games, no falsehoods, no matters of the mind to address— at least none to be addressed in the moment. Our love was pure, unsoiled by the needs and desires of the lower nature that so often leads to the path of lower expressions, and regrets. No, we were set upon a higher path, a greater course; and if it were our destiny to know more, I would have to trust that it would be so.

Trust. The longest bridge man would ever construct. Or perhaps merely the stringing together of 432 bridges over which one must travel to arrive at such a place. No short-cuts. A long and enduring path to the very end.

I watched as Li's water taxi took her away from me. She glanced back, several times. My heart hurt. My eyes welled with the notion I may never again see her, know her. Li's sunglasses shielded the same emotion. I said goodbye once more inside myself. There was more to this story—more to hers; more to my own. It would not be resolved, not here; not now.

For only the tapestry that tells the tale of our time here could offer such a clue. All we could do—all we could ever really do—was let go. Let go, and trust.

So I decided to do just that.

Amore or less.

Share with me, oh Master... the many teachings of the loving heart. *Revealed through you, my Friend.*

8
A BITE OF THE FORBIDDEN APPLE

'Do every act of your life...
As if it were your last'
– Marcus Aurelius

There are moments—defining moments—when the setting and story that surround us are there *for* us, or so it seems; a moment in time orchestrated by some higher form conspiring for a higher good. Our job is merely to show up, open up, and be open to moving up. It is not an easy job, but it is *our* job, and no one else's.

A Christmas Carol, by Charles Dickens, is the story of such an awakening. The Geary Theater in San Francisco provided the setting for the setting, the story in its un-folding. Ebenezer Scrooge was the co-conspirator as well as co-beneficiary, a character played by an actor who was just another character himself. For if we are all actors upon the stage of our own existence—and we are—what is left for us but to choose our role and create from there? False or true, we are choosing which self to bring center stage. True or false, we are creating from the foundation chosen. It has been and always will be *our* choice.

'God bless us... *everyone!*'

Tiny Tim concluded the production in a manner quite familiar. I had the giddiness of a young school child as I made my way through the doors of the theater and spilled onto Taylor Street with the rest of the patrons. I felt the rejuvenation of the main character, awakened to the goodness within, to another chance at this production called life. What to do with it? That was the question. My encounter with Li, however brief, had served in opening up a chamber of my heart that had remained dormant for some time. And I was trusting more in that inner voice—and outward signs—which seemed designed to point the way. But to where? To what end?

For now, New York. A new home, a fresh start. And a date with a man with a propensity for making both wine and wisdom with equal mastery.

A concoction, perhaps, for a greater connection.

'Heading home?'

This query came from the poor chap who had been

damned to the middle seat for the past four hours of our five-hour flight. What compelled someone to begin a conversation with another fully armed with a set of headphones and book in hand I never quite understood. Ignore him, and suffer the torture of perceived selfishness. Engage, and be subjected to the mental anguish of coming up with a polite but pointed exit. Serve, and perhaps the kingdom of the unknown is availed to us. I chose service. I really had no choice in the matter. The universe made certain of this.

'Home? Sort of. Will be in New York the next few months. On business.'

'Oh, what kind of business?'

Here we go.

'Consulting. On a wine project.'

'Oh, wine. I love wine. Thought about getting into the business myself. Thought about many things over the course of my life.'

He paused. I did not fill the void with more words.

'You know, I've given my whole life to my wife, my kids. Kids are now graduated. Wife and I are considering all possibilities, including divorce.'

Why is he sharing this with me? Service, Jeremy. Remember.

'Have a nice home, good job, enough money. Lived the dream, one might say.'

There was a sadness about him, in his voice, his gesture.

'Lately, I've been thinking. What if this were not my life

at all? What if, all this time, I had been living someone else's life... someone else's dream? My father's maybe.'

I was immediately reminded of a poem Cassandra had shared with me, by Rumi; a brief collection of words with a mere lifetime of meaning.

'*There is one thing in this world which you must never forget to do. If you forget everything else and not this, there is nothing to worry about; but if you remember everything else and forget this, then you will have done nothing in your life.*'

I wondered. Did this man in the middle seat get swept away—as with so many of us—to the middle of the pack, another number with no real calculation of the effects of merely plugging in as opposed to stretching out, expanding, finding the answers to his own questions? Did he remember everything else but forget the one thing, the one thing he came here to know? Have I?

I did not need to plan my exit from the conversation. The man in the middle seat had already checked out on his own, craning to see out the window and presumably into the vast nothingness in search of a sign.

I felt for him.

I felt for us all.

———

'Follow the signs to the taxi station. It should take you about forty-five minutes to get to the city,' the attendant at the information desk offered.

Unfamiliar with Newark International, I did as she

instructed and followed the signs. After all, when in unfamiliar territory it was best to do so, I was coming to learn. Making sense of them, well that was another talent altogether. I understood "stop" and "proceed with caution." These were quite clear. But I seemed to have difficulty adhering to the "detour" signs in my life, the ones that would help me to navigate around both the natural and quite human impediments that made for a more arduous journey—and recovery.

The combination of a driving rainstorm and a Ukrainian cab driver with a heavy foot made for a not-so-pleasant journey into the city. Stomach in my throat, we made our way toward the Holland Tunnel.

It was eerie. Something was missing. Something rather substantial. The last time I was in New York, the Twin Towers were still towering. Erased by one swift stroke of fanaticism, the city had lost its feeling of invincibility, on a day—9/11—when clearly not all signs were pointing up. Victims? Sacrifices? The jury would deliberate for some time, with the final verdict still unclear. What was certain was that this one reflective moment, along with those that followed, had taken a bit of a bite out of the forbidden fruit. This left "The Big Apple," and humanity in general, exposed to the core—the way I felt these days myself.

There was no avoiding my rendezvous with myself. I could choose the path—timing even—but not the destination. And as with my new host city, whether I played victim or sacrifice was entirely up to me. For to choose the path of victim would be to choose the road of dis-empowerment, and therefore con myself into relinquishing the power of creation we have all been bestowed. And I could con with the best of them—others, as with myself. My intellect allowed me such privilege. The stronger the mind, the better the con. Inevitably, I would be forced to face my greatest adversary, the part of me that benefited in this world—or so it would seem—from the charade I played so well. The one that would play out the same scenario time and again, as if stuck on an oh-too-familiar tune—unattuned to a higher note.

I left neither my heart nor my body in San Francisco—just a whole lot of old baggage. Of this, I made certain. What was not so clear was the source of my preoccupation with procrastination—along with a desire to be desired—that seemed to delay my scheduled flight plan on many an occasion. Under this newfound spirit of trust, however, I decided to fold self-trust in there as well. If God was big enough to love all of His creation, then surely I should be willing to add myself into the mix.

I was in desperate need of a transfusion the likes of which few cities could provide. New York still had an energy about it; one of manifestation. Different cities, countries, regions of the world have a different energy to them, and bring forward different sides of us. This I learned along the way—and the long way, across cultures and continents. And I was in the market for a greater version of myself. I felt a burning desire to create something other than a mess. It was time for me to part ways with old ways––and *go it alone* for a while. Li remained in my heart. But there was something else stirring inside. As I arrived in Manhattan and made my way to my new sanctuary of the moment, I found the separation from my past to be the easy part, when compared, that is, to coming to grips with myself in the present.

My first day of renewed liberation, I was quickly re-acquainted with the city. My mind took note as I left my building and eventually made my way onto Church Street.

New York was dreary in January.

Doormen were trained to be pit bulls.

New Yorkers rarely looked you in the eyes.

The city was a mecca for foods that fatten.

Only the black side of the Black and White Cookie was actually edible.

I needed a new umbrella and a comfortable pair of shoes.

New York was dreary in January.

It was not cold enough to snow; just rain on any parade of my heart, and dampen every part of me—winter coat and gloves included. I forgot to layer up, but was too far along to double back. I would have to make do with what I had. It usually works out that way.

I arrived at Mocca Lounge. The place was lively. The space was cramped. The food was exotic. And Luca was sharing stories again.

'Jeremy, my family has been in the wine business for

many generations, as you know. We have been at it for quite some time, harvest after harvest. Our wine, it was okay. It was a good wine, but it was not a great one. Until one day, my great grandfather discovered one small detail. In the soil, there were traces of limestone. Sediment that was affecting the grapes, their taste. This sediment had been there its whole life. There was no moving the sediment. So my great grandfather, after much thought, picked up and moved. He moved the winery to where it is today, near Venice. He just picked up and moved. To achieve excellence, he had to make a change.'

'Did he consider just changing professions?'

'He considered many things, had many ideas. But he did not consider that. One cannot change what they are. The limestone is what it is. My great grandfather was what he was. He only had one choice really. To keep moving until he found what he was looking for... until he found a better wine.'

'I have been on the move for quite some time myself.'

'I know. You have said. But some men, they are running from something. Usually they run from themselves. You... you run toward something. It is in your eyes.'

'Well, there are only so many places one can run.'

'To me, Jeremy, I think there is but one. I think a person can only run home. Anywhere else, he will feel like a visitor, a stranger. Visiting, it is nice. But home, it is the only place where we can feel we have arrived.'

I sat there for a moment, for a very long moment. Luca

was playing guide once again. I wondered if he even knew this was the role he was playing. Perhaps he was just sharing with me the history of his family, the winery, so that I would understand his business better. Or perhaps he was doing *His* family business, handling God's matters, where the matter of me was involved. It mattered little, Luca's purpose. It mattered only that I was paying attention.

In the weeks that followed, Luca and I managed to create the foundation for the expansion of his business into North America. His family would be pleased with the success that would result from a purposeful plan and willful execution. The greater purpose at hand was the continued systematic peeling back of the layers that stood between myself and perhaps a greater version of me.

I could only trust that I would be pleased with the result, as well.

The Legend of Sleepy Hollow took place just up the Hudson River, at least in story. It was the legend of the Headless Horseman, a violent personality not of the flesh, who made it his business to terrorize the small town whose fear just fueled his flame for vengeance. Off went the heads of many a victim. The fear associated with it turned the town near crazy. All the while, the ghostly creature was merely searching for what was rightfully his—his head that had been stolen from the grave. So many had to lose their heads, so that one could find solace once again with his own.

I walked along the Hudson by way of Battery Park. The winter chill and not-so-subtle breeze played reminder to a season that had not quite had its final say. Spring would someday arrive, offering an answer to hope for one who was willing to let go of his head, with the promise of a more intelligent guide, and smoother ride. This I believed, which was much closer to knowing than merely thinking.

My journey—my ride—had brought me to this moment, this place. Every decision ever made; every move along the corridor of my content and discontent; every character played and received on this stage—*my* stage—had served its purpose. For so long, I had given my mind dominion, asking my heart to take a back seat on the very journey that perhaps my heart itself held the secret to—the one thing I came here to know.

I thought of that "man in the middle" on the plane ride from San Francisco, and in living a life that was "not his own." Seemed kind of backward, I arrived at, while sipping my third cup of Moroccan tea. A backward process, until we dared to do it differently and chose to expand beyond our imposed constrictions—by self and through others— and live the life we were born to live. Easier said than done. But that was only until we did it. And, quite frankly, was my life really "easier" by choosing not to?

'What can the heart know that the mind would not?' My conscious self began the debate.

'*It can know what the mind can only think, at best*,' the higher self retorted.

'Yeah, but without the head, how would one live in reality?'

'*A greater reality awaits…* '

'And frankly this current one hasn't been all that easy.' The basic self finally got a word in.

The conscious self—that part of me that thought. The basic self—that part of me that felt. The higher self—the one who knew. They all played their role, and played it well. After a lifetime—likely many lifetimes—where the head had had its way, it was clear the other two forces that governed me were casting a vote for something greater. For now, we were working toward a measured détente as we made our way back toward the apartment. A peace offering would only be struck with something we could all agree on.

'I'll take a 'dog and a Coke, please.'

Words spoken every day in every dialect imaginable to the street vendor who teased us with the scented allure of our greatest childhood memory. The little boy in me was onboard with *this* decision.

'Ya want mustad and ketchup wid dat?' asked the man in a hard, New York accent. His clothes were laced with samples of condiments, along with a complement of street grime.

'The works.' Translated—*everything!*

I watched in savory anticipation as the street vendor prepared my dinner—like a dog awaiting the scraps from his tableside view. The vendor's hands spoke of the elements that proved most unkind to these weathered warriors. His simple face, having traveled the world without leaving the corner of Church and Chambers Street, concealed a wisdom that no time in school could manifest.

I took notice of a wooden statuette of Lord Krishna just behind the salt and pepper shakers on his cart. There was even a tattered picture of Vishnu—a Hindu god and the preserver of the universe in Indian mythology—hanging by a worn piece of tape near the register. This man seemed like your "average Joe," but he was apparently so much more.

What a story this man had to tell, I thought. And what a difference between our first impressions and our lasting ones.

'That be all mista'?'

'Yes, thank you.' Short of a million questions, that is.

I imagined his life. Not a life of predictable patterns at all. He was probably once in the military, stationed abroad. Or perhaps a former teacher, retired from armed duty as captain of his classroom. Maybe, on some exotic vacation, he came across a Hindi goddess who captured his heart and awakened his soul to new worlds. So many possibilities.

Of course, the statue and picture could have been merely a series of collectibles for a street merchant with a penchant for finding things. The romantic in me would stay with the other scenarios. I thought to strike up a conversation with the old chap, but decided against it. My time in New York was dedicated to me, and I was determined to spend more of it in introspect, and less in inspecting the lives of others.

As I stepped back to enjoy my hotdog—and allow those queued behind me the same privilege—I observed the subject of my latest fascination as he reached for his cloth and began wiping down the stand he kept so tidy, such pride on display. Playing in the background, but clearly distinguishable as crescendo to the noise of car horns and jackhammers, was the mood of the moment as graced by Bach himself through the man's CD player.

Johann Sebastian Bach was a master at capturing a characteristic emotion and maintaining that mood throughout the work. And in this moment, he managed to compose the perfect expression, of a man that would serve hotdogs with his masterful hands, and feed his soul through such devoted service.

The chirping noise in my ears returned, quickly drowning the music of the latest master to make a timely guest appearance. I stepped onto the street. A bus driver laid on his horn and frightened me back onto the curb. Just another pedestrian not paying attention, as the warning from the little red man on the electronic crosswalk sign went unheeded. Apparently this cricket sound made its presence felt not only within a defining, loving moment, but also when I played both deaf and blind to my surroundings. It acted as a sort of protector of this character known as me.

New York offered many examples of duality, through the dual nature of humanity. Rarely could you find such high energy that could be slowed to a single breath, through a single exchange, from and with any person of any position, awakening the heart to a meaningful moment through conversation.

New York not only "never sleeps," but served in stirring the soul like few others.

January gave way to February. February to March. And March yielded to its sister April. Three months passed. I was no longer present. Missing in action. Unless one would consider cocooning an action. New York may be a mecca for manifestation, but it was the last place on Earth for the "lost" to be "found."

The city stirred the soul like few others. This was true. But I was like no other, capable of going long stretches without including the soul in conversation. There really was no explanation for such foolish behavior; unless one's intention were to devise scheme after scheme for delaying any return to source, thus sourcing my return to this realm.

I awakened—finally—with the intent to do it differently. I found my way to Church Street—this was nothing new. Strapped to my ears was my iPod. Pumping through its wires was a selection of Krishna music. I walked to a slightly different beat. Church Street formed my pilgrimage. Step by step, I awakened more and more. I found myself in unison with the streetlights, the movement of the crowd. The clouds above played due reminder that what stood between the gray of day and the light above was merely a temporary shade of ourselves to be lifted. From the buildings above to the earth below, I experienced the folly of man's innate creativity in concert with the hand of spirit itself. I saw possibility. And I was open.

Moved by one note, one voice, it was time to do. It was always time to do.

Of course, I had little idea just what to do. But I knew Mocca Lounge had something to do with it. I knew this on some level where knowing waited, patiently, for my emergence.

I entered the café. I placed my coat on the rack. I kissed Angelica (the waitress) on the cheek. I made my way to my favorite table, tucked away but in full view of all passersby. The light drizzle outside just added to the mystique, the moment in its unfolding. I sat there, peering out at the crowd of fellow travelers, wondering if they, too, were on some long and lonely journey to nowhere in particular. The city provided all with a million opportunities for self-reflection. Question was, were we ready to look?

The reflective moment was aided through the grace of another. It usually was.

Maya glanced in my direction on more than one occasion. As if the heavens conspired—and the loyal forces desired—to test my resolve once again, this island princess of Jamaican descent made clear her interest in my presence.

'You look like someone,' she shared as if dialed into the *always open* sign of my ego. 'I know that sounds like a pick-up line, but it's not. You really do look like him.'

'Like whom?' I queried back, a bit discomforted with the notion I might be so easily displaced by another face.

'I don't know, but bizarrely familiar. I wish I could remember his name.'

The familiarity of which she spoke was likely a bridge contrived by the universe—connecting two in one moment, for one singular purpose. I was curious how this would play out.

'Hmmm, I think he is an actor.'

An actor, I thought? Oh, I was an actor alright. I mean, weren't we all? I acted like this, then like that. Maybe even like this *and* that. A whole closet full of characters that served in overdressing while not addressing:

The self-confident... who masked his underlying issues with self-worth.

The successful... who effectively hid the fear of failure in the next endeavor.

The giver... who seemed to give only when he would benefit from such benevolence.

The lover... who knew not how to love himself (sometimes even *like* himself).

The man... who was reduced in truth to a mere boy, hurt by the world through his own choices.

The rather odd beginning gave way to an all-day adventure over tea. The dialogue moved from shallow, safe waters to the depth of new discoveries both in ourselves and with each other. Maya was attractive. Her sunkissed skin and wavy, caramel-colored hair was an eye-turner for anyone who possessed such—eyes, that is. Her charismatic smile would captivate any room, and many a heart. Once again, spirit knew just how to grab my attention, even when I was determined to walk Church Street as a monk for the moment. Her attractive ways, however, were more in the manner by which she expressed herself. Maya had this way of getting one excited about pretty much everything. She was like a little girl with her unbridled enthusiasm toward tea, tablecloths, subways, and skylines. She took it all in, and let it all out—like breathing, but much cuter.

We talked about love. We talked about sex, food, family. We talked about Walt Whitman. Maya was a big fan. And why not? Whitman was a master in capturing the underlying passion and overarching purpose of life and love, through poetry and prose alike.

'And whoever walks a furlong without sympathy walks to his own funeral drest in his shroud.'

Maya offered this Whitman quote in the moment, and thus set in motion a series of thoughts and reflections in my mind.

Sympathy? Had I been showing sympathy toward others? Toward myself? I had left quite a trail through my own attempt to traverse the slippery slopes of love. I had hurt others. I had hurt myself. And all in the name of love——a very human love. Certainly no way to live. And, as artfully captured by Walt, a great way to pave a living path to a dying state.

Yet there was hope. My mangy little friend in India would provide testimony to this. Perhaps others, as well.

'Let's go,' Maya insisted. 'I've got a place to show you.'

We settled up with Angelica and were on our way. After all, there was no denying this little girl in a woman's frame once she had a new picture in mind.

Skipping—literally—down Church Street, Maya and I made a sharp right on Chambers, and within minutes found ourselves at Kitchenette. The friendly little cupcakes in the window beckoned us in.

'Oh, these are my favorite!' Maya shared.

'They look like Hostess cupcakes. I used to eat them by the box (those and Ho-Hos during my youth).'

'Yeah, but these are *sooo* much better!'

We grabbed a couple and were out the door. I bit into mine.

'Why is it that these bakeries just can't seem to get the cupcake right?' I asked. 'The icing's always a bit too hard, and the cake is kind of dry.'

'I know. I remembered this a bit different myself. Not quite like mom used to make.'

'Okay. That's it. Come with me.'

I grabbed Maya by the hand and led her into a nearby market, where we proceeded to seek and collect all the makings required for—*the ultimate cupcake.*

'Duncan Hines vanilla mix.'

'Check.'

'Chocolate frosting. Make sure it's Betty Crocker.'

'Check. Ooh, better get the French vanilla, too.'

'Good thinking. Ebony and ivory and all. Eggs, milk…'

'Wait. Do we need these?'

I glanced over the ingredients. 'Yep. Butter too.'

'Tray, holder, mixer… and a bowl. I'm assuming you have none of these.'

I smirked.

'I'll take that as a *check*.'

What we didn't purchase, but were clearly present with us, were these purple flashes. Need to have my eyes checked, but not today, I thought, as we giggled right through the checkout counter and all the way over to my apartment. We spent the remainder of the afternoon making cupcakes, licking mixers, and sharing stories of our childhood. And the bridge to the fountain of youth—and of the youth-filled spirit—was restored. Not through the incessant self-examination as conducted through the contours of the mind, but through the freeing of the soul through the simplest of exercises: making—and eating—cupcakes. Not one, not a couple, but *all twenty-four of them!*

On this gloriously dreary day, Maya and I together consumed all twenty-four of our little black and white, baked buddies. Some with simple smiley faces. Some with more elaborate designs. All with the pleasure of two pups in the playground of our youth…

Swinging *freely!*

Back and forth. Forth and back. From earth to sky and back again. *Flying.* With the sound of the chain-linked swing providing a rhythmic pattern that cradled the consciousness. Free from thought. Free from worry. *Free.* Just the pure flight of spirit through the fresh scent of Mother Nature herself. One, with the trees, the flowers, the clouds that waved hello as they continued on their own journeyed course. And perhaps, if so fortunate, the opportunity to share in the moment with a best friend, sister, brother; swinging, in unison; giggling, uncontrollably. Giggling just like Maya and I throughout an afternoon that served in awakening ourselves to the simple nature of our inner nature—our sole awareness of soul awareness.

Maya and I spent the day contained within a conversation between our basic selves, the little girl and boy in us that needed to be heard. It was a conversation that would change the course and lives of each from that point forward. Maya needed to free herself from a marriage that had gone the route of abuse. And I had to give myself permission to be my *self*, and not some other form that had posed as an imposter for far too long. It was not our minds in discourse this day, but rather our hearts—more accurately, our souls—that once given just a crack in the seam of our false encasements, took full advantage and pleasure in unleashing the will of two, aligned as one, in the moment when truth came to make its case.

I found no choice but to love myself whenever my soul was given center stage. What's not to love? I was in my pure joy, pure loving, pure truth when I lived in this world through my heart. It was of a childlike essence, carefree—as in free of care. It cared little of the judgments of yesterday nor the worries of tomorrow; but for the peace that awaits us all in this, the present moment. Like the peace proposed by Li one enchanting day in Italy, by simply *being* wherever we are.

The thought of Li flashed over my screen. I wondered where she was, when I might hear from her again, see her again. It only served to distract me from the moment.

Unfortunately, the ecstasy of this day would not guarantee a lifetime of eternal bliss for this lad. For my mind had an arsenal of distractive tools at its disposal, and I found the distinction that truly served in separation of each of us from the masters themselves was not in what was our rightful place, but rather in how we chose in each moment to displace ourselves from our right, our truth, that place. As memory served on what was likely the one day I was actually paying attention at Sunday school, the master known as Jesus the Christ once shared such a revealing message:

'He that believeth on me, the works that I do shall he do also; and greater works than these shall he do.'

Paraphrased I understood this as: *"everything I am you can be and more."* And while I was certainly no expert in the teachings of all that is truth, everything in me that could recognize truth—like a child that knows whom he can and cannot trust through an intuition, an inner guide—was learning through my own experiences that the principles of loving, forgiveness, and grace were available to each of us, at any time and under any circumstance or condition. All we had to do was choose in, choose up, and perhaps we too would be walking as masters in the world.

Master Jeremy. Has kind of a cool ring to it, I thought.

'That's your ego talking, Jeremy,' the universe quickly reminded.

A slippery slope indeed.

It was a beautiful spring day in the city. I was reacquainted with the fact that nearly eleven million people flow in, out, and through these streets. The mandatory winter hibernation period was officially over. The cherry blossoms and other colored arrangements from nature told us so. Partly cloudy, the weatherman called it. How they determined which part was sunny and which was cloudy I wasn't quite certain. But there was sun enough for me.

The supermodels of SoHo were out, their legs in full bloom. Yet I barely noticed. I was on a mission. The trees of enticements were merely a distraction, if one allowed it so. I had been distracted long enough.

The scent of a city rich in its array of savory flavors had me make haste to my lunch appointment at Novecento. Maya had arranged for me to meet a friend of hers, Nina Adelina Garcia Moreno from Ecuador. Nina was a talented violinist in the orchestra pit for the Broadway hit *The Phantom of the Opera*. She was also clairvoyant. She had a gift, Maya would explain—one that I apparently was in need of.

From the very beginning, it was like something out of the movie *The House of the Spirits*. We met. She knew me. In what form or manner it did not matter. She saw me. Past life. As an architect. I came back to finish something. *What* she could not say. It would be intrusive. I was enthralled. She continued.

There was a great love forthcoming. And a bridge. She saw a bridge. But not one constructed by any materials known to this world. She paused to laugh at the table behind us. Told me exactly what they were doing. Talking about. But she never turned around. No mirrors to use in reflection, with the noise in the restaurant far too loud for her to gather anything through the ears. I was fascinated. Glued to the moment. So much so that my skirt steak and fries were ice cold—and Novecento had the best Argentine beef in the city.

Nina was mysterious, but entirely believable. I saw truth in her eyes. Her final words…

'Colombia has a special gift awaiting you.'

Maya and I would spend my last day in New York together. I sat there at the café awaiting her sweet face. She had become one of my closest friends in just a few short months, due to the simplest of connections—from my heart to her own through an authentic series of moments together. I reminisced as I awaited her arrival, of our many adventures together that covered the neighborhoods and cast a special light on this Gotham City.

Our trips across the Brooklyn Bridge to Grimaldi's Pizzeria, the *only* place to share a pie; and to my recollection, the only place where a pizza to go was a *no go*. One must be present to enjoy the gift.

Our late night strolls along the Hudson, by way of Battery Park; in particular, the south end where the sidewalks were lit with a mystical purple glow from the street lamps above.

The many picnics in as many parks. A movie here... a dinner there and... 'Oh my God, has it really been six months?' Maya asked while unbuttoning her jacket.

'At least, since that first day in *Cupcakeville*.'

She giggled. I followed.

'Jeremy, I am going to miss you, luv.'

'I know. To be honest I am not sure what awaits me there.'

'Beautiful women. Colombia is filled with them, from what I've heard.'

'Right. But I'm not going for that... not anymore.'

'Never say never, Mr. Braddock. You are one charming fella. There is no erasing that.'

'Besides, I'll be busy. We're building bridges again. This time, medical supplies, pharmaceuticals. From China to South America.'

'Jeremy Braddock, in the drug trade. Well. I suppose

Colombia is as good a place as any for that.' Maya smiled. I would miss her smile, her girlish nature, her joy.

'And you? What will little Miss Maya be doing?'

'I don't know. I've got to get out of here myself. Too many memories, many of which I would rather leave behind.' Maya had already left her husband behind. I suppose he would now have ample opportunity to look at his own self.

Maya and I sat there, holding hands across the table. We embraced each other through a friendship far more meaningful than any temporal love interest would have ever provided. She and I found a greater version of ourselves through the portal of knowing each other. I suppose one could say through the windowed view into the other we saw our own homes better. And we were the perfect bridge into a preferred world.

The Clapton song "Change the World" was playing across the café's speakers. I winked at Maya. Likely, the universe was doing the same.

'Boy, things have sure changed in our worlds,' Maya offered.

'You know, I once had these grand illusions,' I shared. 'I was going to be President, or UN chief, some post of power that would allow me to, well, change the world. Save it even.'

'The world doesn't need saving, Jeremy. It's in good hands already.'

'What? You mean God's got it covered? Everything *is*

going to be okay in the end? Well, that's a relief.'

A bit of ill-timed sarcasm. Maya wasn't having it. She knew me too well.

'*Be the change you wish to see in the world.*' Maya was quoting Gandhi.

'Hmmm. Well, I want loving,' I thought outwardly.

'Be loving.'

'I want joy… happiness.'

'Be happy.'

'I want to create from my heart.'

'Then know your heart… and create from there.'

It felt like I was right there with *Bapu* himself, relaxing along the banks of the Ganges, sharing some raw vegetables, a bit of rice—and more important, our hearts. I wondered how the universe could keep track of everyone at every moment, and know just what to say or show us at just the perfect time. The colossal order of things, with one conductor leading a symphony the size and scope of all humanity; all living things on all dimensions at all times. The concept was far too grand for my little mind to comprehend. What did it matter anyway, really? For the message itself rang true to my heart, and the information was transforming for *me*.

'I'll write you, dear,' sharing the next thought that came present.

'No, you won't.'

'You're right. I won't. But I'll be thinking of you.'

'*That,* you will have no choice in. I am, after all,

unforgettable.' Maya did not lack in self-confidence. 'Remember that, when you are embracing some hot Colombian *dish*.'

'I told you... '

'Oh well, then, off with you, Jeremy, *the builder of bridges!* And when you make your next big splash in the world, don't forget those of us who acted as the ingredients in your...'

'Cupcake?'

'Yes, cupcake! You know, it takes many ingredients to make the perfect cupcake... the perfect life.'

'I will remember one in particular, who made my reunion with my soul so... so... '

'Delicious! Yes, I am! And don't you forget it!'

Saying goodbye to Maya would prove more difficult than I imagined. She was, after all, a playmate for my soul, simply and completely. And that was a rare gift indeed.

This day, and the travels that followed, would provide me with the playground—and classroom—to test my new arsenal of information. As if in harmony with each adjoining neighborhood that made Manhattan uniquely grand while entirely connected, we were all provided with a set of gifts that, once uncovered, polished up and presented, became the neighboring jewel that both reflected that which it was not, and illuminated, from the very same light, that which it was and ever shall be.

Through Maya, I experienced the gift of a love that played timely tutor for the recalcitrant—but increasingly willing—student. We made love, not through the embrace of the physical, but through the liberation of two souls through the playgrounds of our truth. We found love, not from a place of human need, but as disciples of a love within the love, one that beckoned us as did the Ghost of Christmas Present with Scrooge himself.

"Come with me, and know yourself better, man."

The creak of the swings as I made my way down West Broadway, past a small park, and back to my sanctuary one last time were drowned by a greater noise—the laughter of children. They were giggling while swinging freely through the air, reaching with each new thrust for something higher, something greater. The sky was not the limit, but merely the next frontier for these young travelers.

The little boy in me joined in—in spirit.

I was no longer envious.

Does it require another?
All is required and none still.
For the Love... is.
Your discovery is what remains.

9
PURA VIDA

Pure life…

And the treacherous track…
To the sanctity of soul.

———

I awakened—in Costa Rica. Not immediately, but
eventually. It began with a phone call.

'Jeremy!…Cassandra. How are you, sweetheart?'

Cassandra. A most tantalizing taste of my past. A
conference in Lake Tahoe years ago provided proper cover
for the ski vacation that served as everyone's true
inclination. San Francisco provided the encore—many
encores. But it began in Tahoe (and likely lifetimes before).
From the moment she first entered the lodge—a grand

entrance that only few could create—I was captivated, and my heart incarcerated. The midday light from beyond the entrance way cast an imaged silhouette of a choice goddess from Egyptian times. Hair bouncing in concert with the curl of a girl in love with the moment, Cassandra offered a familiar face and way for those who resonated with moxie––along with a more-than-mild propensity for mischief.

'Cassandra. How are you? *Where* are you, in fact?' This was a necessary query, as Cassandra was, in many respects, a female version of me.

'I'm in Costa Rica. Playing, as usual. And you, dear?'

'Colombia. I joined with a drug cartel. You know me, always looking for the next high.'

She giggled. She had an adorable giggle.

'No, I'm actually in New York. But heading to Colombia.'

'Colombia? Not anymore. I have a bed with your name on it. And your *no* will eventually turn to *yes*, so let's skip all the subtleties, shall we? And just get your sweet ass down here.'

She was right. I could not deny my attraction to her distraction. At least that had been my past record. And besides, months had passed without much more than a few e-mails between Li and me. My love for her had not waned. But something was clearly unclear (if such could be manifest). The anchoring of a love with its origin in the heavens was not always to be had in the world of the physical—one masked in illusions. This I knew too well.

The rest of the knowing I would have to leave to the future. For the present moment, I was all in for a bit of free play.

It was the free fall I could do without.

'Hang on, everyone. This is gonna get a little rough. Sorry.'

At least our pilot was polite while casting us closer to our deaths. I could not wait to say goodbye to the tiny bi-plane that shuttled me from San Jose to Quepos, along the central coast of Costa Rica. I must have revisited breakfast a half dozen times, as my so-called free spirit was cast to the winds—literally. I called in the higher powers so often they had likely since changed their number. I was happy to make acquaintance with the ground below in something other than a body bag. *They* were happy that I was happy, I thought, as I made my way through the horde of onlookers at the airport, and to the driver who awaited me.

'Señor Braddock?'

'Si. Soy Jeremy Braddock.'

'I am Antonio. I will be your driver. Please, sir, the car is over here.'

The air was thick. The midday sun baked all that dared expose itself. Beads of sweat began their journey down my temples as we left the fans of the terminal for the dead air of the jungle climate. Perspiration formed above my upper lip. I stopped to wipe, overly aware of my presentation. Antonio neither noticed nor cared.

'Okay, Mr. Braddock, we have a short journey and then we will be there.'

A short journey, and then we will be there. This I had heard before.

The journey up to the Rafiki Lodge where Cassandra was staying was far from short, and anything but pleasant. The roads of Costa Rica reached up and rattled every bone, tested every nerve. An unpaved path to untamed parts, navigating the terrain was a pointless attempt to avoid the more taxing of an endless sea of jarring potholes. There was simply no safe passage, but rather just the better of many difficult choices. Another metaphor for life, as we traversed the minefields with choice again in only which lesson and not whether we had one at all. This I thought, as our Pathfinder maneuvered up the winding trail, our wheels burdened with the soil of the jungle carpet. I gazed out yet another window and into the world around me.

So many places, so many faces, with more than a few questions still unanswered. Could it be that I could cover every inch of soil, play witness to every drop of water upon this planet, and still never reach the shores of my desired continent—my self-content?

Whoa! The terrain shook me from my thoughts, knocking me back into the present reality, and surrounding beauty. I had never seen so many versions of green. The jungle offered the eyes a landscape painted with the imagination, manifest through that which lies beyond. It provided, as well, an example of nature's reliance on itself to create and re-create such pure spectacle.

'One year ago, all of this was not here,' Antonio offered.

'Destroyed by a big storm, and mudslides, *many* mudslides. But the jungle, she is very determined. And now you have this. She is back. She is happy again.'

One year! In one year the jungle had restored itself. Back to its original form.

'Notice the trees. Many sizes, many types. And the plants. The vines. I think you call them *vines*, no? Each needs the other to become what they are. Each requires the other to complete the picture that you see. It is a beautiful picture, would you not agree?'

'Beautiful, yes. Stunning!'

I was otherwise speechless. It was humbling to play witness to the heartbeat of the jungle. The sight of nature intermingling with itself. The sounds of one another, feature of every creature, resonating in accord with the great conductor from above. There was a purity to it, a harmony. One struck while experiencing a jolting ride up a treacherous track.

Our wheels danced with the cliff's edge. The stones that lined the path were cast aside with each shift of our transport, displaced by a set of worn tires. We tempted fate, again and again. Antonio was skilled, but so was the jungle. The river below awaited the outcome.

It was sexy, this dance with death.

It was sexy, this rush with life.

I could taste the jungle upon my lips; its sweat upon my skin; the scent of fresh mud upon my nostrils. I was one with the jungle. It was one with me. There was no other choice in the matter. For to enter the jungle was to enter within its very bowels, and know them as your own.

An hour and a half later our "short journey" concluded. As we pulled up to the lodge, I was reminded of another offering from the jungle. Cassandra came bouncing down the hill, curls dancing, face aglow, grinning from ear to ear. Her smile was her signature, a perfected orchestration from her sparkling eyes to her pearly whites. She could erase any trace of unhappiness through the connection she made with her puppy dog browns, one that simply said, "The joy in me calls out the joy in you."

One suggestive hug later and we were off on our adjoined adventure.

'*Woo-hoo!* Is that all you got, baby?' she yelled, daring the river to up its intensity.

'Careful señorita. She does not have much of a sense of humor today,' Juan warned. By "she," he was referring to the river.

'Oh, she has not met with the likes of me.'

This was true. Few have. Especially, when Cassandra was carrying her personal flag of freedom. Emancipation was her intention this day. Emancipation was her intention *every* day. And may no soul on earth deny her of her *soul* intention.

Our sights were set on the wild in rapid form. We were told the waters were running swift—and deep—this time of year. It was September, the middle of the rain season for this Central American slice of paradise—a paradise made more so as I glanced across the raft at my latest affair with the darling of dare. Cassandra was bathing in the river's spray. Her heart was basking in the moment. Her lips sun-drenched. Her hair bouncing about as if in harmonic accord with the current—both beneath and through her. Cassandra was in her own world, one filled to the brim with a life force that had its origin with the origin of life itself. And the result was pure joy, with me the mere beneficiary of her overflow.

I sat there in both awe and envy, of a woman true to form, living life on her terms, aligned with a spirit within. The river decided to bring us present.

'Holy shit!' She could also mix poetic prose with a vernacular that found comfort at the bottom of a Jack Daniels glass.

'Whoa! Hold on, hun.' Advice I was better to keep for myself, as we approached the first whirlpool.

And in that, the rapid was upon us.

'Shift right, dudes,' Juan barked out in barely distin-guishable slang.

We shifted, only to be met with a bath of blue—more like brown—upon our faces. The spray, a refreshing remin-der to pay attention. The rise and fall through the raging waters, oddly familiar to life itself. Uncharted waters for all but our guide. Another opportunity to put trust to the test.

Cassandra had no issue in this area. Nothing but the

excitement of a child on Christmas morning reflected in her earthy browns. Her eyes—I loved her eyes. Just a moment in those eyes and I would be whisked away to the land of *I believe*. Everything was possible through her eyes. And the woman had no quit.

'More! Give me more! Is that all you got, *pussy!*' Cassandra taunted. The river? Life? Him?

'Watch yourselves here,' Juan shouted. 'This one's gonna rock you.'

We were given a lesson by nature herself—a few lessons. In one swift motion we were offered a crash course in the laws of physics. Force, motion, distance—beginning and ending with gravity. Good met with evil in one splitting second, as Cassandra and I were lifted to new heights, injected with a rush of adrenaline while offering our best impressions of birds in flight, then fish at sea. And from a soul's love to a love's fear.

Cassandra was in the water. The water was moving. She was not. At least, this is what fear saw.

As she lay motionless in the water, the events of the moment prior gave way to the reality of a boulder that had found the most inconvenient place to rest its ageless form. Cassandra's flight from our rubber craft had landed her, back first, on the rock.

The guide quickly picked me up, playing by a set of rules as governed by the river's current and his experience. Cassandra's body was floating down the river. From our angle, we couldn't tell whether she was moving or simply the water was moving her. We paddled fiercely to catch up with her lifeless form.

We arrived. She lay there, the ebb and flow of the waters playing tricks with her body. I feared the worst. My fear was not required.

I was relieved to find Cassandra conscious, albeit clearly in pain.

'Fuck! That hurts!' she exclaimed with that sweet sound of crass fury that had become common partner to unwelcomed events—entirely welcome in this moment.

'Can you move?'

'Yes. Yes, I can... but I don't want to. Fuck!'

'Sorry, hun. No choice in the matter.'

The current was swift. The river was in no mood to be patient. I slid to the right and grabbed her by the arm, lifting her onto the raft with Juan's assistance.

'Shit...! Shit, shit, shit, shit. *Shit!*'

'Cassandra, we have to get you back to the lodge. Find a doctor.'

'Hell, no! I didn't come here to play patient.'

The pain shot up inside her. Her face revealed what her mind would not accept. Cassandra's will would not be her way. Not this time.

'Okay. Okay. I get it. Back to camp.'

Amid the rage of the river, we made our way to shore. This was the easy part. Getting her to the jeep, that would be another story, an altogether unpleasant one.

'Oh, fuck! Stop, stop, *stop!!* I can't...' Cassandra's eyes teared up. This, I had never seen before.

'Hun, there's nothing else we can do. We've got to carry you to where the jeep can pick us up.'

'I know, but damn it hurts!'

'Okay. Juan, stop for a moment,' I instructed. We placed Cassandra on the ground.

'Cassandra, hunny. Remember what Reshma showed us? Her breathing technique.'

'Yes, but...'

'Focus. Up there. The trees. Against the sky. How they move... swaying... flowing... back and forth... back and forth. And your breath... in... and out... in... and out. Deeper still. *Deeep* breaths. In... out... in... out.'

This we did for a few minutes. The world began to slow. It slowed to the speed of our breath. It slowed ever more. And the pain slowed, as well.

'How do you feel?'

'I forgot for a moment. I forgot to feel,' Cassandra answered, her face free of the stress.

'Okay. Juan, let's lift her up. Cassandra, stay focused on the movement of the trees above. They are whispering to you.'

'Yes. I can hear them. They're saying, "Hurry the fuck up, Jeremy! Cassandra is still in fucking pain!"'

We both started laughing. Juan joined in.

'Hey, dude, it worked for *me*. I am much more peaceful now.'

Cassandra laughed again. She laughed right through the

pain. Cassandra had a way of laughing at life itself. It was an invaluable tool, the ability to laugh; to laugh through it all.

We eventually made it back to the jeep and a half hour later to the lodge itself. The local doctor arrived. He was remarkably effective, given how little he had to work with. He prescribed some medication for the pain—played pharmacist, as well—and soon Cassandra was back to her joyful self once again. The doctor spoke of the good fortune her "guardian angel" had blessed her with, as the body bruise—however deep—was only an inch or two from the spine. He also informed us we would have to airlift her to a hospital in San Jose if her condition did not improve in the coming days.

Cassandra dozed off. I sat outside the room, on the verandah overlooking the jungle from above—relieved for the moment. It was late afternoon. A steady downpour from the skies provided a rhythmic reacquaint for the same moisture that once found its home within the dampened earth. The water recycles. Man recycles. But what is it that allows us to break the cycle, our cycle, our reunion with this place time and again? Is it possible we can learn everything we need to know, so that we know we no longer need?

The sun broke through just enough to allow for a rainbow to make its entrance. The colors were clear, defined. Red met with orange. Orange gave way to yellow. Yellow paid homage to green, then to blue. Blue and purple first danced with one another in violet interaction, before giving over to a more mystical purple, one much more attuned to the color I had been seeing for years now.

I thought of my father. Of his death. And of the rainbows that appeared above his home that Thanksgiving Day. The rainbow, its seven rays of colors, each possessing a quality required to aid us in this quest. Could it be the pot of gold, the one at the end of the rainbow spoken of in our youth, was not gold as we would think of it, but rather the Gates of Gold we covet; the threshold between this world and the other? And would we all be welcome? Could such benevolence exist to accept us all, with all our trials, once we have passed the test, and graduated from this form?

Cassandra began to stir. Her eyes opened. Mine were already.

She pulled the covers from over her, revealing a set of bronzed legs that could set a man back a thousand lifetimes by just entertaining the thought of entry.

'Hunny. Come over here.'

I laughed.

'What? You don't find me sexy?'

'Oh, no. Sexy is something you do without any effort at all. It's just… ' More laughter.

'What? *What?* Now you're starting to piss me off. What's so damned funny, Jeremy?'

'Hun, you're slurring your words. "Don't you find me *slexy?*" Too cute, really. How much codeine did the doctor give you anyway?'

'I don't know. But I'm feelin' *fiiiiiine!*'

We both laughed. And, of course, I did join her in bed, resting her head on my chest as we looked out together over the marvel of greens that comprised our jungle view. Her head, on my chest; her hand, in my hand; her leg, wrapped around my own. Where Cassandra began and I ended was barely distinguishable when we attuned to the oneness through our given forms.

It served as bridge if one were wise.

An anchor if less than so.

Cassandra was back on the Río Savegre. It had been nearly a week. The doctor had given her permission to play in the river once again, amazed with her speed of recovery. She, of course, would have it no other way. This was *her* adventure, *her* freedom, *her* stake in the ground that signified in no uncertain terms, "Here! Here is where I declare my liberation!" She claimed it with conviction, and enthusiasm. Cassandra did most everything with such devotion to her inner nature.

I spent the afternoon in a slightly different manner—on horseback through the jungle. My guide Ricardo was determined to blaze an entirely new trail this day. I was up for the challenge. My horse was not.

'Señor Braddock, your horse no want to go?'

'From the look of him, I would say he has not wanted to go for about five years.'

'Maybe he is tired, Señor Braddock. We can take a rest soon.'

My horse was more than merely tired. His pelt was sweating. His breathing, hard and erratic. This boy had nothing left in the tank. Nothing at all. I dismounted.

'Señor Braddock, we only have a little further to go.'

'I will walk him the rest of the way. He's exhausted. Tired. No can go.' And I was feeling an incredible amount of guilt for any attempt at ignoring this detail.

We walked up an embankment. His head bowed to my own eye level. He looked at me. Said nothing, of course, but just looked at me. His eyes were tired, but grateful. He was an older horse. He had been on this planet for many years. There were not many left. He knew this.

I wonder where he will be off to next, I thought to myself as we trudged through the mud, rocks, and old branches that formed our path. Did he know? Did he even care?

'He is an old horse, Señor Braddock. He has been with my family for many years. Has seen many things. My mother leave us. My father not soon after. Both are with God now. I believe he will soon join them.'

'Do you have any brothers? Sisters?' I felt bad for my young guide. I hoped the answer would make me feel better.

'One brother. Older. Two sisters, but they are married.'

'Do you see them often?'

'Every day, Señor Braddock. Every day, in my dreams. I

see my mother. My father. My brother Jesús. My sisters also. They are always there. In my heart, there is my family, much happiness. We are all together there.'

We broke through the jungle brush and into a clearing. There was a small building. We walked our horses over to what I learned was the local market.

'Señor Braddock, do you want anything?'

Want anything? I thought to myself. Less and less these days. There were things I still needed. This was true. But wanted?

'Maybe some water. For me and my friend here. You?'

'I will have some, too.'

I went into the market and found the water. It was a small market, maybe the size of a living room. The matter of choice was made easy. Only one brand to choose from. The local *tica* at the counter was quite friendly. Her face was dark in complexion. Her skin was old, wrinkled. Her smile, void of more than a few teeth. Her smile was much appreciated. It is always nice when the world smiles at you. I smiled back.

As I walked outside, I noticed my guide was assisting another young man with his tire. As was so often the case here in this less than developed part of the world, a spare tire became a monthly repair tire. The rugged dirt roads of the country would ensure such. Ricardo was showing the man how to change the tire, but wasn't actually putting much effort in himself.

I walked over to assist. Ricardo pulled me aside. 'No,

Señor Braddock. Let him do it himself. He will be better off that way.'

The young man proceeded to change the tire. He must have been no more than fifteen, a bit frail, impoverished but undeterred.

'Give a man a fish and you feed him for a day; teach a man to fish and you feed him for a lifetime,' I shared.

'I know these words,' Ricardo replied. 'These are wise words.'

These words have been cited often and by many since Moses Maimonides. He was a Jewish physician and philosopher of the twelfth century, uniquely respected by Jews, Christians, and Muslims alike. And Ricardo was right. This man, however frail, would likely face this challenge again, under perhaps not so fortunate circumstances. After all, who were we to deprive the learning opportunity of another? It would be as though we knew better. Better than *He*. And I was no longer interested in playing such a fool.

I walked over to my horse. I shared my water with the weary warrior. I had only this to offer him. It was all he needed.

I thought to myself, perhaps it is time I take only what I need. Perhaps I have been drinking too long from the same well. Perhaps there is another elixir that quenches a thirst from origins within.

Ricardo and I made our way back...

Our horses walking beside us...

Each thirsting for more within us.

Cassandra and I were the beneficiaries of a love between two that found its fullest expression in the spirit of a greater love. Each of us was on a quest. Both were aware of the role of the other. There was an odd familiarity in the rhythm of each step we took in unison. We were mates from times past—this was certain. Was that enough for the present? Something felt wrong. Something was missing.

I struggled with the desire to express our love in all ways imaginable, with a growing sense of responsibility that apparently accompanied the awakening to a higher calling. There would simply be no ignoring the voice within, as it strengthened in intensity, and I with my clarity. To be free to choose did not mean to be free to not. This was no longer the definition of freedom for me. The voice gave me no choice.

Cassandra and I sat there on the verandah of our room, high above the earth beneath, taking in the sights and sounds of the jungle as it stirred with an anticipation of the evening's adventures. I held her hand within my own, enjoying the comfort of the touch. Only in this world, only in the physical, could we enjoy such a moment. This I thought while Cassandra placed her head upon my shoulder. I would be responsible, yes. I would be responsible to the love we shared, and to sharing this love, this moment. I would be responsible, as well, to the truth that burned within. I would answer to both, as one.

We shared our love in all the ways one had at their disposal. We lived love from the spirit down through the body itself—a gift granted only by this level, this realm. And through it, we declared our emancipation—no longer incarcerated by the love killers of need, jealousy, and expectation. We made sure to steer clear of these.

It was infectious. It was contagious. It was desirous, the times when one chooses emancipation over some self-imprisoned form. Our souls surfaced in applauding fashion of our courage, our conviction, to cast aside all self-imposed obstacles, and bask in the glory of our next breath––as if it were our last.

The time Cassandra and I spent in Costa Rica was pure, unaltered by the jaded finish of civilization in its most uncivil nature. For this nature, this splendor made in His image, served to nurture the most romantic tones played from an adjoined harp of inner loving.

Pure. Unblemished. Untainted by the coldness of the negative that too often clouds the vision of the world, a world in search of a warming light upon the face of the all-deserving that is each in our unfolding. As the *ticos* would remind, here, within the joy of nature's version of Disneyland, we experienced pure life—*pura vida!* And, we knew love better through its compatriot of higher expression—joy.

Cassandra and I expressed our free selves in a manner that we knew not before with one another. I moved over her. Our bodies glistened from the sweat forged from our embrace, and that with the jungle itself. I could feel her body arch as my hand moved to her lower back, ensuring no separation between my chest and her own. Her neck beckoned my lips closer. Her toned legs engulfed me in entirety. I took her, from her lips to her lips. I made certain there was nothing left for the wanting. She made certain I would be left wanting more.

Our love flowed—freely—each movement divulging an inner form of sacredness not of this world. Yet here we were, *in* this world, with our souls allowed to take over and lead us where mere minds could not.

Cassandra and I experienced the highest vibration through the orchestration of a love thread through the many realms available in human form. With each kiss, each canvassed pass along the many curvatures that made her all woman, each embrace of the eyes that dared deeper their travels, we explored all of what was availed on a steamy evening in the middle of nowhere—the center of everywhere.

I lay upon her, balancing the weight of a man nearly twice her own. Beads of sweat made their way from my face to the many destinations to be visited, revisited and then again through the hours of our travels—the timeless-ness of soul. This was not a love shared merely in the physical but one that traversed all layers of light and found a suitable expression in this, the one plane where we may truly know it all. In these moments, there are:

Two bodies, but only one motion...

Two egos, but only one motive…

Two souls, but only the One consciousness.

For it appears it is only in the purity of the loving that we find ourselves in a higher presence, and no other. In these moments, the loving energy of the universe is channeled through the next kiss, the next fluid motion of one with the other. A kiss. *His* kiss. Vetted through the chambers of the divine.

I was lost once again.

This time, I had no intention to be found.

I awakened. I awakened to Cassandra's leg draped across mine. I awakened, as well, to the voice within.

'What are we doing here? Yet, another distraction masked as attraction.'

'Just one more moment,' I responded within. I wanted to wait until eternity had met its final day before saying goodbye to this one.

'Sure thing. We can string together a few more lifetimes of these moments. In fact, we already have. What's a few more. No hurry. It's not like we are going anywhere.'

I popped up. My heart started pounding. What was I doing? Had I not learned *anything*?

Cassandra rolled over, ran her hands across my chest.

'Where are you going? It's early. It's the jungle. It sleeps in the daytime.'

'Cassandra, I have to get going. I have to get to Colombia.'

'What's in Colombia?'

I remembered Nina's words. 'A special gift.'

'A special gift? Sounds mysterious.'

'Oh, it's a mystery alright. It's all a big mystery at this point. But it is *my* mystery, *my* puzzle. And it must be solved. I know this if nothing else.'

The place where words reside became an empty vessel. I sat there, quietly. Cassandra did, as well. Just looking up. As if the ceiling were a barrier. There was something above it all. This was certain. And oddly, it was inextricably linked to the world below, the world of need, *in* need; in need of grace itself.

'Jeremy, I think I love you.' This was delivered from flat on her back, staring up at the ceiling fan as it buzzed with each oscillation.

'You don't love me.'

'No, Jeremy. I really love you. I mean, it feels like love.'

I smiled. I loved love; being love; being loved. I loved it all. But I knew this was not the love I sought, the love she sought.

'I love you, too, sweetheart, but...'

'Why don't you just marry me and get it over with?'

'Marry you? I think you're still swimming in the tequila from last night.'

'No, really. Why don't you marry me?'

'You're serious?'

'I think so. It's not the tequila talking. Maybe the sex.'

Cassandra giggled; then lay there for a moment, as if testing her own words for truth. She loved as I did. She loved many, in her own way. She loved love, in all ways. And she loved her freedom—*always*.

Cassandra continued. 'I mean, I love you. You love me. Whenever we're together, it's wonderful, natural—perfect. I can't think of anyone else, anything else, that I would want. That's it! Marry me, Jeremy Braddock!'

I laughed. 'Okay, I'll make you a deal. If by the end of my journey, and by the end of yours, we find ourselves at the doorstep of one another, then I'm all in.'

'And by journey, you mean...?'

'I'm on a mission. A quest. It's like I have some sort of unfinished business. I can't really explain it. I'm not entirely sure of it all myself.'

'There's no need to explain,' she replied. 'We're all birds... in flight... on our way. Somewhere.'

The thought of my father emerged. I could only hope he found his way—wherever "somewhere" was.

'I get it,' she continued. 'You have questions. And your questions need answers.'

'I think we all do,' I responded. 'I think we all have questions that must be answered, issues that must be resolved, before...'

'Before we can marry?' Cassandra said with a smile.

'Before we can go. Whatever that means.'

'Okay, then. I accept your terms.'

'My terms?'

'Your terms of surrender... to the whole marriage thing.'

I laughed. I really loved this woman.

Cassandra reached out her hand. I extended mine. She grabbed it and pulled me toward her.

'Okay. Deal! Now do what you do best. Make me forget the world for one more moment.'

Cassandra understood. She understood because she also had questions, questions in need of answers. She was not even sure if her question of marrying me was a real question. Cassandra wanted more in her life, as well. Maybe we all did. She knew she felt comfortable with me. I felt comfortable with her. But was it really comfort we sought, or some reclamation of ourselves, in some manner?

I moved over her. She gave me her eyes, those darling puppy dog browns. I gave her my own in return. No more words. The communication from here forward would be from the heart, the sanctuary of a vetted, more coveted loving—the only place where truth may be known.

We made love throughout the day...

As if there were no more love to be made.

———

Costa Rica is filled with riches. It sets one a sail to the remote reaches through a free flow of all that is abundantly available to us. For Costa Rica is not only pure life, it is purely available—whenever, wherever—if one dares to release from the bondage of mind, and allow the heart to lead. In this respect, Costa Rica is not unique at all.

'Whatcha reading?' I asked Cassandra as we made our way to the airport.

'You know what I'm reading. Rumi, of course. Do you remember our first dance together with Rumi?'

'"*Out beyond the ideas of wrong-doing and right-doing...*

"*There is a field.*

"*I will meet you there.*"'

'And we did. Many times. That field remains one of my most cherished places.'

'Mine, too.'

'I can't believe you're off to Colombia. Jeremy Braddock. World traveler. Come join the rest of humanity, and find a home to call your own.'

'I know. It's not the life for everyone. But it's *my* life.'

'It is at that,' Cassandra responded. 'I enjoy the tastes of the world myself. But give me a home, a nearby Pottery Barn, and a yoga instructor—preferably a *hot* one—and I'm good to go.'

'You are, at that. Better than most.'

'We do lead different lives... but with similar passions.'

'And joys.'

'And love.'

'Yes,' I responded. 'We do have love. An abundance of it.'

'Jeremy, sweetheart, you need to find what you're looking for. Don't let anyone get in your way. This is your thing... the "one thing" Rumi speaks of. The one thing you must do. You will never be free... until you do.'

Her words moved me. It was true; all of it. I could never be free unless I fulfilled the one thing I came here to do. It was wonderful to have someone who understood. It was essential I turn my own understanding into vigilance.

Cassandra laid her head on my shoulder. It was her favorite place to rest her head. It was my cherished duty to provide such support for one who was a testament to the joy of love itself. The moment was accompanied by a symphony of approving crickets. I was no longer haunted by its source, but simply appreciative of its presence.

At the airport, we kissed goodbye and set upon our own life journeys, once again. Cassandra lifted to new heights through the momentary emancipation through her own proclamation, and I through the continued awakening of something deeper within. The key to my own liberation beckoned me still.

A promise made. A life at stake.

> This I thought within.
> This I could no longer do without.
> *This*

What is love?
You are Love.

Who is God I choose to know better?
You are God and God is You.

10
COLOMBIAN *HI*

'*The Lord giveth; the Lord taketh away.*'
Was I the lord of my own life, my own construct, deconstruct even? Was there no one else to blame?

'*Though I walk through the valley of the shadow of death, I will fear no evil.*'
Was I to reserve that fear for myself? For that which I did? Did not do? For that which I was?

I crossed into Colombia with a guarded uneasiness as my trusted sidekick. The many faces of love that had been revealed to me appeared quite different from the one I gazed upon as I ran my hands through the chilled water of a nearby creek. In the reflection provided by one of many of His creations, I could barely recognize the face that once housed such varied personalities.

Through my eyes I could not see beyond the emptiness.

'What has become of me?' I wondered in silence, knowing well the distance I had traveled, and the vastness that remained between who I was and what was being reflected back into the world in this moment. So many roads; so many forms; so much illusion. A house of mirrors playing tricks on me for an entire lifetime—longer even.

'Who was I? I mean, who was I *really?*'

I found my way to Colombia, yes. But not before I had strayed in Costa Rica, and lost myself in Panama— physically, emotionally; spiritually, most definitely.

The original plan was to fly direct to Colombia, and claim my "special gift." The freedom I reclaimed while in New York became free choice. I chose Costa Rica. I chose Costa Rica, and the claiming of something else entirely. Now Spirit had other plans. These too were plans made by me, through my actions, and the consequences that must follow. They were not a punishment. God was not in the punishment business. He left that to us, through our own free choice. I was now in the cycle once again. And I had only myself to blame.

An emergency landing in Panama City left me unnerved. My time was running out. Disturbing was the reality that one could cease at any moment. One could cease while on tour. One could cease in detour. One could cease without knowing.

My near demise—and that of my own flight plan—was disturbing enough to set me on a new course; one I would travel by way of motorcycle. It was a dream of mine to bike Central and South America. It was a nightmare once I dared to live such a dream.

I was lost, this was certain. Lost within the jungle of my own creation, my own destruction. Lost, as well, within the jungles of Panama, en route to Colombia. There were nights, in the jungle, where I did not know if day would come. I spent evenings with strangers, with me the strangest one of all. I had taken to scotch as a means of shortening the days and eliminating the nights. In reality, the days grew longer; the nights remained—in silence. The booze served in erecting a temporary wall between me and my Self. There were no voices of greater reason. And I knew the reason.

I was left to reconcile. Left to reconcile the oscillation with a greater expression. Love managed to steer clear of me. Perhaps it was that love knew better than to test its own fate with one whose fate lay in the hands of the devil himself. My business interests slipped; a combination of a recessed world and a depressed man, one who hungered for something more, settled for something less. I was left near broke, and broken—in spirit, and with spirits in hand.

I had lost more than money.

I was losing faith.

Once across the Colombian border, I made my way south, toward Medellín, for some attempt at restoration. Arena grew increasingly worried. She was wise in doing so. It was a chilling revelation when I found myself losing;

losing any balance between integrity and the integration of worlds, realms. The experience shook the foundation I had established while in New York. Work wasn't working. Play was no longer playful; my time in Costa Rica but a distant memory. Giving all I had in so many directions, I left nothing for me. I had lost my appetite for life.

I crossed the Río Atrato—no easy task—and made my way through the jungle terrain. Each new "bed" played avid reminder I had none to call my own. The swampland afforded no comfort, no security. It awaited my retreat, my surrender, ready to swallow me whole within its murky essence. My will was dwindling, as was my assurance all would be okay.

It was a mess; all of it.

I was a mess; all of me.

The bike was a wreck: I left it behind.

I was a wreck; but could not do the same of me. Or could I?

My mind wandered.

Where is the love I covet? *What* is the love I covet? Is it you, Lord, who gives and takes at will? Or simply your will, which allows us each to give and take from ourselves?

Where are you, Li? Is it you I covet; the one who provided me with a glance at true love? Or were you just another of many who played windows, mirrors, providing me with clues but no answers?

It was complicated. I understood.

I made it more complicated. This I stood under.

I gave love a rest, and found only unrest in its place. Perhaps I was only good at one thing—love. Perhaps I was never really good at love at all.

I sat back against a tree that afforded me the only company I had felt in weeks. I was in no shape to take my inventory. So, of course, I did just that.

My shoes. Weathered. Left lace untied. Two strings running counter to each other, refusing to find harmony in one neatly-tied bow.

My pants. Stained with layers of experience. This one, when I slipped along the embankment just moments ago, a fresh new entry into the archives of my Wrangler's.

My shirt. A stench-filled union of aspiration with perspiration, required just to get me to this place and time.

And my face. A veil to conceal, once revealing the many sides of my façade. Now housing only two holes filled with the marbled mystery of the man within as the last hope to my desired unfolding.

I got up. Another splash of the creek's brew provided but a momentary awakening. Each drop made its way back to source, sending distorted waves across the image I had come to see as me. This could not be me. This could not be all that was intended as me. Please, no, Lord! There must be more.

'Keep moving, Jeremy.' I said to myself. 'Keep moving and perhaps...'

I slipped.

A bed of moss-covered rocks made certain of this. I

slipped and banged my shin against another, more sizable one. My leg swelled immediately. It began to bleed. And my ankle—*twisted*.

'This wasn't the *more* I was looking for!' I yelled out. The surrounding jungle absorbed the sound. I was losing my way once again. I was also, for all intents and purposes, lost in the swamp. With nighttime making its entrance soon, this was not a good thing. Not a good thing, at all.

I crawled back up the embankment of the creek; ripped off my shirt; wrapped it around my leg to stop the bleeding. I looked around. There was nothing. Nobody. Just my body. My broken form. Beyond repair.

My eyes filled with a liquid too familiar. I lay my head down upon a soft patch of moss. The swamp waited—patiently—as hope gave way to hopelessness; and my will to lesser still.

I closed my eyes. My mind was giving up, as was my body. My only hope lay with my heart. It was always my only hope.

A series of light flashes awakened me. The trees rose as giants from their roots below, extending to the heavens, stretching their branches in desperation for greater elevation—or merely perhaps to escape the fool at their feet. The creek spoke to me in a language I could not decode. The birds above mocked me as with one another. The resident chatter was more than my mind could handle.

I screamed out for silence. The creek kept on babbling; the birds mocking; the trees judging.

Was I going mad? I wasn't going *anywhere*. Here I lay, and here I would stay. My remains to be lost—forever.

'Not one soul will be lost.'

The voice returned.

'"Not one soul will be lost"? Are you paying attention?'

'Not one soul will be lost.'

'Well, that's great. Except for the fact that I am, in fact, lost... and wounded.' And now, I was arguing with myself. Make that lost, wounded, and insane.

'You are never given more than you can handle.'

'What? Are you kidding? I'm losing it, and you're telling me I've got it all under control?' I was now convinced that even my inner voice of greater wisdom had taken hiatus, leaving me with this pre-recorded nonsense. I could use a hand, and what I received was more words.

'God loves all of his creation.'

'"*All* of his creation"? Well, then I must have been created outside the boundaries of His world.'

I started to chuckle. Even I didn't believe that one. 'Okay, okay. I give. I get it. You love me. I'm not lost. I can handle this. Just point me in the right direction because I actually think I am lost. No idea how to get to Medellín from here. No means to do so.'

The sun was nearly gone. So, too, was my hope. I thought of Africa, how nature claimed life when it so chose. I thought of the questions that remained—*my* questions. They appeared as vultures. Was I delusional, or were there actually vultures looming above? To die without knowing the answers to the questions which remained; the thought brought greater pain to my heart.

'I don't want to die. I don't want to die... without knowing,' I exclaimed, to whomever or *whatever* was listening.

There was still more to do—one thing left to do. I wasn't done yet.

'Please God! Not here. Not now. Not yet.'

'Hola. You lost, *hombre?*' The voice came from a man on the other side of the creek bed. 'You okay? You look lost.'

'Yeah. You could say that.'

'This is no place to be lost. There are better places.'

You could say that again.

The man crossed the creek bed.

'My name is Francisco. Francisco Carlos Días Santana. You can just call me Francisco.' Francisco spoke mainly in his native tongue, testing the limits of my limited Spanish.

'Name's Jeremy,' I answered, wincing in pain.

'You no look so good, hombre. Is it broken?'

'Just twisted, I think.' Ankle as with my life, I thought to myself. 'I'm okay though.'

'Your mouth tells me so, but the rest of you are not onboard with that, amigo.'

I'm sure of that, I thought. Probably reminiscent of the walking dead. A member of the mortuary, just going through the motions, awaiting my final breath. The limp I now acquired didn't alter the image.

'Well, we all go through ruts. I'm just having mine.'

'Hey, amigo, this is no thing you call as rut,' Francisco

responded, while handing me his water bottle. 'You look lost, amigo. It is in the eyes.'

My eyes. The windows to my soul. There would be no hiding what the soul wants you to see.

'This is a search that has not found its treasure.' Francisco continued with such dissection while tending to my wound. 'Perhaps it is not in what you're searching for, but in where you are looking.'

I took a long drink of water.

'Yeah, I guess you could say that. I mean, look, I'm in the middle of nowhere... heading nowhere fast.'

'Especially with that leg. Well, I'm on my way east—to Medellín. You want a lift?'

Of course you are, I thought, as I arose from the embankment, brushed off the remnants of my latest stumble, and grabbed a hold of the lifeline flung to Earth for my benefit.

Francisco slipped under my arm, and assisted me as I struggled to find solid footing. As we crossed the creek together, I noticed how each image of me was washed away with each new step, as if all were temporary reflections of a permanent form. Once on land again, the reflections ceased. I was here, but no reflection was available to tell me so. The "I" was gone. Yet I was not.

The man helped me up the embankment and into his truck.

No soul will be lost.

Not even mine, it would appear.

Any place where there are people, there will be mirrors. Oftentimes, the only question that remains is whether we are willing to perceive with honesty the aspects of ourselves we are here to look at, to work through. And the source of such piercing reflection? As is so often the case, it comes in the form of a friend.

I arrived at Arena's home. I had not seen her since the time I burned a hole in the sands of Avalon. Her art career had taken off, and our respective paths across the planet had not crossed since—until this day.

I knocked. I waited. The door opened. There she was. A fellow traveler and dear friend indeed, arms extended. We embraced, a long exchange filled with the love and appreciation that had ruled our knowing of one another. I missed her. I missed her more than I knew. Her tender, amber eyes. The faint scent of vanilla that graced her body. And her hugs. I missed Arena's hugs. They made me feel like I was all that mattered. And that happened to matter a great deal to me, particularly during times when I was less than thrilled with my own company—times like these.

'What happened to you?' Arena queried with concern. 'Where have you been? And your leg? Get inside. Let me take a look.'

Arena helped me to her couch. She unwrapped my makeshift bandage; then began attending to one of my many "wounds."

'Let's see. Where have I been? Africa. Russia. Finland. Italy. Not to mention a few of America's dearest cities. Everywhere and nowhere, really.' It was sarcasm. It was appropriate, at least from my viewpoint.

And of course Arena knew of my path, my pathology, my dis-ease.

'Oh, and there's Miia. Tessa. Georgia. Natasha. Li, of course. A few of the leading ladies in Jeremy Braddock's life story—a tragic tale of two cities, really. *The City of Broken Promises...*'

'You are wounded. I get it. Let me tend to this one first,' she responded as she cleaned the gash on my leg. 'I think you'll survive.'

'I don't want to survive. I want to thrive. I want to get it right this time. I have traveled...'

Arena interrupted. 'I know where you've been; who you've been... been with, even.' She paused for a moment. 'Well, now you are here. I knew you would find your way. You have much to share, I can see. But first, we need to get you comfortable; acknowledge our surroundings. You are in Colombia. And in Colombia, we feed the moment... and nourish the soul.'

Arena was Colombian, this was fact. She came from a loving home and deeply spirited family. And she always gave me her eyes, the distinction I found with so many Colombians as they pierce your veil and play witness to the truth of your soul through the "windows." From child to elder, male and female alike, every Colombian I had the pleasure of knowing would give you their eyes, providing you with a guided journey to their own truth—their soul. It was remarkable. An experience unequalled as a culture and people by any other place I had walked on this planet.

As for the heart, the Colombian people offered one an opportunity like few others to delve into the far reaches of this vessel. Arena opened her home and her heart, inviting our souls to the altar of the festival to be created. And she, in particular, was a living example of unconditional loving in action. No judgments, just total acceptance of me as me. A sanctuary for my soul—at a time when I could use it most.

Arena moved to the kitchen.

'I would ask you what you would like, but then again it would be a silly question.'

Arena reached into the refrigerator and pulled out two freshly made *arepas*. Both for me, of course, for the savory taste of one of these crispy corn cakes would merely will the little boy inside to beg for another. She worked her way around the kitchen, while I sat back in silence. I sat in silence, but not in ignorance.

She looked amazing. Her dress was an array of festive colors, revealing the full spectrum of the woman. Her jewelry was bold, creative; a statement of content, of character. Her skin was lucent; perhaps from the care she gave to such; perhaps, as well, from the glow sourced from Latin bloodlines. What set Arena apart from the others, however, was not found in the external, but sourced from within.

Radiance. Beyond beauty. This quality reveals itself when the goodness of the soul finds its way past all obstacles of one's persona. As if the light of spirit is given passage through the eyes, the face of such grace in motion. Radiant beauty can be both seen and felt. A pure shot of soul.

Arena was pure radiance. And I was once again in need of her light.

She placed the steaming hot arepas within reach. 'Okay. I'm back with you. So what's been haunting you lately?'

'Something's missing. Something's always missing. It tortures me. I can't find what I'm looking for. I'm miserable in its pursuit.'

'Well, I don't think what you're looking for will be found in *that*.'

'In what?'

'In the misery.'

I paused for a moment. She was, of course, right. Arena was usually right. I adjusted my leg to a more comfortable position; then continued.

'I've just been awakening to a revelation of sorts. It's as if I've been on this quest for, I don't know, a millennium, maybe longer. A quest for some missing piece, that when found would perhaps magically complete the picture of...'

'You?'

'Me. Yes.'

Arena had this uncanny ability to get to the heart of the matter, with few words and great intention.

'Hmmm, a missing *peace*. Sounds peaceful.'

'It's been anything but peaceful, as you well know,' I then caught on with her meaning. 'Yes, peaceful. Maybe that in itself is one of the missing pieces I am searching for——one of the keys. I'm unsure, but there are signs.'

'Signs? What signs?'

I glanced down to gather my thoughts and found on the table a copy of *The Republic* by Plato. I pulled back the cover. An inscription in black ink read…

"*He travels best that knows when to return.*"

'Did you write this?'

'Write what?' she replied.

'The inscription on the inside of this book: "*He travels best that knows when to return.*" Thomas More, right?'

Arena was as much a closet historian as I. We both shared, in particular, a reverence for the various masters who, through quite ordinary lives, had left the world with most extraordinary works. It often required centuries of study to merely begin to grasp the true context and, more important, the source for inspiration. Sir Thomas More was a master who gave his life—literally—standing on higher moral and spiritual ground.

'Oh, yes. I love his work. Had a way with the ladies, too. Maybe you are him, reincarnated,' Arena said, smiling.

'Right, but you see. This is what I am referring to. Signs. Messages. It's like I'm on a treasure hunt. But not just *any* treasure hunt. This is the big hunt, the "big dig." Only I haven't a clue what I am digging for.'

'Oh, I think you do.'

"*He travels best that knows when to return,*" I thought to myself.

But return to what? Was he speaking of a place? A time?

'Okay, so let's assume for the moment we are all on this expedition... fellow travelers... all heading toward the same destination. How will we know when we're there if we're not even clear what we're searching for?'

'Oh, Jeremy, what is missing is what you're searching for.'

'What is *missing* is what I'm searching for? You mean love?'

'Define love. For we both know you have had many to love in this life.'

'Love cannot be defined,' I responded, not entirely onboard with my own answer.

'Especially this one.'

'Which one?'

'The one you seek.'

'Well, I know what it's not. I have had my fill of loves that have left me feeling empty, however fulfilling they may have been in other ways.' The night with Natasha flashed across my screen.

'Go higher.'

'Arena, that's too abstract. This higher love we all speak of is beyond mind and, therefore, impossible to grasp within the mind itself. I do know I have experienced many portals to that loving. Even this evening… '

'Jeremy, my love, look behind you.'

I turned, while trying to keep my leg in place, and found one of Arena's fabulous paintings sitting just above my head. Arena was a master in her own right, somehow blending basic colors and bending common shapes in forming a symphony on canvas. She was an artist before she even knew she was an artist. The world merely awaited her own awakening to her true self.

'You know I love your work, sweetheart.'

'Yes, but before it was this, it was merely a series of simple paint strokes… one upon the other… crossing paths when required… blended together to produce a new discovery, an awakening to what the individual shapes and colors may form when brought into harmonic balance… into oneness.'

'Like pieces of a puzzle.'

'Like the puzzle of peace,' she added.

I sat there considering Arena's words, and more important, the meaning behind them. The world around me, in all its elements—human and otherwise—were providing me with clues. Some revealed what was; others, what was not. All were my teachers. And all experiences, my choices; my lessons.

What it was precisely that wielded its magic wand in formulation of not only a life, but of a series of follies adjoined with another, I did not know. What I did know was that Arena—as with so many others—played the supporting character in the storyline that was me in its unfolding. And presumably I played the same for her. The lead character, playing a supporting role for another. All living the life we were born to live. Or so it seemed.

Arena and I continued in such form until the church bell presiding over the adjacent plaza chimed but a single stroke. One lasting hug, a quick cleanse of the teeth, and I found myself nestled in for the evening amid a wonderland of pillows. There I lay, staring up at the ceiling, with each crack revealing the give and take of man's construction with nature's need to shift even herself from time to time. I began my inward chant as a way of thanking spirit for this evening, for Arena, for the recovery of my better senses— my higher senses. My meditations served in keeping some connection when the litany of my life would leave me lonely and at a loss—when the purpose for even being here would seem pointless.

I began to fade off, observing the traced intersections of the ceiling cracks against the canvas of my eyelids.

How was it possible that something seemed always one step ahead of me, yet always right there with me? I'd felt lonely on many occasions on this life journey. This was clear. And I used others to fill this void. But had I ever really been alone? It seemed a reasonable enough action: to place into question the voice of my imagination, a voice that would have me believe otherwise. In the world, one could feel alone. But in the heart, there seemed another world of possibility existed. And it was a world I wished to explore further.

'*As you will*,' the higher self revealed. '*For the eyes see what the heart is given passageway to speak.*'

'I wish I knew you better. Clearly you are a higher version of me... greater vision of me, perhaps.' I was in a dream. At least, it felt as such.

'*To know me is to know yourself... revealed to you, in time.*'

An image appeared. A face. The face I had seen while on the stone wall in India. It was the image of a man. He looked a bit like Yoda, the wise master from *Star Wars*. Or maybe Buddha. His eyes were indiscernible; like an entire universe resided within them. He leaned forward as if to whisper something to me. I waited. I waited for the words, the words that were meant for me.

'*A true friend is one soul in two bodies.*'

Aristotle. I knew the words. I had seen them before.

The words, the image, were replaced by a purple haze. I rubbed my eyes; opened them. The haze remained; then faded off.

The chorus of crickets was once again deafening, defining.

I remained entranced, until a spider off in the far corner of the room caught my attention. She was going about the methodical act of rebuilding the silk web that had been consigned to history by Arena's housemaid. Interesting, one creature's purposeful act erased by another, both going about doing what they did. I wondered how many times the spider had revisited this situation—and project—as a result of the housemaid's good work? Guilt and innocence in a daily dance of good-natured ignorance; the unwitting act of one teaching another a lesson in perseverance.

Was it possible I could learn, as well, from the stoic actions of a spider? This little being went about building an elaborate tapestry, only to have it wiped away each day. And did the spider wallow in despair? No. She just got back on her feet—all eight of them—and began to build another masterpiece, in the same manner, yet never quite the same result. All perfect, however. Unconsumed by emotions, or by a most active mind. Total allegiance. A model of vigilance.

I closed my eyes again, in deep appreciation for the awareness growing within me; the comfort of the bed beneath me; and for whatever—or *whomever*—was watching over me, guiding me.

> I felt at peace with what was.
> I felt at home with what is.

The aroma awakened me. An arepa awaited me. I made my way downstairs, and found Arena in the kitchen in her lounge pants and nightshirt. She was preparing what a-mounted to a small feast.

'Are we expecting company?'

'What do you mean?' Arena responded.

'Look at the spread you're preparing. It's a meal fit for a king.'

'We are in Colombia, sweetheart. And in my house, there are only kings.' Arena delivered this with a bow, her head lowered to suggest one were graced by royalty. She raised her head and smiled. It worked. I felt like a king.

'And how is the tainted traveler today?'

'Better, thank you.'

'Good. Then would you mind setting the table?'

So much for the title of king.

The "table" was set already. It was for each of us to find our proper place, sit, eat of a most humble pie, and satisfy our taste for something greater.

'Jeremy?'

'Sorry, sweetie. I was… '

'Traveling?'

'Yes, traveling.'

'Some would call it "checking out." But we know better, don't we?'

'Yes, we do.'

Arena knew what I had come to know. My daydreams, my disconnects, were simply an escape, until such time that I began to see more clearly where I was moving toward, hearing more clearly the voice calling me inward.

The kettle had its own voice; one that indicated the moment was upon us. A fresh, almond *rooibos* tea awaited its reunion with the liquid that served in bringing it to life. The tea itself had potential, great potential. But it was only when filled to the brim with life's most essential element that it was able to bring its gift forward.

Of course, the indulgence of tea in this region of the world was pure sacrilege. For we were in Colombia, where only the rich aroma of a Colombian roast, mixed with the sweat of a workforce dedicated to awakening the world each day to its scent and taste, would be acceptable. Arena was merely catering to my preference, as with my needs.

We sat and enjoyed our feast together. I feasted, as well, upon her eyes. Arena's eyes were like windows to some magical place, a place I wanted to know better. She was using meditation as a means to strengthen her connection to a current of sound (as she called it) that served as a highway to another place. What the place was entirely neither of us could say for sure. It was a place of peace. It was a place of union, oneness. It was a personal place.

'Where to next, sweetheart?' Arena inquired.

'Europe. Paris maybe.'

'Paris? What's in Paris? Outside of the obvious.'

'Let's just call it unfinished business.'

I paused; then continued. 'Li is in Paris. She e-mailed me not too far back. She is helping a cousin with her shop in the Latin Quarter.'

Arena became silent. I could feel the energy shift in the room.

'Is something up?' I asked.

'No. Well, just that I thought you had arrived at a different answer. That is all.'

'I thought so, too. But when I was sitting there along the creek side, broken in so many ways, I wished for Li.'

'Careful what you wish for. For wishes they often come true… just not in the form we prefer. Not usually, at least.'

'Arena…'

'You owe me no explanations. You don't owe *me* anything. Now *you*, on the other hand, well…'

'I'm sure *that* debt runs deep. Payback is a bitch, huh.' I tried to be cute, but Arena was feeling something else; perhaps a disappointment with my next direction.

'I know it seems a bit odd, but I need answers. I am being tested everywhere. Maybe Li is just another test. Maybe with her lies another clue. I can only hope the remaining clue, to the mystery—the mystery of me. I am tempted… '

'Tempting fate is not a direction, Jeremy. It's a one-way ticket to a place we all know too well.'

'Arena… '

'Just go. It's not a permission. More like a prediction. You know best.'

Arena was pure Colombian—all heart. She also had little difficulty speaking her mind, another Latin quality. The shortness; this was a first. I was taken aback by it. She was usually so on-target with me that the thought of moving in a direction counter to her intuit was a bit unnerving.

The journey to the airport found us back in more familiar territory.

'Well, we know how it works. Perhaps, you are being courted to Paris for another reason,' Arena offered.

'I know. How often do we experience going somewhere for one reason, and having it play out in an entirely different manner?'

'I can see the future already. Jeremy Braddock... a phone call... "Arena, darling, I need your help. I am caught up in a jail cell here in Paris." Something about a Parisian pimp lord, a stockpile of Russian prostitutes, and some new business venture to satisfy the affairs of the French.'

'Oh, stop it!' She had me laughing now.

'No, it's true. If love is your addiction—sex, even—then maybe some jail time in a rank Parisian penitentiary is just the cure Spirit has in store.'

'Don't even put that out there. How did going to Paris and meeting up with Li end up with me as some pimp lord?'

'Sounds like pimping to me.' Arena was sharp, witty. I loved that about her.

'Stop it. I do have some business to do. Get about the business of me, as well. I may have some demons left in the closet, a closet that needs cleaning.'

'Well, then, on with the exorcism. I want to see Jeremy Braddock "unplugged"... or better yet, plugged *in*. And I wouldn't worry about the business part. The Mr. Braddock I know can manifest diamonds from thin air. Perhaps I will start referring to you as *Le Comte de Saint-Germain*.'

If only I could master such mastery.

Watching Arena drive away left me with an empty feeling inside. I had to travel on; this I knew. But the thread that connected me to all I knew and loved would have to be stretched once again in pursuit of something greater—not in another, but in me.

"He travels best that knows when to return."

I was a traveler. This was certain. What I was traveling toward—perhaps returning to—acted as a beacon, a homing beacon. I was attuning to it through the many that played unwitting guides in my journey, my quest, for the answers to my questions; the pieces of the puzzle; and to a gift, a promise, which awaited me still.

Wherever this road would lead...

I was following.

There was simply no other choice.

Am I?
You are... wherever you are, You are.

How do you know where I'm going in thought?
Unity... One with all... that which breathes You offers this so.

11
LA ROUTE DE LA LIBERTÉ

'Are we running away?'
'No, toward.'

'How do we know?'
'Because our heart is now leading.'

I awakened to the screech of the wheels as our plane
touched down at Charles de Gaulle airport. The conversation with Arena—and a deeper one within me—had
been going on throughout the journey across the Atlantic.
My basic self and higher consciousness were staving off the
queries of a mind programmed according to the laws of this
planet, and not the higher laws of the universe.

The mind feared. The mind worried. The mind required

—demanded even—some logical explanation for the actions of the heart. That was its job. The role of the heart—the spiritual heart—was one of intelligence, whose collaboration with the greater plan dwarfed that of the mind. That part of me that was aligned asked merely that the mind get in line and follow. I had felt a shift within myself while in Colombia, one that unveiled the true captain of my craft, with me as trusting—and for the time being *trusted*—co-pilot. I had set upon this journey long before the mind was privy to such conspiracy. And now it was time for the intelligent heart to take its seat in the cockpit of my own co-creation.

The mind had no other choice...

Than to follow the voice.

The only choice that remained was *when*.

La Route de la Liberté. The road to freedom may be paved with many things, but it required but few when parading through Paris to unleash the spirit within and arouse the senses throughout. Along the stretch of cobblestone that served as a blend of past lore and present activity, I was in discovery once again; this time of the world's finest in subtle pleasantries available to the senses.

The scent of warm baguettes emanated from a nearby *boulangerie*. The mouth watered as it cast its vote for satisfying more savory desires. Café upon café lined the street, serving the needs of the observer. Each passerby played inquisitor, as well as the object of such inquisition. Puffy clouds made haste across the sky, as if in rush to usher in the next spectacular sunset, a firework across the sky, pink in color, inspiring in both design and substance. All added context to the path of the fellow traveler.

Paris held all this and more. Paris held a promise, of an authentic love—within and throughout—for any seeker who brought, as one master would put it, an *"attitude of gratitude"* for the grace of this place.

I was in such a place.

'Ah, monsieur Braddock, welcome to the Hotel Saint Merry.' The melody of the language provided by the front desk attendant only added to the allure of the boutique Gothic-style hotel, tucked away in the famed Marais District.

'Bonjour.'

'Will you be staying long with us?'

'Not sure. We shall see.'

'Sounds liberating. Ah, well, we are happy to have you here.' Sabrina was her name. She was most adorable, mainly due to her pleasant way. I had no time for other notices. I was here on a mission.

'I didn't know this hotel was attached to a church.'

'Even better, monsieur, it is very much a part of the church... or what used to be the church quarters,' Sabrina shared. 'Each room served as the former chambers for members of the clergy, nuns, and other servants. Every room is different. It is part of what makes our hotel so unique.'

Hmmm, a bit creepy, I thought, but I'll give it a go. Sabrina escorted me upstairs, one step at a time. The Saint Merry was like so many hotels in the city, offering character and charm in lieu of such modern amenities as an elevator. Eighty-six steps later, amid the must and mildew of mere centuries of cardinal theater played between the chambered walls of both concrete and congregation, there we were.

The door opened. The eyes ever so much wider.

'Haven't seen something quite like this before.'

'I know. The stone pillars are a bit overwhelming for some.'

Stone pillars? The room had two stone, meter-wide pillars (more like saber teeth) on each side of the king bed, jutting out from the walls and into the floor at the base of the bed frame. A cold concrete creature begging one to swallow whole their greatest childhood fears, when a good night's rest was all I required—and desired.

'Okay, Sabrina, this will do for now. But if I have a nightmare where I am literally consumed by my own imagination, digested into the bowels of my greatest fears, we may have to consider a room change.'

She laughed. I was serious.

I lay there in bed that afternoon, staring up at a ceiling that seemed to be staring back at me. Murals, of angels, floating above, a reminder of the many that had graced my life; no one more so than Li. Images of the many made their way through the memory as my head sank further into the pillow. Something inside always teased me with the return to yesterday. And while there was no going back, only forward, this general rule of the universe didn't preclude us from forming a circle, which could look and feel a lot like yesterday, with a guaranteed return through the *Wheel of 84* (the cycle of births and deaths). It was an awareness that housed a fortress of fresh thoughts, examples, as recent as Costa Rica.

Miia also dominated my awakened state. A recent call from Mikko had placed her in the French Alps, at a Buddhist monastery, studying under a famous monk. Three years of total seclusion. Perhaps Miia had found her path, her way. I was happy for her. Happy for her; and deluged with my own inquisition—mainly my current attempt at love.

Was the act of falling out of love required so that we might find another, deeper love expression? Was Miia finding the answers to her own questions, those which had eluded her during our time together? Was the pain I experienced required for me to break free of whatever bound me here? Did Li hold a key, or was she just another step along the way? Brilliant, I thought, the many paths created to what was likely the same destination, the same home.

The faces and places of many made their way to the subconscious. I saw Sebastien, and courage emerged. There was the compassion of Georgia, her sense of service. A father's purpose, and the opportunity for greater understanding. The humorous path of all bridges leading into— and thankfully out of—San Francisco. The freedom in letting go, trusting, accepting the many varied ways and forms, a lesson most deserving from those on Indian soil. The just reward for simply being present—and loving— with Li in Italy. Arena's clarity. Miia's integrity. Maya's playful nature. Cassandra's sense of freedom. And the timeless wisdom as brought forward by so many masters, through so many members of my community of co-conspirators.

Pieces of a greater puzzle to be solved, re-*solved* or merely resolved? Timely reflections, perhaps, for a man in timeless pursuit of the one truth I came here to know.

> Pieces floating about
> With love in the balance
> And peace at stake

I sat up, flung my feet to the side and remained at the edge of the bed. I looked down at the legs that had taken me across this planet, in pursuit of something that stood between dream and destiny. There would be no rest today. There would be no rest for one who remained restless. The creak of the wooden flooring as I made my way to the window seemed to symbolize the give and take of a life that provided a sturdy foundation, yet remained flexible enough to allow for the variations in how I would choose to distribute my weight in the world.

I opened the windows, and let in whatever was there to greet me. Fresh air. A gentle wind. And the views. Notre

Dame to the west. A sea of cafés below—which would invite themselves into the bedroom through the antiquated windowpanes. The Marais offered a host of opportunities to feed into the eclectic subculture in this part of the right bank. The city in its never-ending love affair with life provided a rightful place to re-connect with a passion for love itself, and unleash the spirit within. I was grateful just to be here. Grateful, as well, for a life that had provided me so many memories that would someday fill the mausoleum of my own making. After all these years of knocking, it was only fitting that I open the door—window even—and stretch a bit.

When I opened, whenever I opened up to *It*, *It* poured through.

Like the light through my window on this particular day in Paris.

The church bells of Notre Dame graced all with the information we required. It was five o'clock. The famed Latin Quarter in the fifth *arrondissement* was already alive with a festival of people that offered the earthly pleasures of good food, good company, and greater appreciation for the persona of Paris.

Step by step, I made my way across the Seine and eventually along rue Descartes to rue Mouffetard. The street was a lively cobblestone stretch of road with a rich history, once pointing the way home to Roman soldiers nearly two thousand years before. Rue Mouffetard was the best street in Paris. It was also where I would find Li.

'Ah, René. We meet again, old friend,' I said to myself as I climbed to greater heights—literally. I studied this famous French philosopher. Descartes always seemed to have such perfect timing for the pervading consciousness of man in his awakening—enlightenment, even—after a steady dose of sleeping pills through much of the preceding Dark Ages. His words blazed the mind and graced my heart, as we walked together up the hill.

'It is so evident that it is I who doubt, who understand, and who desire, that there is no reason here to add anything to explain it.'

'Yes, but what is the value of mind if it does not move us closer to the truth of our Selves?' A fair enough question at this stage, I considered.

The exchange continued within.

'It is at least quite certain that it seems to me that I see light, that I hear noise and that I feel heat. That cannot be false; properly speaking it is what is in me called feeling; and use in this precise sense that is no other than thinking.'

'Granted, thinking and feeling were certainly a part of being, but what of this thing that *knows*, the part of us that is somehow tapped into the universal consciousness from which all questions may be met with the truth in reply. Was this not the pinnacle of man that we may know this part of us as well as we know our own thoughts, our own feelings?'

I was proud of my reply, and of my growing awareness

of such a notion. René took little notice.

'By the name God I understand a substance that is infinite, independent, all-knowing, all-powerful, and by which I myself and everything else, if anything else does exist, has been created. God, in creating me, placed this idea within me to be like the mark of the workman imprinted on his work.'

Thank you, René. A bridge builder between the Seine and sensibility if I ever knew one. How brilliant the use of scientific method to take us on a journey beyond science, and into the spirit of it all.

It was a funny thing, this grand duality of life. This I thought as I made my way past Place de la Contrescarpe, and began my descent into the magic that was Mouffetard. We appear to have at all times one foot on the ground, and one foot in the heavens. Our choice, I suppose, was where we chose to place our greater weight. For now, I set my stride toward the tart shop just down the hill.

'As love leads the way, the steps will be made easy.'

Words spoken once from a master, a teacher. They were his words. They were my words. They were for me.

I made my way down the backside of Mouffetard, grateful for all around me—filled with love within me. I took in the sensations, the expressions of the cheese shops and bakeries; the *crêperies*; fruit and vegetable marts. One quick stop at the wine shop and...

'Bonsoir, monsieur.'

'Bonsoir. *Parlez-vous anglais?*'

'I know a little English. How can I help you?'

'I would like a bottle of wine.'

'But, of course,' the middle-aged shopkeeper responded, already introducing a bit of attitude into the mix.

'Perhaps a Bordeaux.'

And then it began.

'A Bordeaux?' Her accent becoming richer with each corresponding word. 'But what kind of Bordeaux? There are many Bordeaux.'

'Well, I know my American wines pretty well, but am a bit lost with some of the French ones.'

'Ah, but American wines are not French. There is no comparison.'

I saw where this was heading.

'I know. French wines are different... '

'French wines are not only different, monsieur, they are *su*perior in taste. There is no comparison.'

A wine snob I wasn't, but I could certainly recognize one. The wines might be different, but the attitude is the same anywhere in the world.

'I will just have a Bordeaux. You choose.'

The shopkeeper began mumbling to herself as she picked up the closest bottle and carried it over to the register.

'Bordeaux. He wants a Bordeaux. Any Bordeaux, he says. "A rose is a rose is a rose," he thinks. Even when it is *not* just a Bordeaux.'

I smiled, paid the price—in more than one way—and continued on. I could still hear her sharing her tale with the other patrons as I walked away. Yet, there was no attitude

that was going to shake me from the gratitude I was experiencing for everyone and everything around me. And of a
greater love growing within, with each step toward the
awaited.

Out of earshot of Madame Bordeaux, I came upon my
intended destination, a little shop by the name of La
Maison des Tartes. The display in the window was
impeccable, tastefully highlighting a host of savory quiches
and tarts, which captured my fancy. And today, they had
my favorite "dish" of all.

Through the window display I caught a glimpse of her
hand. The hand that once fit so perfectly within my own
was gently preparing a piece of lemon tart for a patron
inside. She glanced up. Her eyes adjusted to the glare from
the sun that shone through the window. Her heart had
already embraced the moment in its unfolding. Her face
filled with joy as reality met with the mind. The next movement was merely the displacement of a door that stood
between an objective in life's daily duties, and the object of
one's eternal loving.

'*Jeremy!*' Li exclaimed as she leaped into my arms. Her
head burrowed between my chin and shoulder. Her arms
trembled. Her heart beat furiously, as if to ensure the blood
which flowed through it—the liquid of life—would serve in
feeding her entire body with the strength to never let go
again. It was an embrace for the ages; an ageless, timeless
embrace.

Li regained her form and looked up and into my eyes.

My hands moved to her silk-like hair. I ran my fingers gently through it as I gazed once again into the eyes of the one who eclipsed all others. Forgetting for the moment that we were center stage for the parade of onlookers, Li and I held one another to the depth of soul. I gave her a kiss deserving of the moment and melody that played within my heart. Her inviting lips ran across my own, the universe conspiring to serve up love in a city that played master chef to such entrée.

'Jeremy, I thought you would come. I wanted to believe it. But to know you are here… '

'Well, you can thank my heart. It led me here.'

'Simply to return mine to me.' Li's eyes began to tear. It was a release of months—many months—of not knowing. I recognized the source of such. My tears had been welled up for some time now. It was painful indeed to not know what we wished to know—needed to know.

Li grabbed my hand. We stepped inside the shop. I took a seat, one of only twelve in the tiny haven.

'My cousin owns this shop, but of course you know this,' Li shared as she meticulously prepared the setting in front of me. 'I'm just filling in for her while she and her husband are on holiday.'

'You know, I've been here before.'

'Many times, I imagine.'

'No. I've been to this shop. This is my favorite pastry shop in all of Paris.'

'Then destiny, once again, has graced us both.'

'Yeah. Destiny. I am beginning to see the pattern.'

Love found a way. Love always found a way—pointed the way, even. In this case, back to Li.

'Give me a moment,' Li asked. She stepped inside the kitchen.

With Li out of view, my eyes took notice of another. My attention diverted to an aged gentleman, grayed with wisdom, squinting for his next sensory experience, style having passed him by for a waistline void of definition. He was sporting a navy blue jacket lacking brand but defining the gentleman he was—and remained still—gray slacks rising with each fading year of his life. He was relaxed, sitting comfortably with a grace and nobility in concert with the city that had played home to him throughout his living days. This man was embracing the gift of the present moment and experience. Nothing more was required or desired. There was an ease about him.

His movements were slow, methodical, manifest from moment to moment. He lifted his cup, graced it with his lips, would sip, then return it to its place, its origin. He would then do the same with his napkin. The world for this warrior had slowed to a series of simple, graceful movements. He was late in his years, but not late for anything else. This man of the ages had nowhere to go, nothing so pressing to achieve, no one to impress. He was there, and he was *here*, in the moment, caring little for what lies ahead or in how he had arrived at now. The need to proceed and the yearning for yesterday had been replaced by a still peace.

My heart stirred, awakening to something inside me, of me, but not only of me. The chorus of crickets emerged. The voice followed.

'*As love leads the way, the steps will be made easy.*'

The old man raised his body to a standing position. He brushed off a speck or two that stood between the imperfect and perfect form, and began to change his vantage point with each calculated step; drawing parallels to our own first steps and learning as perhaps precursor to our last with lasting memories. Cane in hand, having learned to trust in another "friend" in finishing out the journey, my new source for inspiration continued his slow but steady voyage out the door. He proceeded down rue Mouffetard, squinting to hold his focus in the present while providing his pervading gift of example to the world around him.

In his path—as if on cue—entered another aged marvel. Teeth amiss—but not missing the moment—the canine comrade quivered while balancing herself, the chore of merely standing a mission. She was peppered in black and white with a full complement of gray, as if to remind us of those areas of our lives not so easily defined. What had she seen? Where had she been? Did she enjoy the journey? Did she get to come home with us?

'*As love leads the way, the steps will be made easy.*'

I watched the man and his new companion continue on course, step by precious step, upon the cobblestone streets. Amid the clamor of many, there was only silence. One singular moment, with none other to be found, nor required.

I was witnessing completion.

Love in such form was not one of romance, of, with and for another. Love, was the pathway, not the destination. But a pathway of whose construct? To where would this love lead us—lead *me?*

'Have you not played witness to the very answers that you seek?'

The nature of the voice was familiar at this point, as the One that had traveled this road with me since my first gift of breath, and opportunity for life. Whether of the soul, God Himself or his entourage of spiritual support, it mattered not. It was the voice of reason, sourced from the intelligent heart that simply knew beyond all thinking, believing. And it spoke to me whenever—and wherever—I chose *in* to listening. I was listening now.

'Well, I suppose through the very nature of your question, I have in fact been provided with the answers,' I retorted within. 'But I have found it difficult to trust completely in a voice that has no reference point in this world, no place to pacify my practical, if not somewhat cynical, mind.'

'But it has a reference point in this world. The world and everything in this world is its reference point. Ours is to stay present, observe, and be grateful for the learning as presented through our next experience.'

I sat there considering each word that seemed to

represent a universe of meaning behind every letter, every syllable. I had come to understand better what it meant to be present in our lives, not casting favor toward some absentee system void of gratitude for this precious life I have been given. My latest example: a marvel of a man, aged but not upstaged by the most natural giving over of the physical as tradeoff to greater wisdom. He ruled rue Mouffetard with each step, with grace, with ease; as living testament to an everlasting truth.

'*As love leads the way, the steps will be made easy.*'

Love was clearly in the lead. It was simply not the love I thought it to be. It was something more.

'Okay. I'm ready,' Li said. 'I've got the shop covered. Now, let's take care of you.'

'*Us*. There is only us.'

Li smiled. She grabbed a hold of my arm, and we were off.

We made our way toward Luxembourg Gardens. The Panthéon was in the best of spirits this afternoon, majestic as ever, baring its contents to the public while maintaining its greatest treasures within the earth below. Voltaire, Rousseau, Madame Curie were just a few whose remains remained. Above ground, the cafés were alive with a blend of fine roasts and the day's hosts. The clouds above moved with us down rue Soufflot, the grand Panthéon to our backs, the park within our sights. They moved with us as if in anticipation of an event to unfold between two souls who only knew one way when in the comfort of the other.

Once inside, the gardens welcomed with an array of colors, most notably the lavender bouquets that graced the large stone pots that found a home between the series of statues around the basin, carved in honor of former French queens and saints. Li and I made our way to a patch of grass as far from the Medici and other more traveled attractions as one could manage. We lay there on the plush greens, breaking bread and sipping wine while watching the clouds parade across the sky. Li began to peel back the layers through her inquisitive nature.

'Jeremy, what brought you here… to Paris?'

'You did.'

'I mean, what brought you here *really*.'

'My heart. You. The search for answers. I've been haunted by this need to know. And of a promise, one I had made to myself…'

'A promise?'

'Yes. A promise that perhaps can only be answered within—in Spirit. I don't know. But with each new step, each new entry into my own life journals, I am closer to the truth. This I do know.'

'What is truth? What does this mean to *you?*'

I sat there for a moment, a moment of inner reflection. I sat there until words that were not my own flashed across my screen.

'God is Truth… and so are you.

'Seek not what already is.'

'God,' I responded, with little hesitation. 'God is truth.

Love is truth. And truth is love. I see no separation between the truth of me and love in its deepest meaning, deepest expression. *His* expression.'

She smiled. She understood. It was not a mere acknowledgment of my love for her, but of the greater plan played out through such loving. I had written her before, of my quest for love, for truth, the search for another sign, another marker—in the hope for something more. What brought me here? To Paris? The answer was not important. The truth was—to be revealed to me, in time.

'Jeremy, I have owed you an explanation for some time now. For why I have been out of contact.' Li hesitated for a moment; then continued. 'It is not a simple thing.'

'I figured as much. After waiting a mere eternity, there had to be a reason we were awakening anywhere but in each other's arms.'

'I am with someone.'

'Husband? Boyfriend? Both?' I was as quick to respond as I was feeble in my attempt at lightening the moment.

'Husband.'

'I was hoping for boyfriend.'

Li smiled. I had to chuckle, and did so.

'Jeremy, it is complicated. The marriage, it was... '

'Arranged? No, that couldn't be. He's Italian, right?'

'He is Italian. I met him in Rome, years ago. Nine years, in fact. I know this... each time I look into my son's eyes.'

A husband. A son. Complicated indeed. Li was married. She had a child. Cultures and practice in past tradition involved here created complications with a pathway to loving that, at first glance, seemed divinely paved from the moment of our reacquaint in Venice. Divinely paved, maybe. But to what end, this lifetime?

It was complicated for me, as well. I had neither the time nor taste for adding any more to my plate while seeking a stage that could only be achieved by no longer deceiving myself, depriving myself, of something more—so much more—than even I had sense of.

The words returned.

'Do you love him?'

'Yes… but not in the way that I wish. It is a love, a mutual love, but not for each other. It is our son that bonds us, makes us know love. If it were not for him…' Li's eyes migrated to the ground. When she raised her head, there were only tears. She was ashamed for even having to admit to this, to her own truth, to a love that was not bound in such.

I reached out and held her in my arms.

'Li, these are details. Big details, I give you that… but details nonetheless. In the context of eternity, we can wait to see how this unfolds.' I was unsure of the absolute in these words, but they were as honest as I was aware in the moment.

Li ran her hand over mine. Her delicate fingers wanted to point to another solution. It was unclear at this point if another solution was available to her, to us. We would have to wait and see what spirit, the universe, had in store.

Once again, we would have to trust.

A man walked by, holding the hand of his child—a daughter. Her hand rested comfortably within his own. She had no worries to compete with the moment; no concerns that would threaten her in any manner, and move her from her mantle. She trusted in her father, his decisions, his direction. She knew he would eventually guide her home. The soul knew this as well of us, when in the hands of our Creator.

Li broke the silence, 'Jeremy, does it bother you, all the travels, moving from place to place?'

'Bother me?'

'I mean, do you ever feel like a man without a home? Do you ever feel settled?'

'A man without a home? No, not really. Sometimes. Depends who's leading.'

'Who's leading?'

'Yeah. My head or my heart. When my heart is leading, I feel at home with what is... wherever that is. Anything less leaves me wanting... *wherever* I am.'

I thought about this a moment longer, then continued. 'Of course, for some time now I have felt a longing for something more, no matter where I am. It's as if what I seek cannot be completed here.'

'Here?' Li queried.

'Here. On this planet. This world. This lifetime.'

'Perhaps it is in the stars where the final chapter is written.'

'Perhaps it is in the heart where the final chapter will be done.'

Li took in my words as her own. We gathered up the blanket. She took my arm and we ventured on, eventually finding our way to the Seine. We made our way along the river. I felt at peace with the woman beside me, as if she herself held some key to my understanding of the journey I was on, as a result of the many journeys we had taken together, in another life, another form. The river moved in harmony with the current within me. Li strengthened her grip on my arm. I could only imagine what was moving within her.

The love we shared provided a portal to the paradise as can only be known through such unmistakable ecstasy, when we are given a glimpse of the spirit within—in this case through the soul of one adjoined with another. For the afternoon, it mattered little whether this were journey, destination, or procrastination. It mattered only that it was a gift and it was now.

We stopped to take in the setting. The river below seemed to provide a clue as to how smoothly life could flow, when we but allow ourselves to move in symphony with that which is. The birds above used what wind was available as a power to harness, and not a force of resistance. The laughter of passersby a fitting reminder of the joys that surrounded us, when we moved with the sound current that served in unleashing the soul.

As I stood there looking over the embankment, I felt Li's

hand gently touch my arm from behind. It was the touch I had known as a child—a mother's touch—that made all pain subside through a greater knowing that everything has been and forever will be alright. I felt the peace I had been longing for, not because of another, but because I was open to another side of me. The head was quieted, the heart stirred, with truth revealed.

'Jeremy.'

'Yes?'

'Remember that time back in Venice when you mentioned the crickets?'

'Yes. You probably thought I had had a bit too much champagne that day.'

'No. I knew it was real to you, even if I did not have the experience at that time.'

'At that time?'

'Yes. Since then, whenever I feel you deeply in my heart, I hear this chirping sound in my ear. It is not very loud, but it is undeniable.'

'Perhaps it is the sound we know when we feel closest to love—a deeper love. Closest to home.'

It made me think of what Li had shared that sun-drenched Venetian morning. The singing of the cricket was a sign of good luck—when in the home. Was this the source of the sound that formed a current, one that might take us home, wherever home may be?

'Jeremy, when will you know that you have found what you are looking for?'

I stood there for a moment. No words came through my mind. No words were required. Through the silence, the answer was revealed. All words ceased to exist. Only the sound of my intelligent heart could be heard.

'When I am no longer looking… but merely seeing.'

Li smiled, collected my hand, and guided me along the river. I needed no guide in the moment.

I was now hearing clearly the wisdom within me.

The current of sound that was me.

———

The light of day gave way to the dark of night. The night returned the favor in kind. A few days bundled together became one of the most treasured weeks of my life. During this time, I discovered a deeper side of myself. I was in romance with my soul. Every corner of every rue and avenue offered safe passageway to a most worthy pursuit indeed. Happiness, pure and unbridled. Gratitude through a higher altitude. *With* another but not *through* another.

Li and I played within the realm of soul, a place that left us with a childlike giddiness and youthful enthusiasm that had no bearing on any age in human flesh. I was reminded of New York, and Maya. I was reminded of every time I felt alive—when I allowed my soul to surface.

My time with Li awakened that side of me—the gift within me. We honored the spirit in the moment. And the present *was* the future. We took little notice of the realities that awaited. We would have to. There was simply no avoiding the shadows of our own device.

'Bonjour, madame. Bonjour monsieur,' the maître d' offered, dressed in rather formal attire while donning an apron.

'Bonjour,' Li offered back.

The café seemed as good as any for another farewell in the making. After nearly a week amid the stars, Li was off; returning to her husband, her son; her life. And I found myself still in search for the one place I could call home. Our shared destiny—if there was one to be shared—would have to be known in time.

We took in the setting. Madame Piaf provided the background. *La Vie en Rose.*

'You are American, no?'

'Oui, madame.'

The inquiry came from an impeccably dressed lady of maybe sixty-five or seventy I just happened to be rubbing shoulders with. Accessorized with class from head to toe, what completed this woman, however, was not her passion for fashion, but that quality that so often goes undetected, if not completely unnoticed. This new addition to our perfect day exuded grace. The close quarters moved us into conversation.

'You know, I spent two years as an intern in New York. Of course, this was many years ago. I have aged since then. But life offers us pearls in place of diamonds.'

I loved her already. "Pearls in place of diamonds." Wisdom in place of the material we covet before we know of the greater gifts of life.

Li joined the conversation. 'I could not help but notice your smile.'

'I have been practicing it for a lifetime. I suppose I have it down by now.'

'You do indeed,' I added.

'The name's Ariane. Ariane Benoît.'

'Li Giordano. And this is Jeremy. Jeremy Braddock.'

'I noticed you both. You have been busy, watching, observing… taking in everything and everyone. And you have been smiling, too.'

'What's not to smile about,' I replied, glancing over at Li while doing so, leaving out of my mind for the moment the tiny detail of our impending goodbye.

'This week has been a gift,' Li offered, taking my hand in her own.

'"*Aide-toi et Dieu t'aidera*. Help yourself and God will help you." Or some similar translation.'

'Wise words,' Li replied.

'Yes, she was… wise and brave.'

'She?' I asked.

'Why, Joan of Arc. You have heard of her, no?'

'Of course. A true heroine.'

'Joan of Arc—Saint Joan of Arc now—was the national heroine of France who gave her life for her country and its freedom, while giving her faith to God through a most remarkable demonstration of courage.'

Ariane took a sip of her coffee; then continued.

'Through tremendous adversity. She knew only one will... one way.'

I sat there with a new awareness as to the gift before me. Through the pearls of wisdom being offered by this teaching moment, I was reminded of what sacrifice really entailed. Joan of Arc, as with so many of the mortal immortals who have graced this Earth and gifted us all through the ages, was a messenger herself. She revealed—not through her words, but in action—what the path to God would involve. The ultimate sacrifice for the ultimate jewel. True love and devotion in its unfolding.

'It takes great courage to follow your heart,' Li shared.

'And even more, for your heart to follow Him.' Ariane responded. 'It was not a popular move. It was the right move, though. For her. For all of us maybe.'

'Perhaps it's the only move left when all else has been played out in this game of life,' I added.

'All games seem to lead to us arriving safely home. Maybe it is the case with this one too.' Ariane stood up, gathered her purse. 'Well, I must be going. There are others to bother.'

She left us with a smile. She left us with so much more.

It was time for Li to leave, as well. We made our way to the airport. I watched her plane take off amid a rainfall that served in further dampening the moment. I felt the bitter-sweet emotion of knowing love and letting go, once again. Li was returning to China to tend to her ailing mother, and ailing marriage. And while we had committed to keep in contact, I was reminded—painfully so—that love must come without conditions or restrictions. That is, if we seek to escort a higher love into our homes and our hearts.

I knew I loved her.

She knew she loved me.

And that was all we could know for the moment.

As I made my way back to the hotel, I realized that letting go, however painful, was the only way to get higher. Through the unconditioned love of myself or another, I could dispense with the laws of this world, and gain access to the higher realms. Gravity was still in play, yet my weight had somehow shifted. I felt the balance of power elevated, with my cells acting as receptacle to a divine spark that had me lit up inside. I understood better what the many masters who have walked this planet chose into.

They chose into an awareness. They chose into a consciousness. They chose into a direction. They chose into loving. They chose in. They chose up. And the difference between them and us? They chose it daily, with a devotion that eliminated the separation.

I found a park bench to my liking, one facing the same river that guided me into an eternal truth just one week ago. I sat and pondered further. Was it the love of Li or the love in me that made me feel alive? Would Li and I be together someday? Should I want this? Should it matter? What was it that I still feared? Loneliness? Not knowing? What would be the true risk of living loving, a deeper loving, always and in all ways? Had the choice of something less given me anything more? What would be the risk of trying anyhow? After all, life in the penthouse must be better than life in the outhouse. And I'd had my share of "the other end."

Did a kingdom really await us, with infinite patience for our return? Could we really have health, wealth, and happiness just by raising our hands in indication of absolution of any resistance that had only served in returning us to the same place, planet; albeit donning different "attire"' each lifetime? A simple gesture, with corresponding action, of course.

I looked to the heavens once again. Then lowered my head, closed my eyes, and turned my attention to where intention belonged.

'I'm in, God. You got me... I'm yours,' I thought to myself. Or at least I thought it was simply a thought. I had said it out loud. I had said it in the absolute.

I opened my eyes, returned to where I was, on a park bench, in Paris. The river remained in flow. The city, in some circular motion. My heart in its ascension. The street sign nearby told me everything I needed to know, always knew, once knowing was in the known. It was a symbol, a white arrow against a blue background—and it was pointing up.

There has always been only one way; one way really; one direction.

Lord, from this day forward, may I choose wisely the right direction...

With such a pearl in my possession.

Is there a distance between me and you, Lord?
Yes...
As far as the mind will take You...
And as close as You are to Your heart.

12
YOU SAY DUBAI, I SAY HELLO

The more things change...
The more they stay the same.

'Hello!'

The greeting came from the man sitting to my right as we began our descent into Dubai International Airport.

'Hi,' I responded. It was all I could muster for the moment.

'What's your name?'

'Jeremy. Jeremy Braddock.'

'JB, you've been sleeping like baby. I must have jumped over you like four times since we left.'

Zayid Bashara was of Bedouin roots. His family was short on wealth, but rich in virtue and good graces. "Z" (as I would come to know him) was a charming character, and an even better brother and teacher. Our destined reunion was contrived by the universe from the moment my request for a seat upgrade was denied. God had other plans.

'You stay in Dubai or just visit?'

'I am here doing some work for the government.'

'Here is my card. You need anything, you call. You are American? I like Americans. They are so friendly.' Z shared openly and with the purity of a little boy's heart.

He paused for a moment. He paused; then turned to me with a serious face, a benevolent voice. '*Insh'Allah*, I will see you again, brother. Insh'Allah.'

'Insh'Allah?'

'God willing. It is in His hands.'

We deplaned. I had a sense my time with Zayid had just begun.

I had no idea.

The history of the Emirates is one rich in pearl diving and piracy. And my choice to land in the sand mere weeks after my parade through Paris with Li would lend itself to query whether I was truly prepared to dive deeper, or merely looking to take something that I had not earned.

Two women walked by, dressed in *abayas*, accented with precious stones. Their eyes made contact with mine; then quickly looked away. My mind took notice of another noticing me. My heart was left waiting once again.

The deeper we travel, the greater the reward. What awaited at the surface, however, were the many adversaries—those "loyal forces of the opposition"—designed to challenge us for the bounty that was ours from the very beginning.

> Life offers us jewels. It always has.
> Then tests our resolve. It always will.

I was beyond such retreat. At least, I hoped I was.

'Which way you want?' the taxi driver asked.

'The Al Qasr Hotel, please.'

'Do you know the way?'

'No, unfortunately.'

I was kind of hoping he did considering he was the taxi driver and I merely a first timer in Dubai. This I thought, as we made our way along Sheik Zayed Road. I thought it, but let it go in the next breath. I was pleased to see me in another form. I would have once found myself irritated with such matters. Now, I simply found myself, and chose a higher experience. Granted these were small steps, but there was a greater version of me unfolding. And there would be nothing to keep me from knowing myself better.

'I just arrived here. Three days ago. I am from Pakistan. Where are you from?' the driver queried.

A good question. One without a good answer. At least as defined by the mind.

'Not sure anymore.'

The driver laughed. 'It is a good answer. I think I will borrow it.'

My latest guide found our way through his dispatcher. He carried on in conversation—more like a monologue—as we made our way across the city; a city built upon the backs of millions. Sand rising. Glass forming. Reflecting back to us our naked truth. All slaves to something, or someone. I prefer "servants." It was a bit more empowering.

'You are an explorer, yes?' the taxi driver continued. 'There are many of you here. All searching for something. Gold. The jewels of the desert perhaps. Glamour. For the love of the explorer can be found here, in Dubai. So too can the love of glamour, of money, a place where the pretty come to play.'

He paused for a moment; only for a moment. Then continued. 'Ah, but be not mistaken, my friend, as if hijacked from the senses. The true game at hand is the game of deception. What awaits just beyond the horizon is but the oasis of our dreams. Liquid gold, the glistened jewel of our heart's content, discontent, as we seek to fill the void created through the discomfort of a rather unpleasant memory. Perhaps, from our last port of call.'

Through the rear view mirror, I caught a glimpse of his eyes. They sparkled like the jewels he spoke of. I was without words. I envisioned a man of limited education and even less in opportunity, ignorant to the world and its ways.

I was prepared to offer pity as a means of some disjointed good deed. I was not prepared to be schooled by a taxi driver who couldn't find his way to the hotel, yet had his compass firmly positioned toward something greater.

He continued. He had to.

'Ah, Dubai! Where the biggest, brightest, best, grandest, newest, most spectacular of all spectacles finds its home. Where the temptations of the West meet the adaptations of a world that straddles intolerance with adherence to new ways, albeit under old laws. I wish you well here. I wish you well, my friend.'

I was dropped at the hotel—baggage in hand.

He was off to his next destination—trunk empty.

There was still much left to learn.

———

"Whether you're running from or toward, keep moving. It is in the moving that we get our next step."

Arena's words echoed within the hollow chambers of a man who had somehow found his way... *back*. Not to a place of peace I desired, but to a state where peace could not be known.

I was on the move. That was not in question. But where to precisely remained very much in question.

Lost and found; then lost again.

Home was nowhere to be found.

Dubai dared. I adored. "They" delivered. Back and forth; in and out; from nightclub to nightclub; bedroom to bedroom. "Norway" to "Nairobi," "Moscow" to "Mumbai," with an Aussie in between. The downward spiral through countless escapades of the most carnal nature left me in unknown terms with the universe. I had left the planet of the known, familiar, and landed on Mars, coveting only Venus in all her seductive forms.

I loved everyone in every way imaginable. I hated myself in the most unimaginable way.

Six months after my arrival in Dubai I was engulfed in a sea of sensuality, and no measure for a greater pleasure. Up and down the elevator that ran between my humanity and my divinity, pressing every button as if to not miss any and all "levels," I was left on the ground floor, looking up once again. There was no peace to be found when the many pieces I had collected along the journey that was my life—those that formed the picture I was seeking—lay scattered amid a sea of lingerie. My apartment had a revolving door, with each new dialect complexion met with empty words and an erection that only served to stimulate one muscle and silence another. My heart went quiet.

If Dubai was a test, I was failing.

It was. I was.

I had lost my way, once again. Dubai was a parade for the eyes against the seemingly unsuitable backdrop of the Qur'an—a city playing candy store to the many tastes that served in erasing any trace of my prior footprints, escalations, aspirations. A sandstorm was upon me. A mirage before me. Darkness within me.

I awakened each day to a blazing sun that scorched the mind and discouraged even subtle contact with the soul. I buried myself in the bottom of various vodka prescriptions in an effort to forget just how far I had fallen. It didn't work. It never works. My meditations, contemplations, and conversations with any higher self had effectively vanished. My time served between the Persian Gulf and the Sea of Oman left me diving for greater pearls of wisdom, only to surface with a handful of sand that disappeared between my fingers, along with my sense of self. The dark forces were not only in play, but were winning back the right to stamp my return.

How could I have slipped so far? I wanted to blame love for my regress. I wanted to blame all the women whose love was never enough. I wanted to blame love for failing to live up to the stories told to us as children, the fairy tales and "happily ever afters."

I was alone. And I alone was to blame.

It was time to face my maker. It was time to accept my role in my own creation. He already knew what I had come to know. And He waited patiently for my impatience—more like disgust—to come of age.

Evening arrived. Darkness lurked. I entered.

I entered the waters, in need of a cleansing. The sea provided opportunity for such. I waded far enough offshore to create some sense of distance between myself and the city. I lay on my back, floating in the steamy mineral bath known as the Gulf, under the stars, feeling of separation—

and wanting no part of my life. I could turn over, and just end it right here, my wasted existence, I thought, buoyed upon a sea of humility. I could, but I wouldn't. These thoughts had no home with actions; just desperate thoughts from the disparate self; to pass with the next breath. There was only one way out of "the rabbit hole." And it began— and ended—with me. With merely the transcendence of self as soul in delicate balance, I turned to the only one worth turning to.

'God, I feel so unworthy of the conversation I wish to have with you. You have given me countless opportunities to come to a greater answer to the questions inside me. After receiving so much through so many who have graced my path, once again I feel lost, alone, coveting warmth through another, leaving me still in chilling revelation of my ill choices, ill deeds. I am lost. This I know. The question, the only question worthy of knowing the answer to in this moment, is "Are you still here with me?"'

I looked up at the stars from my place upon the mineral sea. The evening was eerily quiet. All I could hear was the rhythmic surf, as that in motion met with that which held in stillness. It was the only sound available. The silence was altogether unnerving.

I stood up in the water, chest deep, resting my palms upon its surface. The rock wall off in the distance served in reminding me of the barriers self-imposed that stood between here and there; between what we knew as life and what awaited us beyond the breakers—as reward for the vigilant.

The reflection of the full moon upon the sea provided an imaginary path of light. To its left, only darkness. To its right, the same. There was something there, in the darkness. It provided mystery. It provided intrigue. Absent of light, it provided no pathway to where I wanted to be.

'*Absence sharpens love... presence strengthens it.*'

The words echoed within. They were the same words once offered to humanity by a master by the name of Benjamin Franklin. They were now being offered to me.

'*Absence sharpens love... presence strengthens it.*'

The voice inside grew louder. Its source undeniable.

'*Absence sharpens love... presence strengthens it.*'

I understood. I understood immediately. It was not the love of another this voice spoke of, but rather the love of myself; the one that I had abandoned for far too long. This Love I must now reclaim in order to reap merely a king's ransom that awaited.

I was afraid. I was afraid I had angered whatever forces were working with me. I was afraid the sound of the crickets that served as a compass to the inner realms would no longer find their home in my ear—and more important, my heart. I was afraid I had been abandoned.

I returned to the beach. I stood upon the solid land. I brushed off the sands of time that were no longer required, nor desired. And did the only thing I knew to do.

I moved.

It did not take long for spirit to test my resolve. It never does.

Another evening. Another chance to dance in the bonfire.

Strewn out on a Turkish rug, smoking *shisha* against the backdrop of the Burj Al Arab and its splendor of ever changing colors, I played the pharaoh. Beyond the haze, an ocean of opportunity swayed to the rhythmic music at Solano. The seas parted. A queen emerged. Her movement graced the desert dwelling, providing another lesson in motion. She was pure magic—black or white, it mattered not. For tonight I was the purveyor of my process. And she, the conveyor of something else entirely.

Love.

Temptation.

Beyond the separation formed by two worlds—as caretakers of one truth.

She was Muslim. I was not. It mattered not.

Perhaps it was the scent of jasmine that emanated from the plumes of *hookah* smoke that filled the air, serving to disorient the senses. Maybe it was the shifting forms that moved with a freedom of expression offered through a beach setting and choice prescription of various mind-altering concoctions. Or simply a craving for one last taste of the divine through humans being less so. Through whatever portal, the goddess appeared.

Her name was Samira. Her look, "ethnically ambiguous" to some. There was nothing ambiguous about her intentions, nor my own for that matter. Or so it seemed.

She moved with a grace, an ease, that left the dance floor wanting more. Our souls embraced as our bodies struggled to keep with a rhythm that had likely begun far before we were *we*. Or was this simply the tale I told myself too often as a way to feel connected to something, someone, *anyone*.

Samira flowed with a sense of freedom not enjoyed too often when veiled from the world through the *burka* she was born into as a Saudi woman. The burka, creating a taste illusion of modesty while, through its very existence, a self-admittance to the vulnerability of man to incomplete himself through his own temptations.

I was vulnerable to such concocted spells. And Spirit knew it.

We moved to the carpet. The pillows offered an appropriate landing for an unsettled spirit, while adding to the sensual setting. The freshly stoked shisha provided an avenue to another addiction. The music faded as Samira's words made acquaintance with my ear.

'Who are you?'

'My name's Jeremy.'

'No. *Who* are you?'

'A question I have been seeking an answer to for some time now.' I paused, in reflection; then continued. 'Who am I? I thought I knew. Had a beat on it for a while. But lately, since I arrived here in Dubai, only darkness looms... shadows of me.'

Samira shifted her body to face me more directly.

'Illusions, the shadows. The shadows are just illusions,' she said. 'They can feel very real. But they are not. Only the Light is real. The darkness is just light, awaiting its moment.'

'I have been awaiting my moment. The answers to my questions. I thought I had found them. But... '

'You are an honest man, Jeremy... a good man. It is written... in your eyes,' Samira paused, then continued. 'I like you. You do not seem as with the others here.'

'You are right and wrong in the same. For when I first saw you, I was attracted to what most men covet. Your beauty. Your movements. Your nature.'

'Oh, you do not know my nature, Jeremy. It is mine to know. And even I am seeking certain truths about me, as you do you.'

'I've been in a free fall ever since I arrived here.'

Samira laughed, 'Dubai is a crazy place. Temptations everywhere.' She paused, looked out across the many that were drinking, dancing, flirting, and following their own nature. She continued again. 'You could see yourself different from the rest, but what's the use. We are all here to learn. We are all here to grow. And by the nature of just being here, we are all far from perfect.'

Samira stopped as if in deliberation over something. Her hands moved to her waist. She began to lift up her shirt. I was not certain whether to look or look away. I had no idea what she was up to.

'Look. Look here. You see.'

She was showing me a scar that ran about six inches across her lower back.

'I was born with two kidneys. Now, I only have one. I have no more kidneys left to give.'

'Were you sick?'

'No. My sister was. She needed a kidney. I had two. I gave her one. But now I must take good care of this one.'

I was moved by the moment, by her courage, her transparency. Samira continued on, as if she had merely shown me a book she was reading.

'You see. I am not perfect. You are not perfect. But it is all perfect, the fact that we are not.'

'Yes, I have come to learn that,' I responded. 'But my imperfect form is keeping me from the perfect ending I am looking for.'

Samira laughed. 'Yes, it can be quite the riddle—life. We are tested, time and again. Not to see what we are not, but to see what we can be... what we have always been. And Allah knows. He knows just what bait to use... to catch the fisherman.'

'Isn't that the truth. When I first saw you, I was attracted once again by beauty.'

'Well, I am a woman too. So with this I am grateful to be seen as such.' Samira finished her words with an embrace with her eyes. Her eyes were like nothing I had ever seen before—before arriving here in Dubai. They were an unnatural, yet lovely marine blue, decorated with jewels. I had come to know of the magic created through specialized contacts—quite popular with women in the Arab world. But that was not all the magic in play this evening. Samira was much more gifted.

'There was more to you that lured me in.'

'What was it you saw... when you were looking?' Samira asked.

'That you were beautiful. That you moved in a mystical way. That I wanted you.' I paused, took in the sound of the crickets, then continued, 'And that you had something for me.'

'Well, of course. I think we all have something for each other.'

Samira smiled at me, an inviting smile. I wasn't certain where this was all heading. She wasn't either, from what I could tell. We spent the next few hours getting acquainted with each other and, in the process, reacquainted with our true selves. She shared with me her challenges as a woman in a world ruled by men. Her experiences were the plight of many; some more specific to her own skin, her own world. I gave her my attention, my support, my thoughts when queried. There were clearly higher laws at work, as we compared notes on what was unfolding.

Two worlds that could not be more diverse.

Two lives that were destined to intersect.

Two hearts aligned by one common purpose: the pursuit

of something greater in ourselves.

Samira was a lifeline. I may have even been one for her. There would be as many lifelines, lifetimes, as were required.

We left Solano and walked along the beach together under the night sky. Flush with possibility for the light to come forward, she opened the portal further.

'Jeremy, I feel compelled to share something with you.'

'A revelation of sorts?' I queried while gazing up at the Burj, now painted lavender by the lights that knelt before it in due homage. 'I had one of my own.'

'No. More of an invocation… as set forth by the prophet Mohammed.'

She paused, closed her eyes, took in a deep breath; then exhaled. She placed her hands over her heart. Her heart opened to that place. His words came forward through her.

'Love of the world is the root of all evil.'

Samira's words—or those of Mohammed—blazed a-cross my mind like a sandstorm of truth across an unsuspecting caravan of thought. I stood there. Frozen. Paralyzed by a truth that could no longer be concealed through wit and well-chosen wording. I had been unmasked yet again. Or maybe, simply released.

As I gazed into her eyes, I saw—*myself*. Through the embrace, I felt my own. Along the passageway of a sacred surrender…

I lay claim to my own kingdom.

'Is there a distance between me and you, Lord?' The

words flowed within.

'*Yes…*

'*As far as the mind will take you…*

'*And as close as you are to your heart.*'

I turned toward the sea. Tears emerged, releasing the emotions stored in the memory banks of years, lifetimes past.

"*Love of the world is the root of all evil.*"

The "evil" was simply what we did to ourselves. We denied ourselves a greater experience, connection, union, by claiming the prizes of this world as the love we sought. I was seeking, but not seeing. I was choosing, but not choosing up. My attachment to the world denied an attunement to something greater. When I chose out in the world, I missed out on the holy grail of the inner worlds. This was the root of the evil in which I condemned myself. I was both jailed and jailor. And I held the keys to my own emancipation.

It was time. It was always time.

It was time to "*set the angel free.*"

Samira embraced me as if compelled through Another. Her gentle touch upon my face provided a warming reminder of the caretaker of my true self that remained still. It was one of forgiveness. It was one of acceptance. It was one of loving. It was from the One.

The light from the Burj reflected back to me the same purple hue that had befriended me. The sea of sound upon my ears I now understood as the awakening of the spirit within, forced all other vibratory notes to the background of my being. Samira pierced into my eyes, as her own danced with the flames of an eternal knowing. She leaned forward.

Was she going to kiss me? I thought. This was not allowed. Not here. Not ever.

She moved beyond my face.

'You were never alone,' she whispered into my ear, her expiration a breath that left me tingling with such truth. 'And it is never too late.'

My eyes welled up, once again. Tears made their way down my cheeks. Each left only a trace of the storied events that had served as the building blocks, the stepping stones to the pyramid of truth I dared ascend.

That which had never left me had returned to me. And with it, the shadows of my own creations—my self-judgments, my guilt, my shames—had retreated by the mere expansion of the Light itself. I understood better through this momentary digression in Dubai that to know the Light does not mean you are the Light. It is earned with each new breath, each choice. We anchor it through living it. We anchor it through loving—*His* loving.

'Jeremy, you give me hope. Hope that all may someday see through the eyes of only One. And live through His heart.'

'Samira, a man much wiser than me once said, "*If your god isn't big enough to include everyone, it isn't a big enough god.*"'

Samira smiled. The universe winked. And I remembered. I remembered why I was here; the game at hand; and the gift that awaited me.

My evening with Samira provided yet another key piece of the puzzle I was born to solve. Here in the desert I was forced to face the reality of my own humanity amid the growing discovery of my divinity. And through it—which is the only direction we invariably must take—a greater acceptance of myself and of those around me was availed to me. Samira's outer beauty had been trumped by the radiance of a higher love at the core of her being, a buried treasure, which by some good fortune had been revealed to me. Our worlds were not the same. But we were from the same world, the same Source. And this Source spoke to us––through us—caring little for the difference created by the human invention of separation.

She was Muslim. I was not. It mattered not.

It never has, when seen through the eyes of the One.

Samira and I embraced one last time. There were no more words. Only a shared silence, filled with the sound of our souls through a glance transcending. She would soon vanish into the desert sands, leaving only a lasting trace upon my heart, and grace upon my mind. The magic carpet had taken us on the great ride from inside, offering each a vantage point high above the walled structures erected through the limited. It offered our minds the opportunity to come along, with only one condition: that the heart may lead. It provided us safe transport beyond the cravings of this world, and into the realm of our true desire. It carried us beyond our bodies, our emotions, our mental ways, illusions of separations, and into the way of the eternal; found within the confines of the unconfined—our souls.

If only I could hold this feeling, this knowing, and not lose my way once again in the search for greater meaning.

If only.

Only if.

'JB. What you doin'?' Zayid had a way of leaving out words that simply delayed the message. 'If not living, then nothing at all.'

And filling in the blanks with greater meaning.

'Z, it's midnight. What do you think I'm doing?'

'*JaayBee!* Come out! Don't be sleep. It's crazy out here. Everybody having fun!'

I was certain that Zayid was put on this planet as Earth's honorary social chairman. He was always out and about. He knew most everyone. And for those he didn't, it was merely a matter of time.

'Alright, alright. Just give me a few minutes.' I had no intention of going out, but with Z you had to leave him with hope.

'Brother, I know you. I call you in ten minutes.'

He *did* know me, and he *would* call me. Again and again, in fact. Not with an intention for disruption, but rather because Z felt he had this mission. Zayid was here to make sure everyone had a good time—especially me.

Thirty minutes later, I was at The Roof Top at the Royal Mirage, chatting it up with my good friend.

'Z, you know you're a bit crazy.'

'I know. But life is crazy. We born. We die. But whether we live… up to us, man.'

He was right. It reminded me of the conversation I had with my brother back in Kenya, reflecting on Sebastien and his choice to live, truly live, until his very last breath.

'Chivas. Double.' Zayid barked out to the nearby bartender.

'JB, what you want?'

'I'm good.' More than good, in fact.

'*JaayBee!* Live it up, man! He'll have a red wine.'

I smiled as I watched Zayid work his magic with the bartender; the group of women to his right; the guy who sought out a place at the bar. He offered him a drink. The man said no. He bought him one anyway. For "no" was merely an unwitting "yes" in Z's vocabulary. He spoke to your basic self that simply wanted to live, laugh, and love. The rest of you he had little time for. Zayid was in a hurry to nowhere fast. He was more than content to extract the life out of each second of living. I loved this about him. His childlike enthusiasm for and amusement with everything and everyone was infectious. He simply had no time for practicalities. He was in the business of awakening us to the simple sensations of the soul. And he did his job well.

'JB, you too uptight, man. Loosen up. Let go. God is in charge. You don't have to be.'

I smiled and made my way over to a nearby couch. I sat down, removed from the crowd and chaos at the bar. The chatter around me was in a language I did not understand. The sound within me I understood better than ever. I was in *that place*. It had—I had—returned. Z was simply misreading my inner experience as in some way a disconnection from the outer world which surrounded. It was a simple misunderstanding. We each had our own way of living our loving.

'He is a happy man,' this comment coming from a rather strange-looking fellow to my left. Maybe five-foot-seven and rather portly, he looked like a cross between a Buddha and Yoda. His eyes were indiscernible, as he had sunglasses on. The evening darkness hardly required them.

'Z? He is a good friend.'

'*A true friend is one soul in two bodies.*'

'"*A true friend is one soul in two bodies.*" Aristotle, right?'

The man did not respond.

My focus was lost for the moment anyway. I was distracted by a rather attractive woman—Russian, maybe—who was clearly in a hurry to somewhere. She brushed by our table. Her scent, physique and stunning beauty reminded me of Miia.

'She looks like her,' the man said.

'What? Who?'

'The woman. She looks like your wife.'

'Ex-wife.'

'Well, that is your choice, how you want to remember

her.'

What? How would he even know her? Who was this guy? I sat there, mouth wide open, as if I were in between a thought and a word that had yet to make its way across my lips.

'Jeremy, my name is, well, I go by many names... and none really. I guess you could say I am a fellow traveler like yourself.'

The man removed his sunglasses. His face looked familiar. I had little time to reflect as he proceeded to look toward me, and directly through me—his eyes piercing the veils of my own windows. All I could see was purple—a myriad of purple flashes similar to the ones I had been seeing for years. It was like someone had flashed a bright light in my eyes. And the chirping. There must have been a million crickets making their racket. It was deafening. I sat there in an almost trance-like state as he continued.

'You are awakening to the Light and Sound within you. To your own soul. You have been on this path for quite some time.'

'What path? To where? It's felt more like a roller-coaster... a merry-go-round even.' I was just happy to formulate a thought. My mind was gone.

The man smiled. 'Your humor is a good tool. Keep it handy. Easier when we find the amusement in it all.'

The words were vaguely familiar. And the message, a good one.

'What of the purple light? The sound of crickets in my

ears?'

'You are awakening to the Spirit. The purple light is sort of a guide. It points the way. It's been there for you—with you. Back when you were finding your courage, in Africa. The journey since… while "taking the little boy with you."'

'How… how do you know all this? So much about me? My life?'

'Let's just leave it as a type of connectedness. There is a place that we can all connect into if we know how. The library of the all-knowing. Available to us all. But you must awaken to it.'

The library of the all-knowing. That's what Reshma had called it.

'I am ready,' I responded.

'Are you? You weren't in Colombia.'

'Yes. I'm tired of this… all of this.'

'When you're sick and tired of being tired and sick, that's when change happens.'

The words. They were the words I first heard back in my apartment, in LA, after Georgia's death. Could it be…

'There have been clues. Many of them. Many more if you would pay closer attention.'

'I hear voices. Sometimes messages. From within usually, but sometimes they come in the form of others. Sometimes even through the old masters. Even then, usually delivered through another, form or figure.'

The man smiled. 'Yes, God speaks to us in many ways. People wait to hear the voice of God. Pray for it even. They never consider that He may choose to speak *through* His creation. Through the many people, places, events—even a timely master—all of which help to unfold the mystery of it all.'

'The mystery?'

'The mystery. The secret. The key to the kingdom. The answers to those "questions" you were speaking of... in Africa, with your brother. Your spiritual promise.'

'How...how do you know all this? How is it even possible? I never spoke of it with...'

'Oh, and don't make me have to pop you in the forehead again. Stay aware and keep looking upward.'

'What about this spiritual promise you mentioned?' I couldn't get the questions out fast enough.

'It's a promise. One you made to yourself, when you entered this life.'

'What was it? What was my spiritual promise?'

The man put his hand on my shoulder. 'Now that would be too easy. Wouldn't be right, either. Spirit is non-invasive. So are all who work with the Light, this consciousness. You are close, anyway. The answer is there. And *you* hold the key. Keep giving over... to yourself...to others... to Spirit.'

The man placed his sunglasses back on; then ushered forth the words once again:

'*A true friend is one soul in two bodies.*'

I put my head down to try to grasp what he was saying, all that was occurring. I sat there, mind blown to bits, heart bursting with what was a super charged jolt of energy permeating my body. My forehead was throbbing. Ears ringing. Feet glued to the floor beneath.

And then it hit me! His face. The image I saw back in India, at the ashram, while on the wall. That purple image against my eyelids. That was *him!* 'How the...?'

I lifted my head, but he was gone.

Distorted, disillusioned, my mind began to catch up to what my heart had already awakened to. This man was anything but just a man. He knew too much. He knew things that no one else could know. Yet, through it all I felt entirely safe, secure, like something was implanted within me to let me know that everything was okay. That it was all fine—perfect even.

Something in me knew of a greater trust through an awakening consciousness. It was that same something—or some *One*—that had been with me through loves, lusts, loss, break-ups, shake-ups and make-ups before; along with the many other situations where reality did not meet with my desired expectations.

'*A true friend is one soul in two bodies.*'

One soul in two bodies. One soul in two bodies.

How could one soul be in two bodies? Maybe Aristotle was not speaking of a soul in the sense we speak of it. Maybe...

Of course! It is that *Friend* of ours that is *in* this world, but not *of* this world. The Spirit that resides within us all. I mean, it's so simple yet so entirely elusive. This man—this strange little portly Yoda-type man—knew because there was no distance between him and *It*. Somehow he was connected in. Somehow he eliminated the separation. Somehow he had cracked the code, no longer apart, but rather *a part*, a part of something much bigger, with the consciousness to know it so.

I emerged from the depths of my mind, holding a jewel––a "pearl" in this case.

'JB, man! Where you been?' Z asked.

'Right here. Talking with that man.'

'What man? I see no man.'

'He was here. I'm not sure where he went.'

'Brother. You seein' things. You need a drink. You the crazy one, now.'

Crazy, maybe, I thought to myself. But it was real. He was real. My head was still abuzz; my body trembling as if supercharged. Zapped. My cells were moving at a frequency that could only be described as an elevated state of—*peace*.

'Z, do you think we get as many chances as it takes, to get it right... to get our lives right?'

'I think God has a plan. And it includes everyone. No accidents, man. No accidents.'

'Right. No accidents. But we can certainly trip and fall. Even after we find the answers.'

'Finding it is one thing. Keeping it, that is something different.'

'I slipped here in Dubai. Messed up big time.'

'Ah, JB! Brother. Did you think yourself better? Better than the prophets even? Abraham. Mohammed. Jesus. All. All faced their shadows, their dark nights. All were given choice, over and over.'

'Yes, but they chose right. They chose up.'

'Eventually, yes. But not always. It is how they learned. It is how we learn. We *learn*, man. We learn more when times require more learning. Usually, when times most difficult.'

'Yes, but how many times do we get, really?'

'As many times as it takes, man. Time is human thing. There is no time with God. Only be.'

'Only be?'

Z took a swig of his Chivas. 'Yes. The mind *do*. The heart *be*. This is why the mind cannot go where heart goes. To "do" is action. To "be" is to know self. And where you are going, brother... where we all going someday... is not a place. It cannot be arrived at. No destination. Only realization. Realization of what is, man.'

Z stood up. He could only sit still for so long. 'You have nowhere else to go, man. You are there. *Insh'Allah*, we all there.'

And in that, he was gone.

He was gone. That strange man was gone. I was left under the stars...

The stars! The meditation. Back in San Francisco. The vision. Under a starlit sky. On a couch. With a strange man; surrounded by a strange language.

319

"Her visions," Wilson once shared of the witch doctor, "Always come true." Apparently, so do mine when I access "the library of the all-knowing" through my own means.

It is a library open to *all*.

The evening began on a rooftop, ascended to even greater heights—under a starlit sky, no less—and later ended in the basement of the Al Qasr, sharing *biryani* and "breaking bread" with Z and the servers long after the restaurant had closed. We looked a bit medieval as we scooped the rice dish from hand to mouth without the use of any manmade utensils. It didn't matter. For we were not "man made," and we had greater tools at our disposal.

I looked over at Zayid, admiring the manner in which he eased his way into everyone's life. He had his worries, his concerns, his own fears perhaps. Yet somehow he was able to rise above them whenever a moment for a higher experience of living and loving was availed—which through Z, I learned, was often and everywhere.

Zayid lived to be only thirty-eight. By thirty-eight, he had cast his bright light around the world. He was granted an early visa to the greater kingdom—I am certain for a job well done. His star remained in the hearts of those graced by his presence, wrapped in a gift of a Muslim man who only knew loving that "*included everyone.*" His light served as yet another lantern along the path of my own awakening.

Insh'Allah, I will see him again.

God willing, it will be so.

'All that spirits desire, spirits attain.'

These were the words of Kahlil Gibran.

Gibran was speaking to the purity in the pursuit that we must attain before we can receive all the treasures that are available to us—the "pearls" worth diving for—with the greatest treasure being Love. This, at least, was my read of it. Kahlil was many things to many people; certainly a master who challenged us with his poetic voice to find the temple within that so many have sought through outer world forms.

And Zayid was a master, as well. One who dared to live life through the simplest of rules:

> Just love.
> And leave the rest to Him.

I watched from the window of the taxi as the heavy winds played havoc on the few that dared to journey by foot. There was a sandstorm approaching, one that would blind in the moment, but not forever. An Indian worker was caught off guard, and knocked from the crate he was balancing himself upon. To the ground he went. He got back on his feet, laughed at himself, and returned to the crate to tie down a sign that had fallen over.

I had fallen here in Dubai. Knocked off my perch like the handyman. But I got back on my feet again, brushed aside whatever ego remained, and returned to the task at hand.

It is our destiny to persevere. To endure until the end.

The palm trees danced with one another, providing kind escort for the desert wind. It's an odd phenomenon this dance we do so often, I thought, as we continued on to the airport. The one of duality—*the great split*—given a choice time and again between the higher and lower roads, the path we have waged and the wager It has made that we will all, someday, find our way home.

'Which terminal, sir?' the driver inquired.

Which terminal? Which transport? Which direction? My choice. It has always been *my* choice.

'Sir?'

A decision that likely seemed an eternity folded into one moment's breath.

'Terminal 1. Air China.'

'What's in China?' The curiosity of my current transporter growing with the presence of silence within the taxi.

'Perhaps the final piece.'

'To what?'

'To a puzzle I have been solving for quite some time.'

'I once had a puzzle,' the driver added. 'Thousand pieces. Many pieces. Took me a long time to finish. So many of the pieces looked the same. Different colors, shapes, but similar. Finished it.'

He laughed.

'What's so funny?' I asked.

'Finished it. Then looked at the picture. Same picture as on the box.' He laughed again. 'All those pieces. All that time. Just to make a picture that was already there. Hah! Funny thing.'

I got the picture.

Insh'Allah.

Is that you, fellow Traveler... calling me?
Yes... and many more times before. Thank you for answering.

13
THE FINAL *PEACE*

'A superior man is modest in his speech...
But exceeds in his actions.'
– Confucius

———

The skies were lit with the splendor of a thousand rockets. None was more lit than I.

The Chinese New Year marked the end of what was and the beginning of what may be. All were given the opportunity to bring closure to obligations past, and to start fresh once again. It was a time of hope. It was a time of reflection, one of projection. It was a time to begin anew.

It was time.

All signs had brought me to this place, this moment; to

China. I had become accustomed to following the signs before me, the voice within me. This voice spoke from a place void of any falseness. It was a voice of reason. It was a voice of knowing. It was also my voice.

'Everything come to a halt.' Dr. Liu shared, as we stepped from the balcony to enjoy the celebration from the warmth of his home.

'All China has gone home to their families. The skies are filled with travelers. The tracks, the roads, pathways home to where the heart belongs. It is a time to embrace what matters most. It is a time to remember.'

As with all chapters in my life, my time with Dr. Liu was the result of a series of events past, all leading up to the serendipitous encounter with this man. Dr. Liu was one of the top botanical scientists in the world (you would have to tell him this, for he would never tell you). He was also my friend; the thread woven through at least a dozen others; and through another dozen or so events over a period of as many years—two paths converging to the point of the present. Life provides such perfect weaving, perfect timing.

There was an instant connection between the good doctor and me. We had been here before, co-creating with the higher, defying the naysayers and gifting the world with new discoveries. It felt so comfortable that the imagination of times past were within reach of the mind, as with the heart. And we were here, now, in this lifetime, together— my good friend and me.

And so was she.

Li was in China. This I knew. My heart remained in some form of longing since Paris. My body and mind did its best to forget in Dubai. My walk through the valley of the shadows had allowed me safe passage to the other side, where the light prevailed. I was intent on seeing Li again, but to what end was less clear.

There was a knock at the door. Dr. Liu arose to answer. His physical features were of a little Buddha (a common image of late) —as was his persona. Intense, yes; but jolly and wise, most assuredly.

He opened the door.

'Ah, Miss Arcova! Welcome, welcome. Please come in.'

Arena entered. My eyes paid homage. She looked beautiful, stunning; her body graced by a most vibrant full-length dress that served in honoring her subtle curves. Her hair was up, exposing a pair of emerald earrings with an Egyptian theme. Her cheeks were flush from the brisk conditions this time of year. Her eyes, her crystal clear amber eyes, had never radiated so much light. She was pure. She was real. She was also my dearest friend. And just so happened to be passing through Asia on her way to New Zealand, creating an impromptu moment for a choice re-connect.

'Jeremy.'

'Miss Arcova,' I greeted her playfully, followed by a kiss upon one cheek, then the other.

'Ah, Miss Arcova, so very nice to meet you!' Dr. Liu shared with the youthful enthusiasm of a young boy discovering the rich properties of life itself. He took her coat and scarf. We made our way to the living room and sat down. I was thankful to have Arena here with us—with me. Dr. Liu continued with his greeting.

'Miss Arcova. *Miss* Arcova. So nice!'

'Dr. Liu, it's *my* pleasure. I have heard so many good things about you.'

Dr. Liu shied from such flattery. 'I am just a man, doing what I know, nothing more,' his reply, with a genuine humbleness I had come to know and admire. 'I understand you have good deeds in your heart, as well. It is written in your eyes,' he responded, while servicing the table with an aged *pǔ'ěr* tea from Yunnan.

Arena's eyes smiled as they graced my direction. The adoration we felt for one another could not be concealed— nor would it serve us in doing so. Dr. Liu picked up on it immediately.

'Jeremy. Such a beautiful woman! Why have you not made her your girlfriend?'

I struggled for an answer. There was no good one to surface. Arena, as usual, saved me from myself.

'Oh, I'm not his type. Jeremy tends to... well let's just say he is a complicated man who enjoys such in others.'

'Well, I have spent many years in the laboratory,' Dr. Liu added. 'And I tell you, there are many simple elements, which when placed together can go *boom* very easily. One must experiment... but be careful when doing so. One must experiment, yes... and recognize when they have found correct formula.'

'I like you already, Dr. Liu,' Arena said. 'You're my kind of man.'

'Oh, I am taken, sorry,' he answered, laughing. 'Been married for nearly forty years. But Jeremy, he is still available.'

'Oh, I know Jeremy's story. And of his pursuits.'

'I like to think of my pursuits as more like Edison's,' I added. '"I didn't fail. Just found 10,000 ways that didn't work"... or something like that.'

Arena laughed.

'Ah yes,' declared the good doctor. 'Very good. Very good indeed.'

The conversation continued between Dr. Liu and Arena. The fireworks continued outside the apartment. The sound of each faded through the growing presence of the sound within me. The choir of a covenant, a pact made with the heavens, was revealed—through the loving that surrounded. The light prevailed as one with the loving unveiled. There was no distance between them. There was no distance between them and us. There never was.

That is, until the mind created such illusion.

I loved Arena, but the idea of her and I together in any form outside of friendship seemed out of sorts—risky certainly. I had been too much of a project for someone who was shining brightly as her own light. Arena's work as an artist set the world ablaze. She was courageous, relentless, a true warrior in spirit; and captured the essence of such through powerful portraits of her countrymen—in particular their eyes.

I looked over at Arena. She glanced my way. Dr. Liu continued with the conversation of me, of us, playing the role of matchmaker—or perhaps simply courier. Her eyes revealed a shyness I had not seen before. I smiled at her. She smiled back. The gods were smiling on us all.

'We have good evening planned. Tonight I will introduce everyone to salted duck egg!'

Dr. Liu emerged with a new point of focus. He would rave on for another fifteen minutes about these unique double-yolk eggs from Gaoyou in northeast China. Like a little boy in a grown man's suit, his enthusiasm was infectious, and his innocence enjoyably refreshing. A little boy, as seen through the eyes of spirit—played out through our soul.

My thoughts moved to the old woman—the witch doctor from Kenya—and to her words that made acquaintance with the truth in the moment.

"Don't forget to take the little boy with you."

She never meant it in a literal sense. This I had come to understand. The little boy she spoke of was symbolic, the nature of the soul itself. As with Dr. Liu, the soul lives in joyous celebration of everyone and everything. It is innocent, pure, removed from the negativity of a planet through the power of the possible that resides within each of us. It is free from it all, that which it is not. It moves freely through this world, and presumably into another.

The only chains were those imposed by my own refusal to see what is; to see through the eyes of a child; and be such as an expression of greater wisdom. As Z would say, to "just *be*."

"Don't forget to take the little boy with you."

I smiled. I understood. I had made my choice. I will not forget. Never again (a claim certain to be tested again).

The dinner was traditional. Whole fish, head and tail intact; to guarantee a good start, a good finish. *Zhāi*, to cleanse oneself. *Jiǎozi* for prosperity. Plenty of greens, served whole, to guarantee a long life. There was more food than there was need for; and not enough to thank the heavens and earth for such good friends, such a good life.

Dr. Liu moved to the kitchen to prepare the *niángāo*. Arena joined him. I remained at the table, transfixed by a thought—a reminder.

"If one is good, then the whole world is good."

It is really not our choice, I thought, as I gazed beyond the forms and into the formless; the sheaths of energy within the light around me an indicator of that which sits between, and connects all that is. It is not our choice as to whether to walk the path we must walk, live the life we were born to live. But it is very much our choice in *how* we choose to experience the journey. The world reflects back to us whatever light we give the world. It always has. It always will.

Dr. Liu and Arena returned.

'So what is it we wish for, on this day where wishes may

be granted?' Dr. Liu queried.

'Peace. Love. More inspiration... and more duck eggs,' Arena answered, gesturing toward the plate of salted eggs.

'Ah! So good!' he responded, while rising to serve her another portion. 'There is more. There is always more... as much as we want. That is, until we no longer want.'

'Or need,' Arena added.

'Yes. No want. No need. Only be... and be good.'

'I have seen the world. It is filled with goodness.' I added. 'Good people... good souls.'

I paused, allowing my heart to reflect. It reflected gratitude, for the many messengers, masters, who gave me sight—and insight. It reflected loving, for whatever gifted me with such. It reflected peace.

'You have had many reflections. We all have,' Arena said. 'Many mirrors reflecting back to us...'

'The one thing I came here to know.'

'It is the great secret,' Dr. Liu added. 'It is the great secret... and the key. The one unknown element that bonds all elements.'

The light around increased in its intensity. Dr. Liu's hand movements slowed. As did Arena's lips as she spoke. The clock on the wall struck second by second; its sound barely discernible—but with its own voice. The tangerine tree that found temporary home in the apartment appeared to move, to stretch. The tone within me played its celestial melody, amid the crickets who summoned me. Every motion, every notion, melody played as symphony. And through the chorus, I found a peace, a solace. Each breath, each note provided a passageway to such.

There was nowhere else to go. There was nowhere else— —no one else—to be.

Dr. Liu's voice beckoned my return.

'Jeremy.'

I heard him, but I did not react. Life was in motion, a slowed motion. I was at peace, an inner peace. There was no need to move, from one place to another, from this moment to the next. All unfolded into one continuous. And in the continuity all was found.

'Jeremy?' Arena inquired.

Jeremy was the character I chose, the one I played, for this lifetime. Jeremy was the platform for the life form. But there was more to this life force than merely Jeremy Braddock. The picture was near clear. And it was greater than me.

'Jeremy, what do *you* wish for?' she asked.

'Yes, Jeremy. What can this year bring for you?'

I remained in the stillness. There was movement around me, but within me there was no movement at all. Through the passageway that finds its genesis in the intelligent One— —bypassing the mind, emotions, the body temple—but a single word emerged. It looked like Love. It sounded like Peace. It came forward as...

'Truth.'

'Ah, you want to know truth.'

'No,' I responded, with a slight gesture of the hand. 'I

want to *be* Truth.'

Dr. Liu went silent. Arena was staring at me. I was just there, present, gifted with an answer. And the one that followed.

'Jeremy, always remember... *"No matter where you go... there you are."'*

Dr. Liu had just quoted Confucius. This I knew. But more important, his words and the pervading energy served in unlocking a very important chamber—a secret chamber. The words that followed were my words, but not mine alone.

'One could travel the world; from place to place.

'One could travel from lifetime to lifetime; from universe to universe.

'One could travel from realm to realm.

'But the traveler in each of us knows.

'There is nowhere else to go. Nothing else to do.

'It has, is, and always will be a matter of simply being simply Loving.

'And in this, we know all there is to know.'

Arena's eyes were aglow. They radiated beyond their normal clarity, beauty. They provided yet another window to the same Truth.

The fireworks outside remained. Their sounds muffled by the current of Sound within. Their light to a greater Light. My thoughts to a higher knowing. A portal had been opened; a soul awakened. And what poured through was pure Loving.

The Longest Distance

For years—an entire lifetime—I had been traveling the world, searching for love and meaning through a series of people, places, events; moments. Years of canvassing the globe for that one gift. So many years. So many miles.

'*No matter where you go, there you are.*'

Could it be that simple? Could it be that everything I have ever wanted, needed, was right here all the time; right in front of me? Better yet, *within* me?

I sat there. My mind was content to remain there. My emotions had other intentions.

It began as a stirring. It moved to something more. Something was shattering—shattering within. A shattering of a crystallization. The crystallization was of separation. The separation but an illusion.

It was clear. I needed no more messages; no more messengers.

The "*One thing.*" Not to be found anywhere in the world, yet everywhere *within* the world. Love. But not love in a human sense. Not the love of another, person, place or thing. *This* was the Love as captured by Rumi, other great masters—an eternal garden seeded with the Love within the love that is the root of all. A Love within, aligned with the Love within. Connected. On target. On purpose. And what shoots forward is Truth, pure and simple Truth.

> *This* is who I am.
> *This* is why I'm here.
> *This*

The Truth was clear. The emotions that followed were more vexing. Joy and sorrow. Confusion and relief. I wanted to scream. I wanted to cry. I began to laugh. Uncontrollably. I couldn't stop…

Laughing!

'Jeremy. Are you okay?' Arena was both amused and confused.

More laughter. *Out of control-type* laughter. Something was moving inside me, tickling me. Tickling every cell of my being. And it was something not to be controlled—*ever*.

Arena started to giggle. Then, she erupted. It spread to Dr. Liu like a wind sweeping about the room. We were all in tears—laughing uncontrollably—with little sense of why.

I knew why. *It* knew why. I had my moment; my breakthrough. But not just any breakthrough. I actually broke through. Broke free. Severed the chains. Shattered the crystallizations, the mirrors that had been reflecting distorted truths for far too long. Shattered them! Shattered them all!

Everything I ever wasn't, melted away. Everything I always was came into perfect view.

I had carved and carved. For a lifetime. Over lifetimes. Carved and carved…

"…*until I set him free.*"

Arena kept laughing. Dr. Liu kept laughing. The current that swept through us, knew us. All anyone could really do was laugh—and smile—and allow *It* to do *Its* thing.

"*What choice do we have, but to go on.*"

What choice indeed.

My laughter began to subside—became more of a giggle. I could have gone on laughing for days. I had finally lost my mind; the same mind that had been stalking me my entire life. We ditched him. Of course he was welcome to join where I was now heading, but he was no longer the leader; just another follower. The heart was now in charge; a most intelligent heart indeed. And the "little boy"?

Leading.

I looked over at Dr. Liu. He looked back at me. Arena was smiling at us both.

I sat there in silence for another moment. The moment was filled with anything but silence. For within the silence was a free-flowing river of gratitude, appreciation, for so many who had given so much to me—as with us all when we choose to open up to its flow.

I turned to Dr. Liu. 'You are a good man, a good teacher.'

'*What is a good man but a bad man's teacher?*' he responded, quoting Lao-Tzu.

'*What is a bad man but a good man's job?*' Arena added.

'Ah,' the good doctor replied, '"*If you don't understand this, you will get lost, however intelligent you are. It is the great secret.*"'

'The secret is in being present with what is. Open to who we are—in Truth.' This I offered, while giving my eyes to Arena in reverence of yet another great teacher.

'Human beings,' she added. 'I mean, could it really be

that simple? Life as a human... simply *being?*'

'I believe that is up to us,' Dr. Liu responded. 'Like with the plants I work with. They sprout. They receive nourishment, sunlight, rain. They take it all in. Give it back, in some form or another. Do all this from one place, one spot. Nowhere to go. Nothing to do. Just *be* who they are. And give back when asked. Like on this table here tonight.'

Dr. Liu giggled.

'There is so much love in that,' Arena responded.

'There is so much love in all things. It is a matter of knowing who you are. This can be seen by what we do. But what we do is not who we are.'

'Nor why we're here,' I added.

'And if we are to be defined by who we are and not by what we do, then what is our job really?' Arena inquired, playing her role artfully in fueling further the discussion.

'Simply to awaken to the reality of our totality,' Dr. Liu answered.

'There's so much peace in that.'

'Perhaps the last piece.' The significance of the moment did not escape me.

'*No matter where you go, there you are.*' There's no escaping that which is.

The conversation of our higher selves continued for the remainder of the evening. I was unsure as to what part destiny played in all aspects of my life. I did know this: if it were destiny or some divine hand that brought Dr. Liu,

Arena and me together this evening, then I was a big fan of whatever forces were at work in such masterful weaving of a single evening, lifetime, or series thereof.

Whether in the arms of a loving embrace…

The glance between eyes that play both window and mirror…

A moment of spirited messaging…

Or a timely offer in time of greatest need…

We need each other.

Lao-Tzu understood. The Love that is the undercurrent of this planet has designed it as such. We need each other, in order to know ourselves better. We need each other, to know Him better in each of us. It is the only time "need" has a place in "loving."

As I embraced Dr. Liu in a long farewell, and offered my arm to Arena, I knew everything I needed to know.

I would be a lesser version of myself…

Without people like these in the world.

The fireworks continued, echoing the sentiment of joyous wonder through an array of forms, colors, and sounds that offered both eyes and ears a breathtaking score from the amateur conductors below.

Arena and I lay there, gazing out through our adjoined window. We grasped for a star, amid the display that served in enlightening the evening in another manner. Our minds were still abuzz with the magic created, and the awakening through a most timely conversation. I knew it was an awakening lifetimes in the making. I knew it was my time. A promise made to me, by me—*for* me.

'Do you think God had all this in mind when he made all this?' Arena queried aloud.

'I think he had a beginning, and an end—if one could call it that—to the story of man.'

'His will.'

'Yes, His and His alone. He was kind enough to give us free choice, though.'

'I'm not sure how kind that was in the end,' Arena offered, giggling a bit.

'Yeah, right. Maybe He thought we would be better students, not recalcitrant children, feet kicked up on the desk, in the back of the classroom...'

'Too cool for school,' she added, with a bit of theater to drive home the point.

We both giggled.

'No. I don't think that was it at all,' I shared. 'I think Spirit loves us so much... that It wanted us to know love— Its Love. Not as an idea or ideal, but as Truth in action. The action of Loving.'

'And there is only one way to know, truly know, anything...'

'Through experience,' I said, finishing Arena's thought. 'This realm is a classroom...'

'And a playground,' she added, smiling.

'Yes. Absolutely. And a playground. A place to play...

and to ground ourselves in the reality of what is.'

I paused for a second, considering all the opportunity that had been granted me with each new breath, each shared breath with another. God gives us our breath. He gives us the gift of our breath, our life; then asks for nothing in return—except that we *be*, and be *loving*.

I reached out. I reached out through my loving, and took Arena's hand. I held her hand in my own, a deserved union for two who felt as one with the One. Her skin was soft, delicate; creamy in complexion; dreamy in nature. I felt a bond with Arena I had not known before. She rolled to her side, and gave me her eyes. I fell into them, the depths of which defined eternity. There was only now. There was ever only now. The past was past; the future unknown and unnecessary.

Arena's hand rested within my own. My hand provided a sacred chalice for which it lay. There was nothing that could break this bond, this moment; this union. Nothing that could trump the knowing that had made its way into my being. Nothing. No one…

My phone buzzed. I pulled it from my pocket.

"Jeremy. Please come. It's my mother. Hurry!"

The message on the screen was from Li. It was a desperate message. The words and their energy told me so.

I had let Li know I was in China, yet had not found my way to Chengdu, where she was. There were many reasons for this. She was married. They were together, tending to her dying mother. I was not the same man I was back in

Paris. The answers I had been in pursuit of, the puzzle picture and its many pieces, were coming into view. I loved Li. But love was being re-defined, refined with each new awareness, each new piece of the picture—the picture of me.

'Jeremy, what is it?'

'Li. She is asking me to come. Her mother... she's dying.'

Silence filled the air. The energy in the room shifted. I could sense a change with Arena, one I had witnessed only once before. Torn between the moment and a sense of duty—each in loving—I didn't know how to respond.

'Arena... '

'I know. Do what you have to do. But...' and she paused for a moment.

In the moment of her pause, I knew what was next. In her words. In my actions.

'Be what you were born to be... what you will always be,' Arena finished.

There was simply no other choice.

She stood up. I followed. I looked in her eyes. She looked in mine. I brushed her hair back; then held her forehead to my own. She closed her eyes. I closed mine, as we opened to something greater. Our Loving. Our Truth. His Way.

Arena gave me the love she was. I gave her my own in return. And in this, we gave each other everything.

A love known. One shared. In the heart. In the Oneness.

And with that, she was gone.

I lay in bed that evening. Once again, I found myself staring at the ceiling above. I wanted to break through it and fly off to wherever my soul would take me. I thought of Arena; what she meant to me. What had taken hold of my heart was not Li, nor anyone else. It was something else. Something more. Something greater. Arena knew this. I was thankful that she did.

I began to drift off. As the mind quieted, the voices within me came forward once again.

"Does it require another?"

"All is required and none still.

For the Love… is."

There were no more words.

There were no more words required.

"Father? Father, are you there?"

My father lay there quietly. In his eyes, in his final moments, was completion—along with a complement of peace, earned and deserved. It left me—he left me—wanting in my own life, yet complete with our time together; whatever it was we came here to do together.

Beyond the misconceptions, mistruths of one with another, we are given moment after moment to shake ourselves free from the web of lies we spin through some false sense of self, masked by illusion, an ignorance lifetimes in the making. This serves in denying the truth to be known—in this case, between one man and his father—setting both on a course where only love may lead. This time I speak of reveals itself when misunderstanding is replaced with greater understanding, and judgment gives way to acceptance—and, if so fortunate, loving in its essence.

My father and I had this moment. It came not too long before he passed, well before his years. It occurred not with a flurry of words, but through the sound of silence. Not by looking away, but through a gaze toward, held in an embrace; his eyes with my own, beyond the varied shades of so many false moments and into the tempered windows of truth.

While my father lay there, testing the waters of living with the proposition of graduating beyond this world and into another, we shared a moment of absolute understanding, and in that, a completion that said simply and with clarity...

The Love in me recognizes the Love in you.

It was the only thing we ever needed to know.

I awakened to the screech of the wheels as our plane touched down in Chengdu.

———

Li's driver picked me up at the airport. We went straight to the hospital where her mother was being attended. I arrived, made my way up to the third floor, and ventured forward. There, in the hallway, was Li.

'Li.'

'Oh, Jeremy.' Li collapsed into my arms and began to cry.

'How is she?'

Li gathered herself as best she could. 'Not good. They don't give her much chance. I think she wants to go.'

'And you?'

'I will let her go when it is time.'

Li looked exhausted. I held her close. I felt the connection again with our souls. Her head rested peacefully upon my shoulder; my head against her own; our hearts but a whisper from one another. It was as comfortable as any place I had known in this world. Li brushed her hair aside. Her eyes made union with my own.

'Jeremy, I am done with my life here. I am leaving my husband. I only held on so as to honor my mother and our name.'

Li's father had passed many years back. Mr. Sun was attuned to a more masculine China, rooted in the past; one that paid little attention to the feminine grace of this place. Like the coal which had no interest in becoming the diamond nor acknowledging the jewel before him. He was a man of tradition, expecting nothing less from his daughter. And marriage—by any means—was a tradition not to tread upon lightly. It was no surprise the imminent passing of her mother would call to completion her marriage—a most displeasing chapter in Li's life story.

'Jeremy, I have to get back. I cannot take you in. You

understand. But I will see you this evening. Thank you so much for coming.'

Li moved nervously. As she was walking away, her husband's head emerged from the room down the hall. She hastened her step. They disappeared together into the room her mother was occupying. I understood. It would best serve all concerned that I do so.

That afternoon, I lay there in bed, consumed by the shift in my ever-changing life. I thought of Arena, her piercing eyes beholding of only Truth. I imagined Li and me, off together, living in the loving we'd be so fortunate to know, with and through the other. My mind raced through the years to come, playing back a picture most attractive. Li had finally been made available. This was the incarnation of my fascination. And what of Arena, my most trusted companion throughout my journey? Or of the deal made with Cassandra, once I had "found the answers to my questions?"

I fell asleep, warmed by the notion of such loving; reminded once again of my reason for being.

There was one deal that preceded all others…

And it came in the form of a promise.

"What is Love?"

"*You are Love.*"

"Who is God I choose to know better?"

"*You are God and God is You.*"

The questions—and more important, the answers—opened up the chambers to the many characters housed within my heart, played upon the stage of one singular lifetime. Windows. Mirrors. Miles upon miles of mirrors. Revelations. Reflections. Of hidden secrets, truths to be unearthed.

It required *Courage*.

Acts of *Service*, *Compassion*.

A dose of *Humor*.

It begged of *Understanding*.

A found *Integrity*.

It asks we *Trust*, *Let Go*.

Move *Freely*, *Joyfully*.

With *Devotion*, *Gratitude*.

Tolerance and *Acceptance*.

That we may know *Peace* as the crown jewel of the kingdom within.

And *Loving* as the King itself.

These and other qualities; all pieces of the greater puzzle in its timed unfolding; picked up along the way of my life journey; reflected back to me through others on theirs.

I drifted. For how long, I did not know. By all accounts, it was awhile. Perhaps a lifetime. Joined only by the sound of the crickets, a purple hue and familiar image that replaced all that surrounded me, and the answer that finally arrived for me.

'*The One you are waiting for and the One you have been looking for is already here, and has been for a long time. You are the [Love] you have been searching to find.'*

The image of the man from Dubai was undeniable. His words, unmistakable. His timing, impeccable. This one, this *One*, was here to reveal to me the one Love, the one Truth I came here to know.

'There is no love or lover. There is only the Beloved.'

Spirit's voice? His? My own? Did it even matter anymore? For the source was the same. It has always been the same Source.

And I knew this. That was the difference. I actually knew *This*. I knew what I was seeking, what I had now discovered. The places covered, faces revealed, distance traveled had all brought me to the singular moment of now. And within it, the moment of seeing—of awakening to— the one thing I came here to know.

A pool emerged. A reflection pool. It held the answers. It held the answers to the questions—to my questions. As I gazed into the depths of its content, the intent was clear. I saw only one thing; the *"one thing,"* and in *This*, I saw everything.

The reflection was of me.

> *I* am the love I seek.
> *I* am the Love I have always sought.
> *I am...* the Beloved.

My eyes were lit with the intensity of a million candles. The next words ushered forward through the channels of a truth undeniable were the easiest words which, bound together, formed the hardest sentence I would utter in this lifetime.

'Where I am going, I cannot take you.'

"Where you are going, nooo one else can go." The words no longer haunting me; their truth awakened to me.

Tears streamed forth. But they did not stop her from seeing, knowing, what was true.

She understood.

She always understood.

It was me who did not know the truth of my own knowing.

It was me who did not know the purpose of my being.

It was me.

And forever shall be.

I awakened. I got dressed.

There was something I had to do.

───

She stood there
Waiting
On us all
And I, awaiting each new breath in solidarity with her own

Her hands danced with the spirit of the moment as she poured the fresh concoction that had its origin in some divine plantation where tea leaves were cultivated with care, caressed with the loving hand, knowing of their own fated destiny upon the lips of a fellow traveler through time and life. I sat in admiration—and remained so moved.

Peace.

Not merely peace with the external, but upon the inner realms where gardens of grace await us all.

The tea master emanated peace through the masterpiece of the moment. And with the early evening sun a befitting backdrop and parading partner in this un-folding event, I enjoyed with each new breath the sight of the golden elixir that poured in symphonic harmony from spout to cup—and from her heart to the very chalice of the soul. The *pí pá* was strummed in accord with the movement of the leaves within the clay-based *zǐ shā* pot. The steam arising made its appearance as it shimmied with the brisk air of this winter solace, through a parade of poets who once graced this soil, and remain still, in spirit.

> Grace offered
> Grace filled
> Grace revealed

Li had invited her brother and his wife to the tea ceremony with us. It was a way of showing respect for her mother, a cup remaining untouched in her honor. Her brother was a kind man, his heart ravaged as well by the latest family crisis. His wife went unnoticed by most, off in a world that sought to satisfy all but herself—therefore no one really. In the world of spirit it was all perfect.

After dinner, Li and I assumed our traditional stroll, this time along the Fu Nan River and not against an Italian or

French backdrop. Arm in arm, there was a familiarity to it, a comfort. Li stopped, and turned toward me. Her face was lit. The nearby streetlight made certain of it.

'Jeremy, I am ready. I have endured years of pain in my heart in knowing...' Li's thought was interrupted by a text message. She checked it; then returned the phone to her purse.

'...knowing you are here, but out of reach...' Another buzz from her phone interrupted her. Li checked it again; this time sending a short response.

'Where was I?'

'Something about "out of reach,"' I reminded, smiling.

Another text message. I started to chuckle. I couldn't help it. Spirit was now swirling inside me, once again tickling every part of me.

Li grinned, 'When I saw you last, you were searching. Have you found what you were searching for Jeremy?'

Another buzz. Another message. The chuckle became a laugh, an uncontrollable laugh. Spirit swirled. Li joined in. We were both in tears by the time our laughter subsided.

'Jeremy.'

'Li?'

More chuckles followed.

'Spirit certainly has its way of, well, sending a message,' I shared as yet another text message arrived. They were from her husband.

'Yes. I believe that, too,' Li responded, as she checked the message.

'Li.'

'Jeremy?'

Another text. More chuckles. This time, she turned her phone to silent.

'You asked me if I found what I was searching for.'

Li smiled. 'You *did*. I can see it in your eyes. Your eyes are like two radiant stars. So much light. So beautiful!'

I paused, taking notice of every detail before me, as if the entire planet slowed to the speed of one singular note.

The street vendor wiped his brow with his forearm, while an assortment of women caressed an assortment of apricots and other dried fruits, sold from the back of his makeshift wagon.

The Chinese lanterns swayed in the evening's breeze, while enlightening the movements of each traveler.

A few good men—with many more observers—presided intensely over a game of *má jiàng*, an old tradition that carries with it an ancient lesson; one of patience while searching for the final piece required to complete the game.

The dance of light upon the river, a breathtaking display of colors as reflection from the nearby buildings; no one color more vivid than the purple streaks that shot forth, providing a compass for the awakening of the spiritual heart.

Joined by a crescendo of sound, as if a sea of locusts had found comfort in an off-season performance; a Sound that unified Li with me—and us with Him.

Everything was moving at the speed of now. The

swirling energy inside me; the joy which accompanied me; the peace within me. Looking deep into Li's eyes, I shared what was present—my heart; my truth.

'Li, I love you. Not merely because of who you are. I love you... because of who I am.'

Tears filled her eyes. My heart, filled with a loving not purely my own, but simply pure in its own, met with hers in the same. We stood there, within the eternal garden of God—where the Love in me knows the Love in you—and replaced the tears with a lasting embrace of souls.

'Li... '

'I know. I have always known. Our love. What it is. What it cannot be.'

'What it will *always* be.'

I held her face in my hands. Her eyes met mine. Our souls shared in one more moment, through a story written in the past, held in the present; to be let go so that each may live the life we were born to live—our spiritual promise.

This chapter would end, so that another may begin. The love would endure. It always has. It always will.

We embraced this. We embraced each other. We embraced the truth through one another.

And we let go.

I made my way to the airport. This time there would be no escort. This time there would be nowhere to go, wherever I went. This time there would be no one to accompany me, as I traveled in good company.

I was good with it all. It was all good. "So good."

I sat there in a sea of traffic formed by fellow travelers. The trees waved; goodbye and hello with the same motion. I thought of the man I met in Dubai, the one whose image I had seen before. I thought of how he could look right through me—through *to* me. I thought of how he knew things that he could only know if he were with me, or could tap into that which was with me, each step of the way. If he was, in fact, some type of guide, and could help me fulfill the promise I had made with myself, then I would follow his lead. I would follow anyone who could point the way—the way home.

Reshma's words graced my consciousness. "You will meet a man. A man who will give you... what you are seeking. It is your destiny."

It is our destiny to find what we are seeking.

It is our destiny to find our way home.

And fulfill our spiritual promise.

My attention moved to a Chinese "flower," a girl of maybe four who was running ahead of her grandfather along the sidewalk. She would run, then stop, then run a bit more—stopping yet again. This went on for quite some time, until I finally caught drift of the game at hand. The little girl was trying to outrun her shadow cast by the streetlights above. She did everything within her power to shake this other version of herself, unaware as to what—or whom—was behind this rather persistent partner. Try as she would to avoid it, the shadow remained as if some guardian of the darkness who had been permanently assigned to this one particular child for one particular reason.

I smiled as I thought to myself how we could never really lose our shadows, no matter how much we tried to avoid—or outrun—them. For how can one lose what does not exist, that which can only find its existence in the illusion created when the light is limited in its capacity by our own doing. There is only one way to eliminate the shadows that surround us; only one way to bask in the purity of light that is everywhere, at all times.

> We must look within.
> And find the Light that dwells within.
> Cast it outward in all directions.
> Connecting with the Light of those around us.
> Erasing all angles where darkness may show its temporal form.
> And simply *be* the very Light we seek.

> This, as well, for Love.

I gazed up at the many stars above on this rare treat of a crystal clear evening in the valley region of Chengdu. The seeming darkness of space itself but a mere co-conspirator for the greater oration in waiting...

> Of a Sound that accompanies an awakening;
> To the greater within ourselves;
> Tweaking our Light ever so;
> The illusion of darkness thus erased by the ever-

expanding presence;
Of the *One* thing, that is the *only* thing;
Worthy of a life lived;
And distance traveled.

The longest distance we will ever know.

'Where are you heading to?' The taxi driver inquired.

'Home.'

What now, my Friend? What next?
Silence...
Listen for the Sound of Silence.

14
HOME

It is said, "Home is where the heart is."
I am now graced in knowing...
Our Heart is where our Home is.

———

C risp is the wind, a fresh coldness I have known
before, but never with such loving embrace.
Within the confines of a mind beholding to my heart, I sit
once again upon the park bench of my reminisce. Each
snowflake upon my cheek, my hand, speaks to me oh so
slowly, yet with such deliberation. For there exists an
eternity of conversation in each final breath I take. A
lifetime of reflection emerges from the ambers within that
warm my soul—and light the way.

Winter holds a special place in my loving heart. Its
peaceful tranquility allowing the thoughts to slow, and
heart to grow. A portal to the supreme, and one of many

loves I have shared through the course of every moment that has led to this one. I am well beyond the twilight of my years, entering the time of both reflection and a destined direction toward what awaits me at the doorstep of the beyond. Thank God, Spirit, the Universe in whatever form thus chosen, for the pleasure, the treasure, of Your hand in mine in this moment.

You in your greatest adaptation have been a consistent sanctuary in my dreams and living testimonies, delivering the ideal to the point of real. Into Your eyes I have known from times past and present still, there is a dialogue ensuing at the moment no attempt at words may soon unravel.

'Do you know what I am thinking? Do you know what I feel in my heart for You? Do you know?' I can hear the sound that speaks through, unspoken to my ear. I understand Your intention at loving me fully by knowing me better, better at times than I have known my own self.

'*Shall we dance this dance together?*' My soul inquires through the same venue of our shared silence.

'*You know it well, the one begun upon the floor of the unwritten, cast forward through the lyrics of many, as Sound made by such heavenly dictation.*'

In as many instances of past, these lyrics of my life as reflected through another voice have made their journey from heart to mind, in memory still. And this Ruler that sits upon the altar of the garden kingdom has been with me for only an eternity.

Who is He really, but a representative of the greater

awakening Spirit within, cast forward through the flawless spectacle of the One before me now, as the One before us all.

All others are just the others, imperfect in the world yet perfect in the moment. As with so many, they play true to a representation of what lies beyond and in between. I have known of Love's many faces, places; Its giving nature and painful discoveries. I have known of joy, willingness, and acceptance; of tolerance and understanding; of service. I have known of these qualities of loving as with others, perhaps not in this order, but in an order that has led me to this very moment, and this form revealed through varied forms.

Your face... speaks of a winter's ice in transparency that awaits the thaw in each of us, that we may someday recall the hills of green amid a sky blue, colored in such fashion through the most friendly manner by which the sun shares its joy in perfect harmony with an accepting earth and its covering.

Your lips... still luscious in their offering, beg to be heard and not merely seen, as the winds of time have swept forward a wisdom that dares replace a skin that once defied the ages, with ageless knowing.

Your eyes... a spectrum of colors that remind us of the many choices we have made, and subtle shades that color our world and view thereof.

You have been a symbol of integrity since the moment I first gazed into the Truth of my own soul—decades previous, yet a mere second in the context of eternity.

And so here we sit, today, the familiarity of Your softness as conveyed through the touch of Yours with my own. Aligned, as if with an old promise of distant lives renewed in the flesh once more. The safety I feel is not in the personality that has offered me so much as mirrored reflection of myself in life. Rather, it is through the window of a sacred Truth that has allowed me to know You better, through the living peace that now shares this splintered bench, restored to its original nature and beauty through the bond of One with all as bridged through our coveted reunion.

The trees dance for us, with the wind providing both music and motivation.

The clouds, a chosen reminder of the beauty that comes and goes before our eyes and lives.

The snowfall blankets us with the sweet softness of your touch.

Another example of what life holds for each, an accumulation of millions of moments—billions even—that together act as necessary threads for the new coat to be worn, in symbolic capturing of the many strands of *This*, through Your divinely woven tapestry.

So many strands, so many moments, so many choice discoveries. Reflections of a journey with so many mirrors, required angles, capturing the many forms of loving that point the way.

The trees offer in shade a choice from sun.

The wind, a refreshing new share of air.

The man on the street corner, a new means.

The woman of my loving, an old way.

Through our family, an adjoined fate.

Through our friends, the brutal truth.

Through Your many creations, an opportunity, to re-create my life anew.

By way of Your view of what I am, not what I do.

> Reflections
> Choices
> Truths
> Love

Not the love that has proven a worthy reflector and director, pointing the way through a series of sentences with little meaning and no true ending; but the Love found through the One through the collection of the many pieces of peace along the way. The pathway to peace in the world requiring us to travel the most arduous of trails, through the inner sanctum of the heart, with a willingness to face and erase that which we had been predisposed to believe. And this, so that we may one day *believe*, and through such bridge simply *be*, simply *live*, to our soul's content, the contents of which are ours for the re-discovery, our rightful heritage.

I have reclaimed the One thing that was mine all along.

The One thing I came here to know.

The cold of a winter's late afternoon provides the motivation to move. We arise as One from the bench that served as a peaceful palace for a sweet embrace. We begin our sojourn along the banks of the bay, walking in unison and at a pace that will allow this moment to endure. Time has often stood still when I have allowed myself to live through each successive breath, absorbing all the sights, smells and sounds that have been available to me since birth. And this, no exception—as vetted through the heart as final door to the everlasting.

It is as if the world of time stilled itself, a caress of the coveted within the safe sanctuary of an inner Loving. In the moment, I find a place where peace exists. Peace exists within the moment of the moment. When we are in the wholeness of our loving, and all things fold into the essence where only Love is present, all-consuming and all giving in One. This is where I find peace, a place where all that stirs about and around may knock but may not enter.

The password?

As stated.

Loving...

His Loving.

If not living the password of *This* Loving, we may not enter into *This* kingdom.

'God, I have searched the world in pursuit of this moment. I stand here at the altar of all I wish to know, and find myself both worthy and unworthy of this Love.'

'*My friend… you have been and forever shall be worthy, by the nature of your very nature. For I am the Love you seek. For I am the God that is you, that breathes you still.'*

Peace. Love. Joy. All within the chambers of our heart; a palace where all are invited, and too few choose to enter.

'Shall we go,' I ask, as the pace and flow of the snow quickens.

'*We shall continue,*' the voice responds, again with the wisdom of One who knows of a journey that has no end in sight, through the greatest insight.

The snow beneath my boots provides a soundtrack with each new step, the crunch a fitting metaphor for the sound that makes its way forward through the collapse of the temporary as it gives way to a more solid and fitting structure, one more sturdy for the traveler. And in a city that personifies peace itself, a city that may be any city when traveling within one's own portable paradise, even the trees whisper so as not to disturb the solitude when at one with nature. The wind calls forward the weather, yet does so with a deserved respect for such calming ways.

What respect does the Universe have in the actions of all its creations! It never ceases to amaze. It creates in its perfect image; then allows all Its creation to go about its own course and action without interference, through our own invention. Infinitely patient in the process, we are allowed to manifest to our heart's delight; then bear witness to the result. And when we are no longer marveled by our own majesty, we wrap ourselves in humble clothing once again, and make haste to our awaiting heaven.

The Longest Distance

We make our way along the sea of our imported tranquility. I hear my own thoughts spoken back to me. There are moments in our lives when we are in absolute synchronicity with the Other. And in these moments...

There are no secrets, no illusions.

There are no games of and by the mind.

There is no separation, no distinction.

There is but One voice; One heart; One beat.

And it is to the tune of a Sound not of this world, yet avails itself *to* this world when we choose to tune in, to turn on. And once you have a piece of Peace, a knowing Loving, and a lasting Truth, you can never return to the world of without and be satisfied within.

Moved by the roar of the crowd of my own content, I play witness to the masterpiece of Sibelius as yet another master messenger of His word. What more fitting end to the symphony of sounds and sights so graciously granted this lifetime than through the composition and divine creation of Jean Sibelius through a most imaginative mind, and divine heart. The sound of Sibelius carries with it the grace and glory of all creation, through the power that comes from poetic solace, and the note that emerges from the Sound of silence itself.

The chimes ring within the chambers of my heart.

Signaling the end of one love story.

And the eternal tale of the only Love we will ever really know.

I sit, waiting, alone but not alone. The movement of the trees beyond the frosted windowsill appears to beckon me forward. The rays from the sun create a prism of reflected light, a rainbow of colors—the most prominent as purple. It dances; a violet flame with but one purpose. To illuminate the pathway to the everlasting, to the only place that ever was—the object of my soul intention.

My mind stills...

While moving at the speed of Light.

My heart slows...

To one final Sound.

One final gaze

Into His eyes

Into My own

Returning

Home

Are We to close out this process?
Open always.

Is there a message You wish to share through Me...
with Me, oh Lord?
In time.
Keep still Your mind... open still Your heart each day...
Embrace Me with Your willingness... the courage to reveal
Your true essence.
I give You what You seek... as reflection in who You are.

Love

'There is one thing in this world which you must never forget to do.
If you forget everything else and not this,
there is nothing to worry about,
but if you remember everything else and forget this,
then you will have done nothing in your life.'

– Rumi

ACKNOWLEDGMENTS

This novel has been a journey, not only for the character it depicts but for the character that is me. And as with all journeys we set upon, there are the many that play voice, ear, hand, and heart along the way. I am most grateful to you all, indebted as service in return.

I thank the Spirit within me for the co-creative process in its unfolding. It is and shall forever remain the Source for all that inspires.

In concert, I am a greater version of myself due to the masters, my teachers, J-R and JM. Thank you J-R, for your words, your wisdom, for showing the way. Thank you JM, for your humility, your humanity, the blessings through the knowing. You have gifted me with opportunity, to travel, and return in the same. I love you both for the Love you are.

To my daughter, Pook—yet another teacher—I thank you for being you, and for once again traveling this road with me. Your creativity is divine. Your sensitivity, embraced within my heart of hearts.

And a profound debt of gratitude for my editor. Lizzie has presented us all with a gift: a novel that moved to point, when the author at times was moved by something else, romanticizing his way along the country road of the co-creative. You made sense of it all, and kept the nonsense—where it belonged. It has been a joy and a privilege.

To the many friends, family, loved ones, colleagues, and fellow travelers around the world: you have been *my* windows, *my* mirrors; guides at times and Friends indeed.

With the greatest and most cherished of them all, my 'Puppy,' the one who reflects back to me, time and time again, what Love is—in Truth. I adore you and all you represent. Most of all, It through you... and a Love without conditions.

I thank you all. And know myself better by simply knowing you.

ABOUT THE AUTHOR

David Scott has spent his career in the field of education,
his life in the field of service. His travels throughout the
world have provided a cross-cultural perspective on
relationships of a human nature. His discovery of the inner
worlds through meditation and study of various teachings
has offered a glimpse into the power of the possible that
resides within. David may be recognized in the world for
his contributions to education. Yet, he remains humbled by
the many lessons—the gifts—the world has bestowed him.
He now remains at your service as an author.

For more information on David Scott, visit
www.authordavidscott.com

Made in the USA
Lexington, KY
04 January 2015